I0764663

Wooing Gertrude

Jodie Wolfe

This is a work of fiction. Names, characters, places, and incidents either are the product of the author's imagination or are used fictitiously, and any resemblance to actual persons living or dead, business establishments, events, or locales, is entirely coincidental.

Wooing Gertrude
COPYRIGHT 2023 by Jodie Wolfe

All rights reserved. No part of this book may be used or reproduced in any manner whatsoever without written permission of the author or Pelican Ventures, LLC except in the case of brief quotations embodied in critical articles or reviews. eBook editions are licensed for your personal enjoyment only. eBooks may not be re-sold, copied or given to other people. If you would like to share an eBook edition, please purchase an additional copy for each person you share it with. Contact Information: titleadmin@pelicanbookgroup.com

All scripture quotations, unless otherwise indicated, are taken from the Holy Bible, New International Version(R). NIV(R). Copyright 1973, 1978, 1984, 2011 by Biblica, Inc.™ Used by permission of Zondervan. All rights reserved worldwide. www.zondervan.com

Scripture quotations, marked KJV are taken from the King James translation, public domain. Scripture quotations marked DR, are taken from the Douay Rheims translation, public domain.

Scripture texts marked NAB are taken from the *New American Bible, revised edition* Copyright 2010, 1991, 1986, 1970 Confraternity of Christian Doctrine, Washington, D.C. and are used by permission of the copyright owner. All Rights Reserved. No part of the New American Bible may be reproduced in any form without permission in writing from the copyright owner.

Cover Art by *Nicola Martinez*
White Rose Publishing, a division of Pelican Ventures, LLC
www.pelicanbookgroup.com PO Box 1738 *Aztec, NM * 87410
White Rose Publishing Circle and Rosebud logo is a trademark of Pelican Ventures, LLC

Publishing History
First White Rose Edition, 2023
Electronic Edition ISBN 978-1-5223-0420-3
Published in the United States of America

Other Burrton Springs Brides Books

Taming Julia
Protecting Annie

Dedication

To Joshua, Jeremiah, and David with many happy memories of 'Aunt Gertrude' and her love of guinea pigs.

To Janice – thank you for being my first reader. You encourage me along the way.

To David who always supports me in my writing. You're my hero! I wouldn't be on this journey without your continual faith, love, and encouragement. Thank you, my love!

To my Lord and Savior – who provides peace in the middle of our storms.

1

Peace I leave with you, my peace I give unto you: not as the world giveth, give I unto you. Let not your heart be troubled, neither let it be afraid. John 14:27

Burrton Springs, Kansas

August 4, 1877

Gertrude Miller's life couldn't get any better. She grinned, patting her pocket. Her fingers traced the two skeleton keys. After months of planning and preparing she finally had moved into her own place a week ago, away from the overbearing reach of her mother. In two days, she'd be opening the clothing shop beneath her apartment.

She studied the trail leading into town hoping for a wisp of dust indicating the stagecoach was on its way, but saw none. Smoothing the light blue flowered fabric of her skirt, Gertrude's hand settled against her churning stomach. What would George Witt think of her when he arrived? Would he see past her faults and still find her loveable? Would he like the place she picked for them to live?

The many letters he'd written to her crinkled in her reticule, as she clutched it close to her heart. His last missive declared he planned to marry her shortly after arriving. Mama would have a conniption, which was why Gertrude hadn't breathed a word to her mother that she'd marry tomorrow after the church service. Mama would try to do everything in her power to prevent it. Gertrude didn't plan to say anything to her until they were sitting side by side in the church. No use creating a stir ahead of time.

Her dress hung from a hook in her new place waiting for the blessed event. She'd spent hours sewing it and adding yards of intricate lace she'd crocheted.

A group of women had stopped in front of the mercantile down the street, but they seemed more interested in the wares in the window than in who might be arriving on the stagecoach.

"Howdy, Gertrude."

She turned. "Hello, Sheriff. Although I guess I can't call you that much longer. I hear Doc Adams is retiring soon, and you'll be taking over for him. Annie must be pleased, especially with…"

Joshua Walker chuckled and hitched his Stetson high on his forehead. "With Annie increasing more and more each day, she can't wait for me to take over for Doc, so I'll be available when the baby makes an appearance. She's not too excited about me still being the sheriff."

"Are there any prospects of someone taking your place soon?" Gertrude glanced toward the outskirts of town again but still no sign of the late stagecoach.

The sheriff leaned against the hitching post and crossed his arms over his chest. "Not a fulltime replacement, but one of the cowboys from the Williams's ranch stopped by interested in a part-time job. I guess things aren't going so well for Ellie Lou. She's had to sell off some of her herd."

"Oh, no, I'm sorry to hear it. I'll have to stop by and see her when I get a free moment. I can't imagine what it would be like to lose a spouse."

He cleared his throat, his Adam's apple bobbing. "I can't either. Hope I never have to…"

She reached over, giving his shoulder a light squeeze before withdrawing her hand.

The tall man shifted his Stetson and glanced toward the edge of town.

Gertrude didn't think she'd hear a more welcoming sound as that of the rumble of the approaching stagecoach. Her heart hitched in her chest as the vehicle come to a halt. She stood a little taller. *Here we go, Lord. By this time tomorrow, I'll be Mrs. George Witt.*

The door creaked open. The local banker stepped down, turning to help his wife.

Sheriff Walker edged closer.

Gertrude resisted the urge to stand on tiptoes as an immaculately dressed young woman stood in the doorway.

The woman waved aside the driver's hand. "You don't expect little me to jump, do you?"

"No, miss." The driver instead gripped the woman's trim waist and swung her to the ground.

Color stained the woman's cheeks. She withdrew a fan and snapped it open.

The driver shifted toward the door and helped an elderly lady from the stagecoach. Gray streaked her hair making it difficult to tell what color her hair used to be. The woman went to stand beside the younger lady. A relative perhaps?

Gertrude refrained from elbowing past the driver. Goodness. How many people were on the stage? Most days not a single soul traveled to their little town. A few seconds passed before a dashing young man with a silk top hat and black cane stepped into the doorway.

Her heart skipped a beat. *George.* It had to be him. His actual appearance far outshone the small tintype he'd sent in his last letter. Lord knew looks weren't everything, but it would be pure pleasure to be married to such a handsome man. She smiled and waved. Should she wait for him to come to her? What was the proper response? After all, he was her fiancé.

A smile spread across George's face as he hopped to the ground.

Gertrude rushed forward along with Sheriff Walker.

"George Witt?" Joshua fished a pair of handcuffs from a pocket. "Or is it Allen Peterson? Or perhaps Joel Abernathy? Or then again, it could be Jeffrey Fordham."

What was he talking about, and why had George's face turned gray?

"You're under arrest." The sheriff clapped the iron bracelets on her fiancé.

"W...what? I'm Gertrude Miller's fiancé," the man said. "You have the wrong man."

"No, I don't," Sheriff Walker's tone was final.

This couldn't be happening, not on the eve before their wedding. *Please, Lord.* "T-there must be some mistake..." She fidgeted with her handbag, waiting for George to somehow explain away the situation.

"Do you know this swindler?" The sheriff's brow rose as he studied her.

She couldn't stop her face from heating. "I…that is…"

"This is an outrage!" George struggled against the constraints on his wrists. "Is this how you treat all your newcomers? I demand you release me at once."

"That won't be happening anytime soon." Joshua tugged her fiancé's arm. "I have a jail cell waiting for you. There's been word sent all along your trail here about the women you've swindled a vast amount of money from." He glanced at Gertrude. "He hasn't taken any money from you, has he?"

Her gaze darted toward George who took a sudden interest in his fancy shoes. "Women? I uh, well, you see…"

Josh ran a hand along the back of his neck. "I guess you'd better come with me too, Gertrude."

"But…" She hung her head. She'd never live this down if word got back to her mother.

~*~

Enoch Valentine patted his mare's neck. "What do you think, Fee? How can we convince Sheriff Walker to take me on full time when I've never had any experience with the law before? Question is, do I really want to be a lawman?"

His horse snorted and tossed her head.

"We need to find a way to make some more money to send home... and to help the boss's wife." Maybe one day he'd do enough to feel worthy again. He shoved the thought aside.

Fee snorted again. The horse had taken to answering in her own way when Enoch was puzzling a problem…or at least he liked to think the mare understood him. Of course, he'd deny it if someone asked him about talking to his horse.

Mrs. Williams hadn't said anything about funds being tight, but ever since her husband had died, she'd slowly been selling off the horses. If things didn't turn around soon, she wouldn't have any left. He wouldn't have a job on the ranch either. Who'd have thought he enjoyed working with horses when all his life he'd been around cattle? He shook his head and shifted his worn Stetson.

Fee's pace quickened as they reached the edge of town. The stagecoach driver was on the carriage tossing baggage to the ground. Enoch pulled back on the reins. "Howdy. You haven't seen Sheriff Walker, have you?"

The burly man shielded his eyes from the sun. "Help me with this, will you?" He handed over a small cage.

Enoch shifted the reins to one hand and reached for the cage. Two small fuzzy creatures stared back at him. "What are they?"

The driver jumped to the ground. "Don't know what the fella called 'em before the sheriff carted him off to jail. I reckon you can find 'em over there still. I'd appreciate you toting the critters with you if you're planning on heading in that direction. The fella said something about 'em being a gift for his fiancée. Course she may not be that much longer. Not after what he pulled." The man tipped his beat-up Stetson before climbing on the high seat of the stagecoach. "You might want to mention to the sheriff the fella's baggage is all there." He nodded, and the vehicle pulled away followed by a cloud of dust.

Enoch stared at the pile of crates, cases, and satchels. All that was from one man traveling? What did the fella need with so many things? "Come on, Fee. Guess these critters need to get to their owner…or at least to the sheriff."

He clicked and Fee trotted toward the center of town. The critters scuttled around their tiny cage. He tried to keep them level as he dismounted and set them on the ground before tying off Fee to the hitching post. He debated about knocking on the door to the jail or just walking in. With a quick rap, he pushed the door open.

A beautiful brown-haired woman with eyes the color of bluebonnets in springtime stood beside the sheriff. A tear glistened on her cheek. She twisted her hands and bit her lip. "T-there has to be a mistake…I would know if he was a…scoundrel."

Enoch removed his Stetson, interrupting the exchange. "Sorry to barge in, Sheriff Walker. The stagecoach driver asked me to bring this to you. Said it belongs to the man in custody." He glanced toward the jail cell. He'd read about a dandy once before, and the man sure fit the description. His clothes were flawless, without a spot or wrinkle. Although they seemed in opposition compared to the smirk marring the man's face.

"Thanks, Enoch. You're just in time. I can show you the ropes with processing a criminal." The sheriff searched through a stack of paperwork. "Now where did I put that paper?" He appeared to be half listening as he continued to flip through pages.

"Sounds good, although the stagecoach driver also wanted me to tell you that a whole mess of this fella's goods are at the depot." He held up the cage. "I'm not sure what these critters are, but I guess they either belong to him or his fiancée." He studied the young woman who was trying to control her emotions and not doing a good job of it. Enoch fished in his pocket until he found his handkerchief, handing it to her. Thankfully he'd put a clean one in his pocket earlier that morning.

She accepted it without a word, shifted sideways, and swiped her eyes.

"What are you holding there?" Sheriff Walker glanced up from the paper he was filling in. "I'm sorry, did you tell me that already? I've been a bit distracted as of late."

"Those are my two guinea pigs." The fella in the jail cell leaned forward and grasped the bars. "Well, actually they are a gift for my intended." He smiled at the woman.

Sheriff Walker's brow rose as he glanced at the tiny cage. "How do I know they aren't stolen from some other woman?"

The young lady's shoulders quaked as a fresh set of tears streaked her cheeks. Should he try and console her?

"I'll have you know they were a gift given to me when I resided in England." The prisoner huffed. "They are a prestigious present for my intended. In fact, I've been told Queen Elizabeth herself had one as a pet."

"You brought them for me?" The young woman came closer and peered into the little cage. "What are they? I've never seen anything like them."

Sheriff Walker pushed back his chair and came over to take a gander at the critters.

One of the animals let out a high-pitched squeal. Enoch nearly dropped the cage.

"They're called guinea pigs." The man from the cell held the iron bars.

"They sure don't look like any pigs I've ever seen." Enoch poked a finger into the cage and touched the furry body of one of them. "Sure are soft."

"I'll have to check, Gertrude, but if his answer is truthful and they aren't stolen, I guess they're yours to keep." Sheriff Walker smiled. "That is, if you want them."

Gertrude. It was a right pretty name. Fit her too.

"You can't just turn them loose." The fella shook the bars. "I'll have you know they are worth a lot of money. They'll die if left to their own defenses."

"I...I'm not sure what to do..." She crumpled the handkerchief Enoch had given her.

"I think I have all the information I need for now, Gertrude. I'll let you know when I require your statement for the full report. For now, you can go on home." The sheriff returned to his desk.

"It'd be my pleasure to see you home, miss. As long as you don't mind my being gone for a few minutes, Sheriff." Enoch glanced at the lawman.

The sheriff nodded.

Enoch prayed she'd say yes. He'd do anything he could to make things easier for her, especially after the scoundrel had lied to her...or at least from what he understood of the situation.

2

Gertrude startled when the cowboy touched her elbow as he steered her from the jail. "I'm sorry. I don't think I caught your name. I saw you a while back at Mr. Williams's funeral. Were you close to him?"

The man swept his black Stetson from his head. Dark hair tumbled across his broad forehead. "Name's Enoch Valentine. I'm the foreman at the Williams's spread." His dark eyes glittered.

"Gertrude Miller." She shook his large, calloused hand. "Josh mentioned you worked at the Williams's ranch." Heat sprang to her cheeks. "I would think being foreman at the ranch would demand your whole attention, especially now with Mr. Williams's death."

"Truth be told, there's not much for me to do at the ranch right now. While I don't know much about being a deputy, I figure I can learn." He kept pace with her as they walked along the dirt street. The small cage dangled from his left hand. "If you don't mind me asking–"

Gertrude puffed a breath. "I might as well tell you about it. I'm sure it'll be the talk of the town before long."

His brow furrowed before he hid it with his hat again. "I don't pay attention to what others say, and if you'd rather not tell me, that's fine too."

She studied him for a moment. There was something about his eyes that put her at ease. Made her feel she could trust him. But then, what did she know about trust when she'd totally misread things with George...or whoever he was. She sighed. Maybe she was becoming as fickle as a teething baby.

"Miss?"

"Sorry." Gertrude once again swiped away at the moisture pooling in her eyes. "I don't know why I'm shedding tears over that scoundrel." Her lip quivered. "He...he said he cared about me. Promised we'd marry when he arrived. How was I to know he'd swindled other women and went by different names?"

"The fault's not on you."

"Sure seems like it. I was the one who was fool enough to send him money for his trip here." Money she could have used to set up things in her new shop. She shook her head. "I should've known no honorable man would ask such a thing. But he said he was low on funds because he was helping to pay off bills for his parents. That's probably a lie too. Silly me to think any man would desire me. My mother always had to tell possible suitors about why I'd make a good wife. Nobody was ever interested in me..."

"If nobody ever took notice of you, Miss Miller, they're the fools, not you." Enoch squeezed her elbow.

Her pulse sped up at the touch of his hand and her breath caught.

"Just because the man's a scoundrel, doesn't mean you're responsible for his behavior." He gently tugged her to a halt, turning her to face him. "The best you can do is try to put it behind you and keep moving forward. If others talk about you, don't pay them no heed. Likely there will be another tumbleweed of gossip to draw their attention before long. It's the way these things usually go."

Her heart lightened. Could it be true? Would the town forget about this instance? The better question was, would her mother? The heavy weight returned, dogging her steps.

The small animals in the cage whistled and squealed. Enoch lifted them up and stared between the tiny bars. He chuckled.

It was a deep-throated manly sound. One that brought a smile to her face.

"Wonder what causes the critters to do that." He shifted the cage so she could see them better.

She shrugged. "I have no idea what I'll do with them, let alone feed them." She scraped her teeth across her lower lip as she contemplated it. "I...I guess I'll have to ask..."

Enoch lowered the cage. "Don't you worry about it, Miss Miller. I'll ask the good-for-nothing and let you know what he says. That way you won't have to talk to him again if you don't want to."

A lump clogged her throat preventing her from answering right away. "Y-you'd do that for me?"

"Certainly. Figured it's the least I can do to ease your pain." He stared back toward the center of town. "I know I'm new to the job, but I'll see if I can convince the sheriff to let you make your statement somewhere other than the jailhouse."

This time she couldn't stop her lip from quivering. "W-why are you being so kind to me? We've never met before a few minutes ago."

He shifted the cage and tipped his hat back. A smile pulled the muscles of his tanned face. "I figure everybody deserves a kindness when the world has knocked them in the dirt. The way I see it, you might be in the dust right now, but it only means things will be looking up before long. At least if you're asking God to direct your steps." He licked his lips.

Her gaze settled there for a few seconds. "Sounds as if you should've been a preacher."

The cowboy didn't answer right away. "That was my path a long time ago, but then I realized there's other ways to serve the good Lord."

The man certainly was a conundrum.

He studied her face. "I just realized. We've been walking all this time, and I don't have any idea where to escort you home to."

Warmth spread to her face. *Relax, Gertrude. The man has no intention of getting to know you better.* She shook her head to rid the thought and sighed. Perhaps her mother was right after all, and she'd never find someone to share her life with.

~*~

Something had caused Miss Miller to frown and pull away from him. Enoch didn't think he'd done anything to warrant her reaction, but he wasn't sure. He didn't exactly have experience when it came to women, especially not beautiful women like the one hanging on his arm. Well, to be honest, she barely had her fingers touching the crook of his arm. She was the closest he'd get to escorting a lady any time soon.

He gave her a moment to compose herself. Poor thing. Who wouldn't be upset to find the person they thought loved them and wanted to spend the rest of their life with was no more than a common thief and swindler? No wonder she was floundering like a trout on the bank of a creek.

When she still hadn't directed him toward her home, he cleared his throat. "I'm not trying to pry, Miss Miller. I figured the least I can do is see you get home unharmed…"

Moisture lined the edges of her pretty blue eyes. It went against everything his ma had taught him to leave her in the middle of the street instead of seeing her home. He wouldn't press her though if she didn't tell him. She'd had a hard enough day as it was.

She blinked causing tears to trail down her pale cheeks.

It took all his effort to refrain from brushing them away and cupping her face. He shook his head. What had come over him? If he wasn't careful, he'd work toward intertwining his life with the beauty standing before him. He knew better than to get involved with a woman. Besides, all Miss Miller needed right now was a sympathetic friend. He could do that. He patted her cold hand.

Her gaze drifted toward him. "I'm sorry, did you ask me something?"

"If you tell me where you live, I'll make sure you get there without any mishap."

She bit her lip. "You asked me that before, didn't you?" She glanced at their surroundings. "Good heavens. I wasn't paying attention to where we've been walking."

"It's understandable, considering."

"Right." She stood a little taller.

Good for her. He couldn't hold back a smile.

"It looks as though we'll have to backtrack. I don't live far from the jail." Her chin trembled for a second before she gripped his arm. "We'll need to head toward town again. I'm sorry; I hadn't realized we'd traveled all the way through town."

"It's no problem, Miss Miller." He guided her as they turned back.

Her lips lifted upward a smidgen. "Please, after all you've done for me, call me Gertrude."

He couldn't help wanting to see what she would look like with a real smile on her face. One that spread to her eyes. He cleared his throat, thrusting the thought aside. "Thank you, Miss, er, Gertrude. It'd be my pleasure if you'd return the kindness and call me Enoch."

"Enoch." She patted his arm. Gertrude didn't say anything else as they strolled through town until they stood before a shop with women's clothes in the window display. "This is me…I mean, this is where I live and my new shop."

He studied the store. "I didn't realize you were a business owner."

"It's been a recent acquisition. Monday will be my opening day." She dropped her hand from the crook of his arm. "Thank you for seeing me home, Enoch."

"It doesn't look like a home." He handed her the small cage.

"My place is above the store." She took a deep breath. "I appreciate your kindness."

"My pleasure, Gertrude." He tipped his hat. "I'll find out more about those critters and let you know."

She nodded, slipped a key from her pocket, and shifted the small animals.

He waited until she went inside the shop. His gaze followed her as she went to the back of the store and then disappeared. He hesitated a few seconds longer before he turned toward the jail again.

Thoughts of the brown-haired beauty teased him as he nodded at people he passed on the street. *Lord, be with Gertrude. Soothe her heart as only You can.*

A few minutes later he pushed open the door to the jail.

"I was beginning to wonder if I needed to send out a posse to find you." Sheriff Walker glanced up from his paperwork. His brow quirked.

Should he share Gertrude was distracted and forgot where they were heading?

The sheriff smiled. "I'm joking. Glad you could be a comfort to Gertrude."

"That's my job." The miscreant from the cell shook the bars.

"Keep your distance from her. I'm sure I'll be out of here in no time."

The next few hours were spent learning the ins and outs of the sheriff's office. Enoch's brain swirled with all the information. He hoped he'd be able to keep it straight if the sheriff was ever unavailable, or if he had to fill in for him.

Next, they read through stacks of accusations against the prisoner. The man refused to answer what his real name was. Not that it mattered since he'd be transferred back east and would stand trial there.

Sheriff Walker signed the last paper.

Enoch sauntered to the bars separating him from the prisoner. "You said those critters are called guinea pigs? How do you care for them?"

The man studied his fingernails before he answered. "They need plenty of water and fresh hay or grass. They like vegetables too. You'll have to let my intended know they are a treasured gift. I wanted only but the best for my fiancée."

"She won't be your fiancée any longer." Sheriff Walker pushed back his chair and stood. "The only time you'll be seeing her again is when she comes in to make her statement."

"About that..." Enoch nodded toward the door. "Could I see you outside for a moment?" He followed the sheriff and closed the door behind him. "I told Gertrude I'd ask if she could make her statement anywhere other than here."

The tall sheriff studied him for a moment. He was tempted to fidget under the man's perusal, but Enoch kept his stance frozen.

A grin played across the man's face. "Gertrude, huh?" He chuckled. "That won't be a problem. I should've thought of it myself. Maybe you want to be the one to take down her version of the story."

"You think I'm ready for something like that?"

"I think you're exactly what she needs."

3

The saddle creaked beneath Enoch. He studied the dry grass but didn't see evidence the six escaped mares had travelled this way. He reined Fee to the right. Enoch wished it was as easy to bridle his frustration as it was to direct his horse.

It hadn't helped he found the break after Mrs. Williams and Jim Malley, the other ranch hand, had left to attend church in Hutchinson. Enoch typically would've gone with them, but he'd intended to worship in Burrton Springs today. Mrs. Williams's brow had quirked when he told her his plans although she hadn't shared her opinion. He told himself his wanting to change his church attendance had nothing to do with Gertrude or checking to see how she fared. It was about getting to know the people in the town employing him as deputy. Enoch couldn't help it if he happened upon Gertrude. It wasn't as if he planned to make a point of seeking her out.

He kneed Fee to a gallop. The quicker he found the mares, the faster he could get into town. He should've asked Sheriff Walker what time church service started.

~*~

The sun had climbed high in the sky by the time Enoch found the mares and herded them back to the ranch.

Jim, who had returned from church service, tilted his Stetson, staring in his direction. A moment later he opened the gate to the corral as Enoch approached. "Saw the torn fence. Just finished repairing it. Was planning on heading out to help round up the herd when the mares crested the rise. Glad you found them." Jim closed the gate behind the last horse.

Enoch dismounted and led Fee to the barn.

Jim followed him. "I can take care of her." He stepped forward. "Boss's wife said she'd keep a plate warm for you. Said to come in the house when you returned."

He handed the reins to Jim. "Thanks."

The younger man nodded and started to unbuckle the saddle.

Weariness tugged at Enoch's shoulders. *Must be getting old.* Riding in the saddle for hours at a time never bothered him before. He crossed the yard. Grass crunched beneath his worn boots. Sweat beaded between his shoulder blades. His gut sent out a protest as he rapped on the back door before entering the kitchen. "It's Enoch, ma'am."

Feminine voices sounded from the interior of the house. Best help himself to the chow and slip away. Mrs. Williams hadn't had many visitors in the past few months. Perhaps company would do her some good. He snagged a towel from the dry sink and pulled a heaping plate from the warming oven.

His gut gurgled as the scent of mashed potatoes and roast beef smothered in gravy and roasted corn wafted to his nostrils. He settled in the chair close to where the missus had placed cutlery and a cloth napkin on the table. Bowing his head, he said a quick prayer thanking the good Lord for the food and for directing him to the mares. Enoch shoveled a big helping into his mouth.

"I thought I heard you come in."

He lifted his gaze from his plate.

Gertrude Miller stood beside Mrs. Williams.

He stood, sweeping off his Stetson.

"Sit, Enoch." Mrs. Williams crossed to the stove. "I'm sure you're famished. Heard the horses a few minutes ago. Did you find them all? Oh, forgive my manners. This is Miss Miller."

"We've already met," Gertrude murmured.

He chewed and swallowed, but remained standing. "Yes, ma'am. They're all in the corral." He sent a smile in Gertrude's direction. Enoch guessed she hadn't slept much. Her face was pale and dark circles smudged beneath her sad eyes.

Mrs. Williams seemed to study the interaction between the two of them but didn't say a word as she stoked the embers and added a chunk of wood to the stove. She shifted the kettle. "Sorry I don't have any fresh coffee, Enoch. Miss Miller and I will have a cup of tea. Would you like one?" She motioned again for him to sit.

"No, ma'am." He sat this time and started eating even though it went against the manners Ma had drilled into him as a young boy.

"Take a seat, Gertrude, while the water heats." Mrs. Williams fluttered around the small kitchen, setting fancy cups and saucers on the table.

Before he could get up and hold the chair for Gertrude, she'd already settled in the seat across from him.

"I can't figure how the fence got a hole in it. I checked it two days ago." Mrs. Williams rubbed a hand across her forehead.

"Must have been wearing thin and none of us noticed it." Enoch shifted, glancing at his employer. The woman had enough to deal with. He'd do whatever he could to ease her concern.

She tapped a finger against her chin. "Still. You sure it wasn't cut?"

He scrubbed his hand along the tight muscles in his neck. Had he somehow missed a cut? What kind of lawman was he? Enoch shook his head. "I really don't think so."

Some emotion flickered across Mrs. Williams's face, but he couldn't identify it. He'd never been great at such a task except with… He tamped down further thoughts on the matter.

"Is something wrong?" Gertrude's words startled him.

"No…it's just…no." Mrs. Williams lifted her head.

Enoch speared a piece of roast beef and shoved it in. He studied the widow once more. What made her think someone was trying to harm the stock?

"It appears you both are in the middle of something." Gertrude pushed back her chair. "Perhaps I should leave."

"No." The word slipped from his mouth before he could halt it. Surely, she didn't think he had intentions toward Mrs. Williams. He hadn't given that impression, had he? And why did it matter to him what Gertrude thought?

~*~

Gertrude headed toward the sitting room to gather her reticule. It was a mistake coming here. Her only intention had been to check on Ellie Lou. But when she'd walked into the kitchen and had seen him sitting there, it was as if all manner of coherent thought flittered away. Seeing the two converse so easily brought back her humiliation Enoch had witnessed. It would've been better if she'd stayed in bed, but the sun finally rose and brought her restless night to an end. By then, she was sick of seeing the walls of her tiny home. Instead, she'd risen, dressed, and slipped outside as the morning light sent a menagerie of colors across the sky. She'd walked until her feet complained.

Church services had already started when Gertrude managed to slip into a seat in the back. She'd left as Pastor Montgomery prayed at the end of the service. Choosing to visit Ellie Lou had been two-fold – she truly wanted to see how her friend was faring, and it gave her an excuse to not run into anyone in town, particularly her mother.

"Please don't leave." Ellie Lou's hand settled on Gertrude's shoulder. "I'm sorry I was distracted. I really could use the company. Besides, it's been a while since I visited Burrton Springs, not since–"

Gertrude withdrew a handkerchief from her reticule. She gave the widow a brief hug then handed her the slip of cloth. If she remembered correctly, her friend hadn't been in town since her husband's funeral last fall. While it was difficult to think about George's betrayal, she couldn't imagine losing a spouse. "How many years were you and Mr. Williams married? I'm sorry. If you don't want to talk about it..."

Tears escaped Ellie Lou's brown eyes and rolled down her pale cheeks. "I appreciate you asking about Charles. Everyone inquired about him while he was alive but since then nobody mentions him anymore." She dabbed her wet cheeks and sat on a fainting couch.

Gertrude sat in an overstuffed chair. She waited for the widow to continue.

"We were married ten years." A smile flickered. "We both were barely seventeen when we wed. Our parents thought we were far too young, especially when Charles had just inherited his grandfather's farm. This land." She stared out the window for a moment before she continued. "You probably heard of George and Charlie Williams who live in Burrton Springs."

Gertrude flinched at the name of George, even though he wasn't who Ellie Lou was talking about.

"George and Charlie are my late husband's cousins. If you happen to know them, you've likely heard of their propensity to pick fights. Those two have never been very nice. They weren't happy when my Charles inherited the land they'd expected their grandfather to deed to them, since they're older. Those two were furious when Charles decided to turn the farm into a horse ranch." Ellie Lou twisted the handkerchief. "It's been a struggle, but Charles was making great progress with turning it into a productive ranch. I'm afraid I don't have the head for business like he did."

"Nonsense. I'm sure things will turn around soon." Gertrude cringed when she realized Ellie Lou hadn't shared about her financial concerns. She didn't want to be the brunt of gossip and here she was talking about something she hadn't heard firsthand. "Forgive me. It's not my place to interfere."

"I shouldn't be surprised word of my struggles has been shared in town. I was hoping it wouldn't since we regularly only did business in Hutchinson." She sighed.

"Why did you choose to have the funeral in Burrton Springs?" Gertrude smoothed the skirt of her navy dress.

"Because Charles grew up there. It's where his parents and grandparents are buried. And even though his cousins never got along with him, they are the only family left besides me."

"Do you think you'll ever marry again? Oh, I'm sorry. I shouldn't have asked you that." She swallowed. When would she learn to keep her mouth shut?

"Fiddlesticks. I want you to feel free to ask me anything. Will I ever marry again?" Ellie Lou's gaze travelled to the window once more. "I won't go looking for it. If God ever wants me to marry again, it will take some convincing." She chuckled.

"I can't imagine losing a husband after ten years together." Gertrude cleared her throat. "You never had any children?"

A shadow crossed Ellie Lou's face. "We'd always longed for a big family, but it never happened. Charles always made sure I knew how much he loved me. Even when children never came." She smiled. "What about you? Do you have someone in your life?"

A throat being cleared interrupted their conversation. "I'm sorry to butt in, ma'am." Enoch stood in the doorway, filling it. "Just wanted to let you know the water's hot."

"Thank you, Enoch. I completely forgot about it." Ellie Lou stood. "Did you get enough to eat?"

"Yes, ma'am."

Gertrude's gaze darted toward his. Would he bring up yesterday?

"I didn't get a chance to ask how the little critters are doing."

The day before he'd sent a short note via a local lad with a brief explanation on how to care for the guinea pigs.

She'd completely forgotten about them earlier. Would they be fine on their own for a little while longer? "I'm sure they're doing as good as can be expected." She prayed he wouldn't say anymore.

His brow furrowed, but he didn't make any more comments.

"I'll just get our tea." Ellie Lou hurried into the kitchen.

Enoch nodded and followed her.

Gertrude released a breath. She waited until she heard the outside door open and close before she strolled into the kitchen.

"What critters was Enoch talking about?" Ellie Lou set a cup of tea on the table, and then poured hot water into the other cup.

Gertrude closed her eyes for a few seconds. How much should she share?

"If it's something personal, don't feel pressured to say anything."

Except how could she not share when Ellie Lou had just opened up to her? What kind of friend would she be if she didn't reciprocate? "I…I thought I had someone special. He arrived on the stagecoach yesterday."

"That's wonderful. I'm happy for you, Gertrude."

She blinked away the sudden tears.

"Is something wrong?"

"No. Yes. Oh, Ellie Lou, I've made a mess of things."

Her friend leaned forward and patted Gertrude's arm. "I'm sure it's nothing you can't fix. Disagreements are part of a relationship. Charles and I would disagree from time to time, but we always made sure we talked things through by the end of day."

Gertrude shook her head. "There's no working through things. It isn't happening at all." She sniffed. "Turns out he's a scoundrel. Sheriff Walker arrested him just after George arrived."

"Oh, my. You poor dear. Is there any chance it was a mistake?"

"I'm afraid not. I don't know what I'll do now." She flicked a piece of lint from her sleeve. "He brought along two guinea pigs, and I haven't the slightest idea what I will do with them."

"I never heard of such a creature. How big are they?"

Gertrude held her hands about ten inches apart. "They're kind of cute. They have floppy ears and make the most interesting noises. Enoch says they're soft, but I haven't held them yet. I wasn't sure if they would bite me or not."

Ellie Lou's brows rose, but she didn't speak.

Should she have not called him by his first name? "I imagine I'll get all sorts of questions about George when the dress shop opens tomorrow morning."

"Dress shop? I hadn't heard Burrton Springs had a dress shop. Will you be working there?"

She nodded. "It's *my* shop. I've always wanted to open one." And she wanted someone to love her, but that wouldn't be happening.

"How wonderful. It will provide something for you to focus on. Don't pay any attention to those who want to gossip about you. I've found the best way to combat a gossip is re-direction."

"I'm not sure I'm following you."

"Like this. Say someone says, 'I heard your beau was arrested.' Instead of answering the question try commenting, 'This blue dress will bring out the color of your eyes.' Or something like that." Ellie Lou smiled. "Of course, if someone keeps pestering, I give a short answer and turn things around and ask them questions. Most times they forget what they were asking me."

"I'll keep it in mind. I just wish my mother was easy to switch to a different train of thought, but she's like a starving dog with a meaty bone when it comes to yanking out information."

Ellie Lou chuckled. "I've had a few run-ins with your mother through the years. I imagine it's much worse being her daughter."

"You have no idea." Heat rose in her cheeks. "Don't get me wrong, I love her dearly, but sometimes–"

"She can be a handful."

Gertrude smiled. That was an understatement.

"I'm sure God will go before you. Even though I miss Charles every day, I trust the Lord to intervene in my situation and my struggles."

"I think you're stronger than I am."

"Nonsense. With the Lord's help, you're much stronger than you can imagine. Ask Him, and He'll provide the peace you need to get you through this situation."

"You think so?" The invisible ropes squeezing her chest eased for a moment. She may no longer have a beau, but at least she had the dress shop. It was something. It would have to be enough. She'd make sure it was enough.

4

The sun had just crested the horizon as Enoch headed toward town on Monday morning. Jim had promised to check all the fences while Enoch worked as deputy. Maybe he should mention something to the sheriff. No, that wouldn't do. No sense appearing as though he didn't know what he was doing and give the man doubts about hiring him on.

A few minutes before hitting the edge of town he noticed white flowers growing along the trail. He swung down from Fee, switching the reins to one hand as he picked a few of them. Wouldn't hurt to drop by Gertrude's new shop and give her something to make her opening day special. He shoved them in his saddle bag and mounted his horse.

Several folks were on the main street as he entered Burrton Springs. He wasn't due at the jail just yet. He dismounted in front of the dress shop, tying Fee to the hitching post in front. The sign on the door still said CLOSED, but he could see Gertrude scurrying around inside the building. He pulled the flowers from the saddlebag. The blooms were a bit squashed. He rapped on the door.

The window shade lifted, and she peered at him. Her brow furrowed. A moment later the key grated before the door swung open. "Good morning. Did you need something?"

He shoved the crumpled flowers toward her. "Thought these might help to… That is, I wanted to wish you well on the first day of your shop opening."

Color rose to her cheeks. It was much better than the paleness he'd witnessed ever since he first met her a couple days ago.

"Thank you. It's very thoughtful of you." She reached for the flowers and took a big whiff of them. Several petals fell to the floor.

He glanced down. "Sorry. I guess storing them in my saddlebag wasn't the best idea."

Her blue eyes sparkled for a second. She was right pretty when they lit up like that. A shame the scoundrel had broken her heart.

"I don't mind. I appreciate you thinking of me today." She stepped back. "I'd invite you in, but I still have a lot to accomplish before I open in a couple hours."

"No need. I'm on my way to work. Hope you have a great day and lots of folks stop by and purchase dresses." He sent her a smile. "Well, I'd best get on my way."

"Thank you, Enoch." She sniffed the flowers again. "Nobody else has ever done something like this."

"As I said before, the men in town must be blind if they haven't taken notice of you by now. Any fella would be proud to have you on his arm."

Her cheeks got as red as a berry.

He tipped his hat. "See you later."

She gave a small wave and closed the door.

He had to be careful, or she'd think he had inclinations toward her. Wouldn't do to give her the wrong impression and cause her to be hurt again. Enoch had no intention of taking on any filly, no matter how pretty they were. He just wanted to help her through this rough patch. He'd best keep his distance for a bit, so she had time to heal.

He untied Fee and walked toward the jail. The extra moments gave him time to put her away from his mind so he could concentrate on the day ahead of him.

A minute later he shoved the jail door open and stepped inside the small room.

"There you are." Sheriff Walker stood. "I was hoping you'd be here early. A federal marshal will be arriving on the stagecoach this morning to transport the prisoner back east. I need you to get Gertrude's witness to the facts before the fella gets here. I'd do it myself, but I promised Annie I'd be here if she needs me. She was feeling peaked when we woke this morning. If need be, she'll send word to me here."

"What all should I do with getting her account?" Enoch studied the prisoner, snoring on the small cot in the cell.

"Anything she can think of about their communication, how much money she sent to him. Things like that. He's refusing to say anything else. Write down everything she says, and we'll send it along with the marshal."

"Got it. Do you have paper and a pencil?"

The sheriff handed him the items.

"I'll be back as soon as I get all the information from her."

"Appreciate it."

So much for staying away from Gertrude for a while.

~*~

Gertrude flitted about the shop, adjusting garments on display, making sure there were no wrinkles or lint marring the fabric of the dresses. She rearranged a box of bonnets for the third time. Next, she moved on to a pile of drawers and chemises. Some were covered in lace and ribbons. She ran her hand along the lace-trimmed chemise she'd planned to wear on her wedding day. Warmth rose in her neck. Perhaps some other young bride would appreciate it since she'd never have need of it.

Her gaze travelled to her wedding dress she'd placed on display. She should sell the thing, but for now she'd attached a sign to it stating her availability to make wedding garments to order. Hopefully it wouldn't cause questions. If it did, she'd take it back upstairs to her apartment.

She crossed the room to the small counter checking again to make sure her pencil and paper were there along with her scissors, cloth measuring tape, and pins. Everything appeared to be in order.

Gertrude tapped her upper lip with her index finger. What else needed her attention? Ahh, the rolls of fabric. She hurried over to the two tables that held a myriad of colors and types of fabric to choose for dresses. While she hoped to have ladies order dresses from her, she also wanted to have fabric available for purchase for those who couldn't afford her services. She'd sent for fabric all the way from New York City. It was a costly purchase that she prayed would pay off since Hiram Martin, the town's storekeeper, only had a few selections of serviceable fabrics.

She placed a hand over her fluttering stomach. *Dear Lord, please help my shop to take off and be a blessing to many of the ladies around these parts. Could You see that it provides for my needs, so I don't have to move back home?*

What else was there to do? Oh, the flowers from Enoch. Her stomach fluttered again as she thought about him standing on the boardwalk earlier. He'd looked as uncomfortable as a naughty student having to stand before the classroom. He hadn't meant anything by bringing her flowers, had he? She'd have to make it clear she had no intention of getting involved with another man. After her experience with George, she'd resolved not to let another fella sway her into thinking about foolish things like love and marriage. Being a spinster couldn't be that bad, could it? At least she had the shop to keep her busy.

The flowers. Should she keep them here where others could enjoy them when they entered the shop, or would it invite more questions and speculations? She scooped them up and took a big sniff. Might as well enjoy them while they lasted since she wouldn't be getting flowers from anyone else ever again. They were her first and last. Decision made, she hurried upstairs to get a glass and water to put them in.

By the time she entered the shop again, someone was knocking at the front door. She set the flowers on the counter and scurried to the door, pulling up the shade. *Enoch.* Her heart fluttered. What was he doing here again? Best let him know while she welcomed his friendship, that's all they could ever be.

She opened the door. "I'm not open yet. Was there something you forgot?"

He removed his Stetson. "Sorry to barge in when I'm sure you're busy, but Sheriff Walker wanted me to get your testimony. I guess the prisoner will be transported back east this morning, and the marshal will need to know everything."

"Do we need to do this now? Are you sure it can't wait?" She glanced at the street. More and more folks were out and about and would soon be visiting her shop. At least she hoped so. She didn't want to be tied up going over the whole debacle with George.

"Afraid so. I promise to write as fast as I can so we can be finished before the shop opens."

She sighed. "Come in, then." She stepped aside, closed the door, and pulled the shade in the shop window as soon as Enoch was inside. Motioning toward the back of the shop, she led him to the place where she'd set a couple chairs in case someone got tired while waiting.

Enoch settled into one of the chairs. His frame filled it. The wooden chair squeaked under his weight. "Let's start at the beginning. When did you first learn about George? Or whomever he is?"

She sat on the edge of the chair, arranging her skirt for a second before she answered. "I uh, first got acquainted with him through the advertisements in *Matrimonial News*." Should she tell him she'd advertised for a husband? "Most of the announcements are for brides, but there are a few men who also submit their information." She squirmed. That wasn't forthcoming. She cleared her throat. "I'm the one, that is, it was my advertisement that he answered."

Enoch's gaze swung to hers. He made a notation on his paper.

Heat curled its way up her neck and into her face.

"I assume you started corresponding after that?"

Gertrude nodded. "We wrote for a couple years. I wanted to make sure he was who he said he was. I thought the extra time would show he was serious about me and also prove whether he was a man of his word. So much for that."

He wrote a few lines. "He didn't want you to come to him?"

She shook her head. "No, he said he'd always wanted to see the west. He just needed money for the train fare. I told you before he said he didn't have funds since he'd been paying off bills for his family. I doubt it was true."

The sound of pencil against paper was all that could be heard in the shop. She glanced toward the front window. At least nobody was lining up at the door yet. She could be thankful for that much.

"How much money did he ask you to send?"

She quoted the amount and shifted on her chair. How foolish

she'd been.

Enoch wrote the number down but didn't make any comment about it. "Did he make it clear he wanted to marry you after he arrived?"

"He was anxious to wed as soon as he got here. He asked me to make sure we had suitable housing, and he'd reimburse me once he found a job."

"Did he have something in mind for work before he came here?"

"No. He never did tell me what job experiences he'd had in the past. I'd asked in one of my letters thinking I could inquire around town before he arrived, but he never answered my question. In fact, there were many times I asked him things and he either didn't answer or he was evasive." She twisted her hands in her lap. "I should've noticed the signs."

"As I said before, this isn't your fault. It's his." Enoch's face grew stern. "Don't take on responsibility for his indiscretions. He took advantage of you and your kindness and openness. No man should ever do that."

"Yes, but…"

He reached across and gripped her hand for a second. "Look at me, Gertrude."

Her gaze dragged toward his as tears pooled in her eyes.

Enoch released her hand, and she felt a deeper sense of loss. It made no sense. Had to be all this talk about George.

"He's the one who's in the wrong. No man should ever take advantage of a woman as he did. I realize you still have feelings for the fella, but I say he's not worth another thought. He definitely shouldn't make you believe you're the one in the wrong. Do you hear me?"

Her chin trembled. So why did it feel as though she was the fool? Any other woman would've been able to see through his lies.

"And don't be thinking you're foolish because you didn't see his lies."

Her mouth gaped open. How had he known her thoughts? If George hadn't turned out to be a scoundrel, would he have been able to realize what she was thinking without telling him?

"He's obviously a smooth talker considering he's left a string of women he's taken money from."

As if that made it any better.

"What I'm trying to say is, don't be so hard on yourself. I know it may not seem like it now, but you're better off because you didn't get to go through with the marriage."

She cringed. It would've been awful if she hadn't learned of George's misdeeds until after they were married. At least she could be thankful for that. It wasn't much, but it was something.

"I'm sure your heart will mend in time, and you'll find another fella who's worthy of you." Enoch smiled at her.

Perhaps it was time to make sure he knew where she stood in that regard. "About that. I think it's better if we are only friends."

A confused look passed across his face followed by his cheeks deepening in color.

The front door burst open.

She groaned realizing she'd forgotten to lock it behind them.

"What's this I hear about you having a fiancé who is in jail?" Her mother stood with hands planted on her ample hips. "Why am I the last one hearing about it, and who is this young man?"

5

Gertrude longed for the floor to open and swallow her, providing an escape. She didn't want to deal with her mother's questions, or talk to Enoch about George. She yearned to forget everything about the swindler. She wanted to open her shop, have the community be excited about it, and the ladies in town to see the value of dresses made to order. Was that too much to ask?

Enoch rose to his feet and stood in front of her.

Was he trying to protect her?

"Howdy, ma'am. I'm Enoch Valentine, and I'm afraid you'll have to come back later."

She bit back a giggle. Nobody told her mother what to do. Not even her father. She glanced around him to catch her mother's expression.

Her mother's mouth gaped open and then closed like a fish a couple times. "You have no right to tell me what to do, young man."

"Except I do, ma'am. I'm here on official business."

Oh, no. That would only lead to more questions. But before her mother could say anything else, Enoch stepped forward, hooking her mother's arm through his and leading her to the front door of the shop.

Her mother blustered and swatted Enoch's arm. "I never met such a reprehensible man. You haven't heard the end of this. I'll be sure to make a report to the sheriff."

"Feel free to do that, ma'am." He closed the door behind her mother, locking it.

Mother glared at them from the door window for several minutes. Enoch stared her down and didn't budge from the spot until she stomped off in the direction of the jail.

He turned toward her with a grin. "Sorry about that. Figured it's best if we finished here before you need to open." He glanced at the clock on the wall. "I assume you're opening at eight?"

She nodded.

"If we're blessed, she won't come back for a while. Sheriff Walker won't give her any answers." He crossed the room and settled in his seat. "No guarantee what George will say, though."

"I'm afraid she'll get you in trouble with Josh."

Enoch waggled his eyebrows. "Don't worry about me. It's nothing I can't handle. Now, where were we?"

Should she reemphasize her desire to only be friends? She nibbled her lower lip.

"Ahh, yes. Did George ever say anything else about his background? Where he was from? What experiences he's had?"

"No. He wanted to know about Burrton Springs. How many people live here. Where the closest large city is. What sort of transportation came in and out of town. Where the nearest train station was. I figured he might want to do something that involved shipping of some sort, although he never mentioned anything."

Again, Enoch made notations on his paper. "Can you think of any more information you forgot to mention?"

She considered his question for a moment. "I don't think so." She swallowed. "Would it be helpful to have the letters he sent?"

He ran a hand across his chin. "It might. You sure you're willing to part with them?"

"I have no reason to read through them again." She stood. "If you wait here, I'll get them." She hurried upstairs to her bedroom. One of the guinea pigs sent out a squeak as she passed by the cage. If she got a break during the day, she'd have to see if someone could build them a bigger cage so they had a chance to stretch their little legs.

Scooping the box that held the letters from the table beside her bed, she headed back downstairs. She'd been tempted to shred them to bits when she got home from visiting Ellie Lou yesterday but had refrained. It would be good to be rid of the reminder of him. Lord willing, she'd never see the man again. Good riddance. "Here." She thrust them into Enoch's outstretched hand. At least he wouldn't be reading the personal things she'd written in her letters to George.

Unless they also confiscated them from the man. Maybe George hadn't kept them or brought them along. Best not make mention of it.

"Thanks. Anything else you forgot to share about him?" He took the box of letters and stood.

"I don't think so." She glanced at the clock. Only ten more minutes before the store opened. *Please, Lord, don't let Mother return until after the shop closes for the day. Even longer would be nice. Is it too much to ask for weeks or months?*

"I'll let you know if we need anything else." Enoch pocketed the pencil and paper. "I hope you can put all this behind you now and have a great opening day." He glanced around the shop. "Looks as though you have all manner of things women might like. I'll be praying your business takes off."

"Thank you." Her gaze travelled to the clock again. Just a couple minutes before eight. She could see a few ladies staring in the door window.

Enoch must have seen them too. "Perhaps it's best if I don't leave through the front door. Might cause more gossip. Is there a different way out?"

"Let me show you." She walked toward the back of the shop and made a left turn that led to a small corridor. "If you go to the doorway there, you'll be in the alley."

He placed his Stetson over his dark hair and tipped it. "Have a great day, Gertrude."

"Thank you."

He exited the building.

After locking the alley door, Gertrude hurried back into her shop. Smoothing the front of her bodice, she took a deep breath before lifting the shop window shade and unlocking the door. Gertrude plastered a smile on her face. "Welcome, ladies, to Ruffles and Stitches. Let me know if you have any questions."

The older woman and younger lady she'd seen arrive on the stagecoach smiled and stepped into the shop along with Sarah Brown and Jules Montgomery.

"Never seen a shop with just ladies' clothes." Jules plopped her fists on her expanding waist. "Don't suppose you have somethin' for someone in my condition."

"I have a few garments there against the far wall for women who are increasing." She motioned in the direction.

Jules' eyebrows rose before she let out a chuckle. "Never could figure out why you folks call it increasin' instead of expandin' or spreadin' since it's all my waist has been doin'."

Gertrude smiled. The preacher's wife always had the ability of looking at things in a different way. Perhaps because she'd had limited time in a town or around people much until she'd married Pastor Drew a couple years ago.

Sarah chuckled at her sister-in-law. "I'm sure we can find something pretty for you to wear. Gertrude's a wonder when it comes to creating flattering dresses. Maybe we can purchase something special for you as a belated birthday gift." They headed toward the dresses for women who were expecting.

Gertrude strolled toward the first ladies who'd entered the shop. "Is there anything I can help you with?"

The elderly woman smiled. "I'm browsing today. I'll let you know if I need something."

The younger woman was pulling dresses out one at a time and studying the seams.

Her gut clenched. Had she forgotten to stitch something? And why did her first thoughts go to doubting herself and her abilities when someone inspected her work? Living under her mother's constant disapproval hadn't helped.

"Your designs are rather simplistic. But I suppose living in the middle of nowhere, women don't know about the fine designs from New York and Paris."

"Now, Betty. Mind your manners." The elderly woman smiled. "I'm Mary Scott and this is my niece, Betty Hatler."

"Gertrude Miller." She shook each of their hands. "I believe I saw you both arrive on the stagecoach over the weekend. Are you passing through town or just visiting?"

Miss Hatler continued to peruse each of the garments.

"We've moved here from New York City. Please call me Mary."

"Do you have family here?" Gertrude straightened a pile of

handkerchiefs.

"No. Betty's father, my brother, recently died. Years ago, he passed through this little town and always said how nice it was. Betty and I decided we needed a change. An opportunity to make some new memories."

"I'm so sorry for your loss." Her heart quickened. So many were hurting from recent deaths. Her problems with George seemed small in comparison to them. She must see what she could do to comfort those who were hurting. "I hope you'll enjoy living in Burrton Springs. Please let me know if I can help you learn more about our town. We try and help each other however we can."

Miss Hatler flicked a glance her way. "Do you happen to know of any place available in town?"

Sarah and Jules joined them. "I think I heard the Zeller family were heading west. Perhaps you'd be interested in their farm. Hello, I'm Sarah Brown, and this is my sister-in-law, Jules Montgomery. Her husband, my brother, is the pastor of our church. We'd love for you to join us this coming Sunday."

Miss Hatler wrinkled her nose. "Farm. Ugh. I can't imagine living on such a primitive domicile. Why anyone would do so is beyond me."

Sarah stiffened and Jules frowned. "Since yer new to town, I'll try and be nice. Just so you know, livin' on a farm isn't somethin' bad. Sarah here lives on a farm, and it's right nice."

"I didn't mean any disrespect." Miss Hatler took a tiny step backward and bumped into a display of shirtwaists.

"I'm not goin' to slug you." Jules tipped her ever-present Stetson. "But you should do a better job at bein' nice to folks if you want to make friends here."

"Honestly, Betty. Your father taught you to have better manners than this." Mary shook her head. "You'll have to forgive her. She's been testy from the long trip."

"Long trip or not, don't seem right to have poor manners." Jules glared at the young woman.

Gertrude bit back a smile. She felt the same way but wouldn't have had the gumption to say it. Jules always had to state what was on her mind.

"I'm sure she didn't mean anything by it, Jules." Sarah patted her sister-in-law's arm. "No sense getting upset. Not all people like farm living."

The young woman had the decency to look apologetic. "Forgive me. I didn't mean to put you down in any way. I had no idea you lived on a farm. Please, call me Betty."

"I don't think there's anything available in town for places to reside." Gertrude thought for a moment. "I can let you know if I hear of something."

"We'd appreciate it." Mary smiled. "For the time being we're staying at Mrs. Walsh's. We should've made living arrangements before we arrived, but we both were ready to leave the city."

"*You* were, Aunt Mary. I told you I'd rather stay there." Betty frowned. "I was perfectly happy living with Mildred and her family."

"Nonsense. We don't take advantage of our friends. Besides, your place is with me." Mary pierced her niece with a fierce look.

Betty mumbled but didn't say anything more.

The door to the shop burst open. Beatrice Smith pranced in along with Amelia Evans.

Oh, no. The two had a penchant for spouting the latest gossip. And they'd been in front of the mercantile when the stagecoach arrived.

"Welcome." Gertrude plastered on what she hoped was a smile. "Let me know if you have any questions."

Beatrice giggled and whispered something in Amelia's ear.

Gertrude's eyes flickered shut for a few seconds. *Please, Lord.*

"We don't plan to buy anything. We just wanted to find out if it's true." Beatrice laughed again. "It's taken you years to snag a man, and when you finally do, he ends up in prison. What on earth did you do, that he'd rather be in jail than marry you?"

Amelia grinned. "It's all over town. We even went to the jail to try and see your fiancé, but that new deputy wouldn't let us in."

Thank heavens for Enoch. If only he could thwart all her problems and the gossip surrounding it.

6

Enoch suspected the two young women who'd tried to enter the jail and gawk at George went straight to Gertrude's shop to harass her. It took everything in him to refrain from heading in that direction to protect her. He didn't know what it was about her that caused him to do everything possible to ease her pain in any way he could. Perhaps because he'd witnessed her distress firsthand. He was just being neighborly–nothing more than that. At least he kept trying to tell himself that was why he couldn't stop thinking about her.

"Glad to have the prisoner gone. Appreciate you getting Gertrude's testimony as well as those letters. Maybe between the ones he wrote and the information she gave you, the marshal will be able to piece together more, although it sounds as though there's already a mound of evidence against him." Sheriff Walker stood. "Think you can handle things while I run home to check on my wife?"

"I'd be glad to, Sheriff. Should I stay here or make rounds in town?"

"Call me Josh. Most folks do. Should have told you that before. Guess I've been a bit distracted between the prisoner, and my wife getting close to birthing. Feel free to stroll through town. Might want to check on Gertrude. Best to keep the peace if possible. Most times I try to head off things that look as if they could become more of a potential issue." He lifted his Stetson from a hook near the door. "Wouldn't do to have trouble stirring, especially on the first day of her shop opening. Don't know about you, but sometimes I think female trouble is the hardest to deal with."

Enoch wasn't sure how to respond. He'd never dealt with female disturbances before. "I guess I could mosey over there." Though he'd be hard pressed to handle things if the women got into a tussle. Did women ever do that? Enoch shifted his gun belt and seated his

Stetson. "Anything else I should be aware of?"

"No. Not much usually happens here. The only reason I needed a deputy was because I wanted to train someone to step in for me at a moment's notice, especially with me soon taking over for Doc Adams. If you find you aren't in demand at the Williams's ranch, perhaps you'll consider taking over as sheriff."

"I'm not sure…"

"Think on it. I don't need your answer just yet. I know you haven't been on the job more than a few days, but I think you could be a good fit." Josh opened the door. "Well, I'd best go check on the wife."

Did he even want to be a lawman? Enoch had never considered the profession. Not that it wasn't honorable. He'd just imagined he'd one day have a spread of his own with a couple hundred head of cattle. He'd given up on having a wife and a family, but it would be nice to have a parcel of property to call home. *Is that in Your plans for me, Lord? What about this job?*

No answer came, so he'd keep praying for direction. The Lord would show him in His timing. He'd always been faithful in the past. No reason to think He wouldn't do so now or in the future.

Enoch adjusted his Stetson to keep the sun from his eyes and headed away from Gertrude's shop. Might as well check things on the other end of town first. Wouldn't do to appear too eager to monitor her situation. Course she wouldn't know he was delaying stopping by her shop.

Folks greeted him as he strolled down the street. A stray dog wandered over, wagging his tail. He stooped to pet the animal. Had Gertrude learned to take care of her guinea pigs? He'd have to tell her the critters belonged to her free and clear. There was no evidence George had stolen them from anyone.

Enoch chuckled. He couldn't imagine giving guinea pigs as a wedding gift to his fiancée. Not that he considered himself to know what a woman liked, but he didn't think a critter spoke to a woman's heart. Not that he ever intended to be in a predicament to give such a present.

He puffed out a breath. As soon as the sheriff got back, and he was free to leave for the day, he'd go hunting or riding. Anything to make him stop thinking about females and marriage. It was enough to drive a man to seek somewhere other than his own thoughts.

The church building loomed ahead at the outskirts of town. Enoch walked up the steps and opened the door. In a few weeks the room would be full of school students during the week, but for now it was empty. He slipped into a seat. The quietness of the room helped to calm his spirit.

The door creaked open.

So much for peace and quiet.

"Howdy." A tall man smiled and reached out a hand. "I'm Drew Montgomery. I'm the pastor here. Can I help you?"

He'd seen the fella at his boss's funeral, but they hadn't had a chance to speak. Enoch gripped the preacher's hand for a second. "Name's Enoch Valentine. Hope you don't mind me stopping by."

The pastor eased into a seat across the aisle. "You're always welcome. Were you wanting to talk to me, or were you just needing some time with the Lord?"

"Just enjoying the quiet." He sat back down.

"I won't disturb you then."

"No reason for you to leave. I shouldn't linger since Sheriff Walker wanted me to make rounds."

The man stared at him for a few seconds. "You must be the new deputy Josh hired. He told me he hoped you'd sign on full time. In case you didn't know, he's my brother-in-law."

"Hadn't realized the connection."

"Guess his Annie will be delivering any day. I'm surprised he hasn't hung up his gun long before now. I know she worries something will happen to him." He chuckled. "I reckon that's not the best thing to tell you since you're new to the job."

Enoch smiled. "Far as I can tell, most any job has its own hazards. Although I expect preaching is less troublesome."

"Well, you never can tell. I maybe don't have people shooting at me, but it can be a struggle to corral folks who are prone to gossip." He rubbed his jaw. "Believe me, I'd rather wrangle a wild horse than deal with that."

"You talking from experience?"

The preacher nodded. "Had an issue a time or two. Don't know why women have a tendency toward it. Not that a man can't get caught up with it too, but in my experience it's not often the case."

"Well, I'd best get going on my rounds."

"Are you sure you didn't have something you wanted to talk through?"

The man's hazel eyes had a way of piercing through to a man's soul. Or at least it felt like it. Enoch swallowed. "For now, I'm praying for the Lord's direction in my life."

"Always a great place to start, putting the Lord in charge of the reins. I'll be praying He makes His answers clear for you. Do you mind if I pray for you before you head out?"

A lump lodged in Enoch's throat. He coughed, trying to clear it. "Would be much obliged."

The preacher bowed his head, and Enoch followed suit, swiping off his Stetson.

"Dear God, I thank You for Enoch and his desire to serve and follow You. He's needing Your wisdom when it comes to knowing what You have for him to do. I pray You make the answer evident in Your timing, Lord. Guide, direct, and protect him as he fills in for Josh. Help him to be like King David, a man after Your heart. In Jesus' name, amen."

The lump returned. Enoch nodded his thanks, not trusting his voice. By the time he'd replaced his Stetson, his throat had calmed. He thrust out his hand. "Thank you, Pastor Montgomery. I look forward to seeing you in church on Sunday."

"Feel free to call me Drew." He returned the handshake. "Glad to hear you'll be worshiping with us. Hope you have a blessed day."

"You, too." Enoch exited the building with a lighter heart even though he still had no answer to his prayers. Sometimes knowing someone else was praying helped to ease the burden. He should tell Gertrude he was praying for her too. Puffing out a breath, he headed in the direction of her store.

A small boy with a shock of hair the color of wheat ran up to him, puffing as he tried to catch his breath. "Are you Deputy Valentine?"

He knelt beside the child. "That's me. What do you need?"

The boy sucked in a lungful of air before he answered. "Sheriff Walker asked me to find you. Said somefing about complations. Wanted you to find Doc Adams." He gasped for air again. "Thought he went fishing."

Enoch glanced at the town. "Do you know where the doc usually goes fishing?"

The boy pointed to the other end of town. "There's a stream down that-a-way. Maybe he's there. I would've gone, but my ma don't let me play around the water."

He grinned and patted the boy's head. "It's always best to obey your ma. I'll find him. Can you let Sheriff Walker know you found me?"

The lad nodded and took off without another word.

Enoch jogged toward the jail where Fee was tied up in front of the building. He swung onto his horse and headed in the direction the boy had pointed. It didn't take long to find the meandering stream. He thought he'd seen a glimpse of a waterway behind the church earlier. It must parallel the town. Ahead he could see a place where it widened. If he wasn't mistaken, a horse was standing in a copse of trees. "Come on, Fee." He urged the mare to go faster.

Within a couple minutes he reined his horse to a halt and dismounted, walking to an area where the stream gurgled over rocks. A fella stood in the middle of the creek with a fishing pole.

"You wouldn't happen to be Doc Adams, would you?"

An older gentleman with shaggy eyebrows turned toward him. "I am. Is something wrong?"

"Sounds like Sheriff Walker's wife is fixing to birth. He sent word to me via a boy to find you because there are complications."

The man already was sloshing through the stream, dropping his pole, and hurrying toward his horse. "First babies are usually the hardest."

Enoch didn't know if the man was talking to him or just thinking out loud. He nodded, not sure what else to do.

The elderly doc swung onto his horse with more agility than Enoch figured the man had. "Would appreciate it if you grab my pole.

Might want to find Jules and Gertrude too. They'll want to know."

Before he had a chance to respond, the doctor was gone in a cloud of dust. Enoch strolled over and scooped up the fishing pole, holding onto it as he swung onto Fee.

Lord, I know where to find Gertrude, but I don't know who Jules is. Help me find her. And be with Sheriff Walker's wife. Help Doc to get there in time. Be with whatever problems there may be. Keep the mama and baby safe.

His gut tightened. What would he do if he had a wife struggling in childbirth?

7

It took everything in Gertrude to stay calm. Beatrice and Amelia had continued to barrage her for a good half hour before they finally took their leave. She'd never been so relieved to see someone depart from her presence. The new ladies, Jules and Sarah, hadn't heard the conversation. She could at least be thankful for that.

She glanced around her small shop. Nothing needed her attention. Maybe she should run up to her apartment and check on the guinea pigs. No, first she'd go out the back and get a handful of grass for them. She'd only be gone for a few minutes.

The sun beat down on her as she stooped to snag a bunch of grass growing near the outhouse. She wrinkled her nose at the smell before hurrying back inside. Poking her head around the corner, she didn't see anyone in the shop, so she ran upstairs.

In her apartment, Gertrude picked up the small cage and carried it downstairs. The animals scurried around their tiny enclosure. She'd just entered the shop and was trying to decide where to put them when the bell let out a cheery ring as someone entered the door.

She frowned. What was Enoch doing here again? If he didn't soon stop showing up, people would begin a new rumor about her.

"There you are." He smiled when he saw her. "I wondered when I glanced in the window and didn't see you in the shop. Doc Adams asked me to let you know Sheriff Walker's wife is getting ready to bring a little one into the world and is having a rough time of it. He said you'd want to know as well as someone named Jules. Do you know how to find her?"

"Oh my. Annie." She set the cage down on the counter, shoving the grass through the small wooden bars. "Jules mentioned going to the general store. You should be able to find her there." She bit her lip, torn between her friend and her first day in her own shop. *If only it weren't opening day. Annie would come for me if I needed her on such an important occasion.*

"I reckon I could watch the shop for a short while."

"You can?" Gertrude stared at him, processing her thoughts. "If you wouldn't mind. I can find Jules, so we both can go to Annie." She hesitated. Would people talk about Enoch watching the shop? She shook her head. It didn't matter. If Annie needed help, she wanted to be there. Besides, she might be able to be of some assistance to the doc.

"Just tell me the prices of things, and I'll keep a tally of what I sell." Enoch glanced around the shop, a flush staining his high cheekbones.

"There's a list on the counter there with all the prices. If you aren't sure of what something is, you can always ask the customer." Gertrude reached for her bonnet and reticule on a shelf beneath the table. She secured the hat, tying the ribbons under her chin. "I hope I won't be overlong."

"I'm sure I can manage." His words contradicted the expression on his face.

"Are you positive you don't mind?" She hesitated. "I can go tell Jules and come right back."

He shook his head. "No. Go be with your friend. I reckon she'd appreciate your being there."

"As long as you don't think you'll be in over your head…" She paused, her hand on the door latch.

"As I said, I'll be fine."

~*~

Enoch was in over his head. Females lined every area of the shop wanting to know where different article of clothes were that he'd never heard of. He stared at the clock on the wall. Surely the thing wasn't working. Had Gertrude only been gone for twenty minutes? Was it too much to hope for her to return soon? To wish that her friend had already delivered the baby. Then Gertrude would get back to her business.

With a sigh he studied the handwritten signs she'd posted all around the store. Why had she only posted prices and not what the items were? He didn't know who was more embarrassed – the women who weren't happy about having a man interfering in their domain, or his having to ask them what they were buying or searching for.

He scrubbed a hand across his jaw. "What were you hunting?"

The red-haired woman's cheeks flushed the same color as her hair. "I…uh…that is…er…never mind." She headed towards the door.

He had to stop her. Gertrude needed all the support and sales from the community she could garner. He bolted in front of her and threw his arms wide. "Hold up there."

Her eyes widened, and she flinched.

Great. Now she probably feared he'd hit her or something stupid. Too bad she wasn't a mare. At least he'd know how to calm her then. Probably was best if he didn't pat her head. He bit back a chuckle. She likely wouldn't respond well to it. "I'm sure if you browse, you'll find whatever it is you're searching for. Miss Miller was called away unexpectedly since her friend's er…struggling with the birthing. Ger…Miss Miller has such a big heart. When she found out, she wanted to go to her friend but with being opening day, she was torn. I knew how much it meant to her, so I offered to fill in for just a short time. I bet you can find whatever it is you need. If not, we can write up an order for you and the specifics, so Miss Miller can take care of it when she returns. Also, if there's a special fabric you're interested in..." He motioned to the bolts of material. "She sure has a mess of them you can choose from." He didn't think he'd ever strung so many words together in one sitting. At least not to a stranger, let alone a female.

The young woman peered back at the shop instead of the door.

He was making progress. "There's got to be something here that'll please you." He reached for a pile of clothing beside him and held it up. "What about this?"

She turned pale.

He glanced at the item and felt the heat rise in his face. He dropped the set of bloomers as if he'd picked up the hot end of a branding iron.

The woman fled to the door, and this time he didn't stop her.

He couldn't help but study the clock again. Two more minutes had passed. Why did it feel like an hour? He moved on to the gaggle of women eyeing him and whispering behind their hands. What made them do something like that? If they had something to say, why didn't they just share it like a fella would? It took everything in him to hold back a groan. He plastered on what he hoped was a smile and headed in their direction. "Howdy. Something I can help you with?"

A blonde smiled at him, batting her eyes as if she'd gotten dirt in them. "I thought Gertrude was the owner. You must be her fiancé. Glad to see you managed to be released from jail."

No doubt she was fishing for information. "I wasn't in jail. I'm a deputy. Gertrude is the owner, but she had to step away for a while. Can I assist you?" Best to keep things simple.

"I don't believe I caught your name." She kept opening and closing her eyes. If she kept it up, he wondered how much she could see with all the fluttering.

"That's because I didn't give it." Maybe not the best way to get the woman interested in the shop. "If you need me, I'll be behind the counter." He scurried away before she could ask him another question. Two boys were pressed up against the long table snickering and shoving each other. He'd almost reached them when an older woman snagged his arm.

"Young man, where is Gertrude? I wanted to see if she had finished making the periwinkle bonnet and polonaise I had requested for my upcoming dinner party." She waved a handkerchief back and forth.

"Peri-what?" He scratched his head.

The woman rolled her eyes. "Honestly. Whatever was Gertrude thinking to hire a man as a worker in a woman's shop?"

"No, ma'am. I'm filling in, she didn't hire me."

"Well, thank goodness for that." She crossed her hefty arms. "Do you know anything about the order or not?"

"I don't ma'am, but if you describe it better, I'll know what to look for."

She sighed. "Maybe I should come back later or take my business somewhere else."

These women sure were fickle.

"Hold your britches." Oops. Probably not the best thing to say.

The women's lips pursed as though they'd been stitched together.

"That is…I can check the back room and see what I can find." He headed toward the back of the store, not sure if there was such a thing, but at least it would give him a few minutes of reprieve. He darted up the steps, hoping Gertrude had additional storage up there. If anything, it would get him away from the onslaught of women. He pushed open the door at the top of the stairs. A small sitting room was all he saw. He continued forward poking his head in each room. With each glance he realized instead of a storage room, he'd found Gertrude's apartment. Heat flared as he scurried back down the stairs. Maybe there was something in the short hallway she'd showed him earlier when he'd wanted to escape and avoid going out the front door. The idea of fleeing was a temptation for sure. No. He couldn't do that to Gertrude.

It didn't take long to discover no other doorways in the hall. He squared his shoulders and went back into the lion's den. He stayed at the back of the shop, trying to see if there were any hiding spots…or places where she might have placed items ordered and ready for pick up. There was a small curtained off area but nothing inside it. He still had no idea what he was looking for. The woman never had explained what the things were.

His gaze settled on the counter in the middle of the store where now a gaggle of boys were gathered around. One thing he knew, when there were that many boys in one area, it likely spelled trouble. He started towards them when the elderly woman barreled his way again.

"Well, did you find it?"

"If you'll just give me a minute." He edged away.

"Young man, will you help me or not?"

Her words caused him to pause. It wouldn't do to chase off

another woman from Gertrude's shop.

The boys snickered and jabbed each other. Maybe they would behave for another minute or two.

He forced himself to stay. "Tell me again. What am I searching for?"

She puffed out a breath. "A per-i-winkle bon-net. You do know what that is, right?"

"Some sort of hat?"

She shook her head. Those lips pressed together again. "A purple hat and a matching polo—jacket since I doubt you know what a polonaise is."

"Yes, ma'am, I mean, no, ma'am."

"Miss Miller said she would have it ready for me today."

"Don't you worry, I'm sure I can find it." *Please, Lord.*

A woman's scream pierced his ears. He turned to see the boys scrambling to leave the shop. One woman jumped onto a chair, lifting her skirts, showing her boots. Another started to sway. He bolted toward her, catching her before she fell. The older woman snagged a broom and started running across the room chasing he didn't know what. Unsure what to do, he eased the woman in his arms to the floor of the shop and headed toward the broom wielding lady. As he scurried past the counter, he saw the open cage that once held Gertrude's guinea pigs. They were nowhere to be seen.

8

Absolute pandemonium greeted Gertrude no less than forty minutes after she'd left Enoch in charge of her dress shop. A group of children barreled past her. Something furry ran along the edge of the floorboard. Mrs. Montgomery chased after it with a boom, and Enoch pursued the pastor's mother. Was that a guinea pig? Sally Russell lay sprawled on the floor like a sack of potatoes. Several other ladies were shrieking and hiking their skirts above their boots. Another stood on a chair. No wonder God had prompted her to return.

Enoch stooped and picked up something. When he caught sight of her, he headed in her direction. He plopped something furry into her hand.

"Here, hold this while I try and save the other one before she gets to it." He didn't wait for her to respond.

Her fingers curled around the guinea pig, drawing it close to her chest. His or her eyes looked as scared as she felt holding it. Its tiny heart beat wildly against her hand. "Shh." She rubbed it between the eyes, and it thrust his head against her finger as if asking her to pet him again. She stroked him once more. "Don't you worry. We'll get your sibling caught."

"Ma'am, put down the broom before you hurt it or yourself." Enoch's firm voice carried from the back of the store.

He'd met his match with the older woman. Gertrude bit back a smile. She'd best do what she could to help get the situation in hand. Crossing to the counter, she found the upended small wooden cage and turned it upright. Before placing the guinea pig inside, she snuggled it close and whispered in its floppy ear, "You be good." She secured him in the tiny enclosure and turned towards Enoch.

He grabbed the broom as Mrs. Montgomery raised it above her head as if to take aim at something.

"No!" She rushed to them. *Please let it be unharmed, Lord.*

Enoch bent down and scooped up the small animal.

"Is it hurt?" She held her breath afraid of what his response would be.

He cradled it in his big hands. It wasn't moving.

"Why did you stop me?" Mrs. Montgomery planted her fists on her wide hips. "I cannot believe you would allow rats to roam free in here, Gertrude." She sniffed. "Maybe I do not want my order after all."

"But…"

"Now see here, there's no call to be mean to Miss Miller." He glared at the older woman. "And you're wrong, they aren't rats. She'd never have something like rodents in this fine establishment. They're guinea pigs. A rare and special animal."

"Looks like a rat to me," the woman muttered under her breath.

"You're mistaken." He rubbed the furry creature.

It shuddered but appeared to be alive.

"Is it…" Gertrude couldn't finish the question.

He held it up for closer inspection.

Her chest constricted.

His shoulders relaxed. "Looks as if it's fine. Scared almost to death I'm sure, but she's still breathing."

"She?"

He shrugged. "Don't know which it is, but I figured it must be a gal to have stamina like its owner." His gaze held hers for a second.

Her pulse stuttered. What would he say if he knew she didn't have as much gumption as he thought she had?

"How's your friend doing?"

Friend? She glanced at the guinea pig in his hands.

"The one you went to check on?" A slow grin spread across his handsome face.

Mercy. How did one look from him cause her to lose the ability to keep track of a single thought in her brain?

"If you two are finished mooning over each other, I suppose I might as well pick up my order since I already paid for it." Mrs. Montgomery pushed in between them. "Put that oversized mouse outside where hopefully something will eat it, and we can put this nonsense behind us."

Enoch frowned at her. "There will be no putting it outside." He strolled over to the cage and placed the guinea pig beside its mate. "I best get on my way before I do any more damage to your store."

"Good riddance." The older woman harumphed and turned her back on him.

"Thank you." Gertrude watched as he headed out, feeling a sense of loss as he closed the door behind him.

"I do not know why you would have those filthy animals in here." Mrs. Montgomery glared at the cage. "I will think twice about making an order from you again."

"If you give me a moment…" She didn't wait for the woman to respond; instead she went to where Sally stirred. "Here, let me help you up." She stooped and assisted the young woman. "Can I get you a glass of water?"

Her brown eyes opened and closed a few times before she stood, smoothing her skirt. "No, I think I'll be fine. What was that thing?"

"A guinea pig."

"A pig?"

Gertrude chuckled. "No. A guinea pig. They're small and furry."

The woman shuddered. "Is it gone?"

She motioned toward the cage. "They won't hurt you. Would you like to browse while I assist Mrs. Montgomery?"

She nodded and headed toward some of the dresses Gertrude had hanging along the edge of the shop.

Gertrude went toward the huddle of women who were whispering to each other. "Please let me know if you need anything." She noticed the woman who had been on the chair was now standing with the other ladies.

Mrs. Montgomery cleared her throat.

She crossed to the counter and searched underneath for the elderly woman's items. She pulled out the paper wrapped bundle and handed it to her. "I hope this meets your expectations."

"I will be sure to let you know if it does not." She took the package and left without another word.

Gertrude sighed. *Somehow this isn't how I envisioned my first day to go, Lord. Could You be with Annie? I know Jules said she'd let me know when Annie finally delivers, but it's hard not being there.* She blew out a breath. "Too bad I can't be two places at once."

The rest of the day passed by slowly. She made a few sales although not as many as she'd hoped. Maybe it would take time for word to spread she was finally open for business. Who was she kidding? She lived in a small community. People always knew what was happening, most times within minutes after an occurrence. Maybe opening a shop of her own wasn't as good of an idea as she thought it would be.

~*~

Enoch stayed away from Gertrude and her shop for the rest of the week. Josh Walker had sent word his wife had delivered a little girl but because Annie was still weak from the birthing, the sheriff put Enoch in charge until he decided to come back. With not knowing when that would be, Enoch made a point to make hourly rounds in town throughout the daylight hours to make sure things stayed calm. As soon as dusk settled each day, he wearily climbed in the saddle and headed to the Williams's ranch.

Jim kept him abreast of what was happening with the mares. The ranch hand had found another broken spot in the fencing about midweek, although he couldn't say for sure whether it had been cut.

With the long hours in Burrton Springs, Enoch hadn't had a chance to ask Mrs. Williams about it since there usually wasn't light in the main house by the time he returned home, and he left before the sun came up each day.

On Saturday morning, he yawned and stretched as he pulled on his worn boots. Somehow working as temporary sheriff was more exhausting than working a full day at the ranch.

"You heading out?" Jim's voice came from the bunk on the opposite side of the barn loft.

"In a few minutes. Sorry, didn't mean to wake you."

"You didn't. Figured I'd get up early to ride the fence line again."

The bed creaked as Jim shifted on it. "Know what time you'll be back later? The missus has been worried. Thought maybe you could ease her fears."

"She still thinks someone is after the mares?" As he sat up and slipped on his boots, Enoch could barely make out Jim's form in the other bunk.

"She hasn't come outright and said as such, but I can tell she's worried about something. Whether it's the break in the fence or something else, I'm not sure. Thought maybe she'd tell you." Jim arched his back as he stood. "Think you could make it home earlier tonight?"

"I'll see what I can do, barring there's no trouble in town today. You think she's upset I've been gone so much?"

"No. She knows you're trying to help out and realizes there isn't much work for the two of us." Jim was quiet for a minute. "I almost think she's ready to let one of us go."

His gut clenched. He hadn't thought things were that bad. Maybe this was God's way of showing him the answer to his prayer about the deputy job, make that sheriff position. Only problem, he'd have to find a new place to live. He wasn't sure how he felt about that. No use worrying about it until he had a chance to talk to Mrs. Williams.

"I can be the one to leave if it comes to that." Jim's voice broke through his thoughts.

"No use deciding anything until she says something to either of us. Didn't get a chance to tell you the sheriff offered me his position if I want it." Might as well get it out in the open.

"You planning on accepting?" Jim snapped his suspenders in place.

"Been praying about it. Not sure yet." With a flick of his wrist, the light blanket fell into some semblance of order on his bunk. "Well, I'd best be on my way." The loft had lightened enough for him to see Jim lift a hand in farewell.

Within a few minutes, he saddled Fee and swung onto his horse. He dipped his head as he rode from the barn and headed towards Burrton Springs. He was halfway to town before the sky was ablaze with pinks and purples. Soon after the sun broke over the horizon.

The day promised to be another scorcher.

He hadn't even made it to the jail before a rider was pressing his horse hard, headed in his direction. Enoch pulled Fee to a halt.

"You Deputy Valentine?"

He nodded. "You need something?"

"Better come quick. There's a brawl at the saloon." The fella didn't wait for his response but instead headed back in the direction from which he'd come.

Enoch reined Fee towards the building on the outskirts of town. He didn't know why towns almost always had a saloon. In his experience, they meant trouble. The sound of glass shattering greeted his ears before he even had a chance to swing down from his horse. Swearing rent the morning air. He tied Fee to the hitching post out front and hurried inside.

Three men brawled in the middle of the room. One picked up a bottle, crashing it down on another's head.

"Stop!" He rushed forward into the middle of the ruckus, grabbing one man by the collar. "That's enough."

"You leave my brother alone."

He ducked as the second man swung at him.

The third man lay on the floor sporting a bloody lip and a lump from where the glass had hit him. "Best to stay out of this, fella."

Enoch shoved the man he'd collared into a chair. "Stay there." He'd no sooner turned away when the second guy charged him. The air rushed from his lungs as the man slammed his mid-section, knocking him to the floor.

"Told you to leave my brother alone." The man glared at him, his nostrils flaring.

The man on the floor beside him swiped his lip and sat up. "As I said, it's best not to mess with the Williams brothers."

"Only problem is, I'm the acting sheriff." He groaned as he stood.

Light and pain exploded in his head as something hard crashed into his skull.

9

Gertrude hadn't been able to sleep. Before the sun rose, she'd pulled on her clothes and headed outside. She'd hoped a brisk walk before it became too hot would help to clear her mind. It had done just the opposite. The sun had risen by the time she made it back to town.

Commotion at the saloon caught her attention as she passed the building. She lifted her skirt an inch so the heel of her boots wouldn't get caught in the hem of her dress as she hurried. She'd almost made it past when a man ran outside.

"Hey. You there, ma'am. Quick, go get the doc."

She glanced around but didn't see anyone else on the street at the early hour. "M-me?"

"Yes'm. The lawman's knocked out cold and has a big knot on his head. Can you run and get the doc? I'd go, but I need to keep an eye on things. No telling what the Williams brothers will do if I step away."

Enoch? Her chest constricted. Surely it wasn't Josh since Annie had said he planned to be with her for the first couple weeks.

"Ma'am?"

"Sorry. I'll find him." She didn't wait for his response, but moved briskly in the direction of Doc Adams's home.

Her breath came in short bursts by the time she reached the small clapboard building. A note was pinned to his front door stating he'd be gone for a few days and if medical attention was needed, to seek out Joshua Walker. With a groan, she headed in the opposite direction where Josh and Annie lived in a small house. The gate of the white picket fence creaked as she opened it and rushed to the front door. She gave a quick rap, hoping she wouldn't wake the baby.

The door opened. Annie Walker stood in her nightgown, her

brown hair slipping from her long braid. Little Eve was nestled in her mother's arms, her lip quivering.

"I'm sorry, Annie. I didn't mean to wake you."

"You didn't. Eve did." Her friend settled the baby on her shoulder, patting the tiny back. "Come in."

"I can't. Is Josh here? Doc's gone away for a few days, and I think Enoch got injured at the saloon."

"Enoch?" Her friend's blue eyes widened behind her spectacles.

The door opened farther. "Something happened to Enoch?" Josh slipped his suspenders over his shoulders.

She nodded. "I think so. The man said something about him being knocked out and the Williams brothers."

Josh strapped his gun belt in place and picked up a medical bag. He kissed Annie's brow and the cheek of his daughter. "I'll be back as soon as I can."

"Did you want to stay, Gertrude?" Annie yawned.

"No. Looks as if you could use some more rest." Gertrude smiled. "I'll check on you and Eve later."

Josh had saddled his horse by the time she'd said her goodbyes. He tipped his Stetson at her as he rode past.

Dear Lord, be with Enoch. Help him to not be seriously injured. He continued to be in her thoughts and prayers as she walked back through town. As she passed by the saloon, a gaggle of folks were standing just outside the swinging doors. Most of them were men, but a few women were in their midst. She bit her lip as she tried to decide what to do.

Melissa Evans motioned her over. "Did you hear the man who works in your shop was in a brawl?" Her brow furrowed. "You might want to think twice about keeping him on."

She couldn't imagine Enoch had been involved in a brawl. But then again, how much did she know about the man? Just because he'd helped her a time or two didn't mean he was a man who could be trusted. For all she knew, he was a scoundrel like George. Maybe he'd only assisted her and had been kind because he was running his own swindling endeavor. After all, why was he even in the saloon in the first place?

"He isn't my employee. He's the new deputy." Had Josh researched the man's reputation before he'd hired him?

Melissa's lips flattened. "Can't imagine why the deputy was in the saloon so early in the morning. I wonder if Sheriff Walker knows the man has a drinking problem."

"What makes you think that?" Her gut tightened.

The young woman motioned to some of the men. "That's what they said. He was drinking with the Williams brothers. You know how nasty they can be. Figured you'd want to know since he was in your shop. Wouldn't want folks to think you're associated with him. Can't imagine how it will affect your sales if word gets out."

Her sales were already slower than she'd like.

"You make poor choices when it comes to men, don't you?" Melissa patted Gertrude's shoulder. "If I were you, I'd stay away from fellas for a while."

Her reputation was already tarnished because of George. Last thing she needed was for more rumors to spread about her and Enoch, especially if he *was* a drinking man.

Melissa was also known for spreading gossip around town, like her younger sister Amelia. Best to squelch the association with Enoch before the woman decided to spread her latest news.

"I don't have any plans to be involved with any man. En…Mr. Valentine only helped me when I checked on Annie when she was travailing with little Eve. He isn't a friend, just someone new to town who helped me for a short time. There's nothing between us."

Melissa's face pinched. "That's not what I heard."

Heat rose in her cheeks. "Then you heard wrong. Now, if you'll excuse me, I'd best get to my shop." She hesitated for a few seconds. "I'd appreciate it if you don't connect my name with Mr. Valentine. After all, we're not even friends."

The woman's brows rose.

She didn't wait for Melissa's response but headed in the direction of her shop. A weight dogged her steps. Why did Gertrude feel as if she'd betrayed a friend?

~*~

Enoch's head throbbed with each beat of his heart.

"How many fingers am I holding up?"

The voice dragged him from the pain, pushing him to try and think past the drum beating in his skull.

"Enoch? Open your eyes."

He'd heard the voice before. He cracked one eye. The light felt like an arrow. The room swam around him. He closed his eyes, praying the pain would subside.

"Enoch Valentine."

He groaned. Why couldn't the fella leave him in peace? He flopped a hand across his eyes, trying to block the light filtering through his eyelids.

Hands probed his temple. He winced and pulled away.

"Come on, Enoch. Stay with me."

Was he going somewhere? Maybe he'd wake up soon, and it was all a bad dream. Nightmare was more like it.

Someone dragged his hand away from his eyes, lifting his eyelids. He growled. "Have pity on a man, will you?"

"Sorry. Can't do that. I need you to open your eyes, Enoch."

He should know the man's voice, but he couldn't for the life of him remember who it belonged to. Didn't care to recall it. All he wanted to do was sleep. "Leave me be."

The fella persisted, poking, and prodding his limbs. "You don't seem to have broken anything. That's good."

He should care that he didn't have anything broken, but right now all he wanted was for the guy to stop his harassment and move on to something else.

"We need to sit you up."

He heard movement but didn't care to see what was happening around him. Next he knew, he was sitting on something hard. The movement caused another spear of pain in his head. He groaned and tried again to open his eyes. The sun streamed through a dirty window.

"That's it. Keep your eyes open."

"Josh? What're you doing here? Where am I?" He rubbed the back of his neck, trying to ease the tension in his neck and head.

"What happened?"

"Let's get you in a chair so I can check you over better." Josh motioned to a couple men who helped Enoch to a wooden chair.

He glanced around the room. A long counter lined one wall. A series of tables and chairs filled the rest of the area. The smell of alcohol lingered in the air. A saloon? He didn't remember coming in here. He'd promised his ma he'd never darken the door of such an establishment. How had he gotten in here? Why couldn't he remember?

"You've got a goose egg on your noggin." Josh's fingers explored the area.

A moan slipped out of his lips before he could halt it.

"Sorry. I'm sure it hurts. What do you remember?" Josh stooped in front of him. He put a finger in front of his face. "Follow my finger with your eyes."

He did his best to obey not knowing if he was doing a good job of it or not. "Not sure. I recall coming to town." Was that earlier today or days ago? It all jumbled in his mind.

A fella stepped into his line of vision. "You need to do something about those Williams brothers, Sheriff."

"What did they do this time?" Josh pulled something out of his bag and placed it around his neck.

The small man motioned to Enoch. "Knocked him out cold for one. They turned on another fella too. Not sure who he was. Never saw him before. Them brothers said something to him about him not following through with what he promised. Then this young man came in trying to break up their fighting, and George brought a chair down on his head. I tried to stop the fight, but you know how they get when they've been drinking."

Josh put the instrument in his ear and held it to Enoch's chest. He couldn't recall what the thing was called. He'd seen a doctor use one before, but he couldn't remember where or when.

Did his heart sound as loud to Josh as it did to him?

The sheriff's fingers held Enoch's wrist for a few minutes.

"Your pulse and heart are strong." He nodded his approval and then put the instrument back in his leather bag. "You still don't remember what happened?"

He shook his head, regretting the motion.

"Let's get you to your feet."

Enoch stood and the room started spinning.

"Whoa, there. Not so fast." Josh eased him back into the chair. "I think you'd best come to my place so I can keep an eye on you."

"No need. Give me a minute, and I'll be fine. Besides, I reckon I should go after the Williams brothers." That was his job, wasn't it?

Josh shook his head. "Not today you're not. I'll pay a visit on them later. First, we need to get you where you can rest for a bit."

"If you help me to the jail, I can rest there." Did he have a bed there? Why couldn't he remember? One thing he knew, he didn't like having to ask someone to help, but he didn't think he could get there on his own.

"No. You're coming with me. Jeb, give me a hand here." Josh directed the short man. "You get his left arm. We'll get him to my horse."

The world swam as the two other men lifted Enoch and maneuvered him out of the building. He groaned as they shoved him onto the horse as if he was a sack of potatoes.

"Sorry, buddy. Don't know if you'll stay upright in the saddle. You'll be better off this way since it's only a short distance." Josh said from somewhere beside him. "Just hang on until we get to my place."

The next minutes were a blur. Soon he was being dragged off the horse and eased to the ground. Strong arms supported his shoulders as Josh helped him stand beside the horse.

"How're you feeling? You aren't feeling sick to your stomach, are you?"

Josh's words caused Enoch's gut to lurch in his throat. It took all his will power to keep from upchucking on the man.

"You've gone all pale."

Enoch didn't need to be told that. He could feel his strength waning. Reaching out to grasp the reins, he missed, and his body sank to the ground.

10

Gertrude had watched from her shop window and glimpsed Enoch getting thrown over Josh's horse and being led down the street. Where they went, she didn't know. Her earlier words disowning her connection to Enoch rose to haunt her thoughts. She paced in front of her window. Peace was elusive. Was he alive? He hadn't moved a muscle from what she could tell.

Lord, I don't know why You brought Enoch, make that Mr. Valentine, into my life when You did. I have no intention of getting close to the man…but I don't want to see him hurt either. Just like I wouldn't want to see anyone hurt. She paced some more. *Help him to be unharmed. Make him give up drinking and turn to You.*

Her prayer was cut short as the front door opened followed by the dinging of the bell above it. She turned and pasted a smile on her face. Her tension eased when she spotted Ellie Lou Williams. "Good morning. How can I help you today? Are you looking for something in particular?"

Her friend pulled her into a hug. "I wanted to see you and your shop. How has your first week been?" She glanced around. "It's quite charming. I love all the attention to detail you've put into it." She fingered a stack of chemises. "You do such lovely work, Gertrude. Anyone would be blessed to wear something you've made."

Warmth spread through Gertrude, heating her cheeks. "Thank you. I don't know that the rest of the town shares your sentiments, but I appreciate your support."

"I take it things haven't been selling as well as you'd like?"

She shook her head.

Ellie Lou reached over and squeezed her hand. "I'm sure things will get better."

Tears welled in her eyes. She blinked to keep them from falling.

"Want to tell me about it?"

She shrugged. "There's not a lot to say. Business has been slow..."

"Perhaps it will take time for women to see the need for pre-made things."

"It's just that the dresses and other items I'd made were selling so well at the general store. I thought for sure a shop exclusively selling my handiwork would be valued by the ladies. And the rest of the community since I also made some items for men too."

Ellie Lou glanced around the store. "Looks like most of your items are geared for women. You might want to have a mix of both types of clothes here."

Why hadn't she thought of it? She bit her lip. "Do you really think men and women would like to shop for clothes in the same store together?"

Her friend didn't answer right away. "It might take a bit for it to catch on, but I believe if this is what God has for you, He'll allow you to do well with your new endeavor. I assume you've prayed about it and have sought His direction in your life."

She had but maybe not as much as she should've. "Yes, but..." Would God not honor her prayers because she'd been negligent?

"Sometimes when I go before God and rush ahead of Him, I find myself ill at ease. Peace and I seem to be distant from each other. I become anxious, fearful." Ellie Lou strolled to the back of the store and sat on a chair.

Gertrude followed her and perched on the edge of one of the seats. "What do you do when that happens? How do you stop from being anxious, or fearful? How do you find peace again?"

Ellie Lou smiled. "I don't think there's a foolproof plan that works every time I encounter a stressful situation or times I rush before God's timing. My mother used to say we're the ones who lose our peace. We choose to lay it down. We give it up. We abandon peace and choose to worry. I especially struggled with this after my Charles died." She flicked away a tear. "It was so easy to worry about my future. What would happen to me, to the ranch. There are so many things that can consume us and cause us to worry, to be afraid."

Gertrude leaned forward in her chair. "What did you do to stop those feelings? How are you able to stop worrying?"

"Well, I haven't completely figured that out, but I'm learning to take things to God when I start to fear or become apprehensive." She opened her reticule and withdrew a piece of paper. "I wrote this verse down to remind me when I have moments when uncertainties feel as if they might sweep me away."

"What is it?"

"It's from the Gospel of John. Chapter fourteen and verse twenty-seven. 'Peace I leave with you, my peace I give unto you: not as the world giveth, give I unto you. Let not your heart be troubled, neither let it be afraid.'" She pointed to the words as she read them.

"But it doesn't say how to not be afraid or troubled."

"Oh, but it does. Jesus promised us His peace. So, when I'm feeling distraught, I tell the Lord. I say, 'I'm not feeling Your peace right now. But I know Your Word promises it to me because of Your Son. Because of that, I'm asking You to help my heart not to be troubled. Help me not to be afraid. I choose to trust You in this situation. Even when I can't find hope in it, I know hope can be found in You.' I'm also reminded what it says in Second Corinthians about 'bringing into captivity every thought to the obedience of Christ.' Not an easy task, but I'm working at trying to do so."

Gertrude pondered her friend's words. "You've given me much to think about. Pray about too."

Ellie Lou smiled and patted her hand again. "Just remember if you've lost your peace, it's because you've surrendered it."

She refrained from squirming in her seat. Was it true? Was she not at ease because she'd chosen to surrender her peace and give in to fear? *Dear God, please forgive me for my words to Melissa concerning Enoch. He's been nothing but kind to me. Help me to truly be a friend to him. I pray I have the chance and that nothing has happened to him.* A tear welled in the corner of her eye as she recalled him slung over Josh's saddle.

~*~

Enoch groaned as Josh brought the lantern close to check his eyes again. "Have pity on a man, won't you? You keep it up, and I'll go blind." He wasn't sure how much time had passed since the sheriff had brought him to his home. Enoch felt bad intruding on the little family.

Josh chuckled. "I'm guessing you're starting to feel some better since you're getting ornerier each time I check on you."

Annie jiggled the newborn, trying to calm the child's cries.

He winced at the sound.

"Sorry," she murmured. She opened the door leading to what he guessed was their bedroom. A brass bed could be seen covered with a colorful quilt. She closed the door behind her.

He sighed. "Please tell her I'm sorry."

Josh took his pulse and checked his heartbeat before the sheriff started probing the lump on Enoch's head. "I know sound can really bother you when you have a headache, especially from a head injury such as yours. Annie understands. It's why she took little Eve in the bedroom. That and…" He didn't continue, his cheeks flushing.

He was about to ask what had the lawman embarrassed until he thought about what the young mother was likely doing. Enoch cleared his throat. "You think I can leave anytime soon? I'm sure you and the missus would like me gone." He glanced out the window where the sun was creeping closer to the horizon. If he didn't leave soon, he'd be riding home in the dark again.

A knock came from the front door.

"Wonder who that could be." Josh set the stethoscope back in his leather bag and crossed the room to open it.

As he swung the door wide, Enoch glimpsed a flowery skirt.

"Gertrude. Come in. Annie will be happy to see you."

Enoch didn't think he ever saw her looking more pretty than she did standing there, color flooding her cheeks. A few strands of hair had slipped loose from the tight knot at the back of her neck, making her face look softer somehow.

"Enoch. Oh, thank goodness. I've been trying to find you. I was so worried when I saw you on Josh's horse earlier this morning." She ran her hand along the skirt of her dress. "I would've come sooner but

I was tied up with the store and when I closed for the day, I couldn't find anyone who knew what had happened to you."

"I carted him here after he was knocked out cold." Josh motioned her to a chair. "Have a seat. Annie will be finished in a few minutes. I'm sure she'll want to see you."

"Someone said you'd been drinking..." Her chin dipped to her chest. "That is..."

He rubbed the back of his neck. What else had she heard about him?

"Gertrude, you know better than to believe what you hear in town." Josh held the chair for her.

Her cheeks flushed even darker. "They mentioned the Williams brothers. Is that part true?"

"Best if we start at the beginning." Enoch cleared his throat. "Apparently, I was called to the saloon because there was a brawl. I don't recall a lot of it. Seems I got caught in the middle of it." He indicated his temple where he knew from seeing in a mirror earlier that a nice-sized goose egg bulged.

The color drained from her face. "I'm so sorry. I should've never listened to... Never mind about that. I'm sorry you were injured, Enoch. Is there anything I can do for you? Did you want me to ride to the ranch and let Ellie Lou know you won't be home tonight?"

He glanced at Josh. "I'll be leaving as soon as he sets me free. Besides, I don't want you having to go all that way in the dark. It's not safe."

Her brow wrinkled. "Not safe? Since when? I haven't heard of any trouble. Is there something you're not telling me?" Her gaze flickered between him and Josh. "If there is, I want to know about it."

"Let's just say it's part of an ongoing investigation." Josh brought over a platter of biscuits. "Help yourself."

He and Josh had spoken earlier about the Williams brothers, how to handle them, and he'd also brought up the troubles with the fencing at the ranch. More than likely the two weren't related, but for now they'd agreed it was best to keep things between them until they could do some more fact-finding. Wouldn't do to get folks upset or worrying over potentially nothing.

She glanced back and forth, studying them both. "Why do I get the feeling there's a lot neither of you are saying?"

The bedroom door creaked open, saving him from having to say anything else. Not that he wanted to keep something from her, but he'd promised Josh to keep the matter close to his chest for now.

Gertrude stood and crossed to Annie and the baby. "May I hold her?"

Tiredness sagged the young mother's shoulders.

Enoch needed to get out of here and give the little lady a break instead of making extra work for her by preparing meals for him. He stood. "I should be on my way."

"Didn't release you yet." The sheriff crossed his arms. "Sit."

He was tempted to push out his lip like a contrary child but figured it wouldn't help him leave any sooner. The man was as stubborn as a prickly pear cactus stuck in his hide.

Annie handed the baby to Gertrude.

Gertrude settled the child in her arms, smiling and cooing to it. She'd make a great mother. Too bad the scoundrel had demolished her chances of settling down and having a passel of children. He'd have to see what he could do to find a husband for her.

11

Gertrude breathed in the newborn scent of little Eve. Her chest constricted. Would she ever have a child of her own to nestle in her arms? She hadn't allowed herself to think or hope about having a family when she'd thought to marry George. He'd told her in a letter he couldn't have children. She'd assumed some injury, but he'd never indicated what that might be. But holding the baby did strange things to her heart. Her gaze flickered to Enoch. His eyes locked with hers. Heat sprang to her cheeks, and she glanced away. What was he thinking?

She shifted the infant in her arms, running her finger along the girl's brown curls at the top of her head. "She has so much hair." Eve let out a soft burp. Gertrude bit back a giggle.

Annie touched her daughter's cheek and smiled. "She takes after her papa." Her eyes shone as she shared a look with Josh.

What would it be like to have a husband? She refrained from gaping at Enoch again. It wouldn't do for him to get wrong ideas about her. Friend. Nothing else.

The baby started to pucker her lips. Gertrude shifted the little one to her shoulder, patting Eve's small back. The child settled down and snuggled into her neck. Gertrude's throat clogged. She turned away so the others wouldn't see her swell of emotions. *Take this desire away, Lord. It doesn't do any good to hope for things that won't ever come true.*

"I'd best be on my way. Did you say you brought my horse here, Josh?" Enoch flinched as he gingerly placed his Stetson on his head.

Gertrude winced, imagining how much his injury must be bothering him.

Josh nodded. "Still didn't clear you yet."

"That may be, but I feel fine to head on home. I promise to take it easy. Can I see you home, Gertrude?" He crossed to the door.

She shook her head. "No. I'll visit for a little while yet."

He hesitated almost as if he wanted to say something more.

"Don't you worry about Gertrude. I'll see she gets home without any harm." Josh snagged his hat from a peg on the wall. "Be back in a few minutes, dear, I'll just make sure Enoch doesn't overdo."

"Haven't needed someone to mother me in a long time." Enoch grumbled as he pulled the door open. "Thanks for everything, Annie. Congratulations again on little Eve. She's a sweetheart."

Josh chuckled as he followed him outside and closed the door.

Had she done something to offend Enoch? He hadn't even said goodbye to her. And why was she bothered by the slight? It was what she wanted.

Annie sank into a chair by the table. Her face was pale.

Gertrude hurried over to her friend. "Are you feeling poorly? You're looking mighty peaked."

"Would you mind getting me a glass of water, please? I just felt faint all of a sudden." She dropped her head to her crossed arms on the table.

Gertrude hesitated for a moment. Should she run and get Josh? Eve let out a whimper. She jiggled her as she crossed the room to the dry sink where a bucket of water sat. Shifting the baby, she grabbed a mug and dipped it into the water. She hurried over to Annie and set the cup in front of her. "Here you go."

The young mother roused and took a sip. "Thank you."

"I think I should get Josh."

As she moved toward the door, Annie snagged her hand. "I'm fine, really. Have a seat."

She glanced toward where the men had left but sat down as instructed. Shifting Eve, she rocked the baby in her arms.

A little color started to come back to Annie's cheeks. "Sorry. Didn't mean to worry you. It was a difficult delivery. Doc Adams said I lost more blood than most women. Said it'd take me a while to get my strength back."

"You should be in your bed." Gertrude reached over and squeezed her friend's hand. "If you like, I can watch Eve until Josh comes back. Rest while you can. I imagine this little missy gets you up frequently through the night."

Annie chuckled. "That's an understatement. She's up every couple hours."

"Oh, my. No wonder you're worn out."

"I'll rest in a bit. First, I wanted to hear about you and Enoch."

Heat sprang to her face. She dipped her head, praying it would soon leave. "T-there's nothing to tell."

"Right. Which was why you kept glancing at him when you thought he wasn't watching; and he was doing the same thing to you."

He was? She hadn't felt his gaze on her other than that one time. Maybe her friend's overtiredness was making her see things that weren't really there. Must be.

"Your silence says plenty."

It did? "You're mistaken. We met the day Josh arrested George. He's checked in a time or two since then just because he feels sorry for me. I mean, who wouldn't after my being practically left at the altar. Any sensible person would have pity on me."

"Maybe. But not just anyone would watch your dress shop when you came to check on me."

She fidgeted with the blanket wrapped around Eve. "A lot of people would."

Annie laughed. "I can't think of any other man who would do that. I doubt Joshua would unless you twisted his arm. Most men wouldn't want to be caught in a woman's dress shop."

Best to change the subject away from Enoch. "I've been thinking about that and praying. Ellie Lou Williams mentioned the idea of the shop having ready-made clothes for men and women. Do you think men would shop there too?"

"Hmm. They might. What if you also had some children's clothes, and maybe a few baby items?"

"You mean clothing for the entire family?"

Annie shrugged. "Couldn't hurt to try. I don't know of anywhere else in town that has something like it other than the new Montgomery Ward catalogue Hiram Martin has at the general store. With it, you have to make an order, and you can't tell how the clothes will look or fit, let alone how long it will take for it to come in. You wouldn't need to have a lot of variety at first until you see what people are interested in."

A surge of excitement surged through Gertrude's veins. "I like the idea."

Annie reached for Eve. "Figured it would keep you busy thinking of something else until you're open to the idea of having a nice man such as Enoch in your life."

~*~

Enoch was dog tired by the time he reached the ranch. He wanted to crawl into his bunk, but he saw a light in the main house. Best to check in with the missus before he hit his bedroll. He groaned as he dismounted from Fee and slung the reins over the hitching post in front of the house. Every bone in his body protested at his movement. He rapped against the side door. No use tracking dirt in her sitting room.

The door creaked open. "Enoch? My goodness, what happened to you?" She held the door wider and motioned him inside. "Have a seat, and I'll get you a cup of coffee."

"No thanks, ma'am. Just wanted to check in with you before I settle in for the night." He stepped inside the kitchen, sweeping off his Stetson.

"Oh, dear. How did you hurt your head?"

"I guess my head got in the way of a chair." Best to keep it simple.

Her brow furrowed. "How?"

"Stopping a bar fight this morning." No use telling her the Williams brothers were involved. She had enough on her mind as it was. "Jim mentioned you've been fretting?"

She hefted a sigh. "Trying my best not to, but I'm afraid I don't always succeed. I have to admit these problems with the mares getting out twice now has been weighing on me. That and the troubles with the fencing. I don't recall Charles ever mentioning struggles like that."

He rubbed his head, wincing when he accidentally knocked against his temple. "There had been a time or two a few years back when the fencing kept breaking down. Don't know if it was an inferior brand or what. I'll make a point of riding the fence line after church tomorrow if it will put your mind at ease."

"You sure? Looks as though you could use a break."

"No, ma'am. It's part of my job." He gripped the brim of his hat. "Sorry I haven't been around as much. I hadn't counted on the deputy position taking so much of my time, but with the sheriff off right now since his wife just gave birth a few days ago…"

"Please don't worry about it. I know you're trying to help there, and I'll keep paying you as long as I'm able to." She fidgeted with the cuff of her long sleeve.

Should he ask about her money concerns? Somehow it didn't seem as though it was his place to bring it up.

"The Lord will see me through. One way or another." She smiled. "Nothing for you to worry about. I should let you go so you can get some rest. Looks as if you're in sore need of it."

"Yes, ma'am. Good night." He slipped out the door. Fee knickered when she saw him. "Come on, girl. Been a long day. I think we both could use some shut eye."

Jim stepped from the barn as he got closer. "You look about done in. Want me to take care of her for you?"

"Would you mind?"

Instead of answering, Jim reached for the reins, patting Fee's neck.

It took all of his remaining energy to climb the ladder to the loft. He kicked off his boots and sank to the bed not even bothering to remove his pants. He barely had his head on the pillow before he fell asleep.

He awoke hours later. It was still the dead of night. His head pounded. It was likely what had awakened him. He shifted on his mattress when a clank came from below him. Was he imagining things? Enoch glanced at Jim's bunk.

The younger man was softly snoring.

"Jim," he whispered.

He snorted and started snoring again.

From the looks of it, the ranch hand wouldn't be any help. Might as well check it out himself. He shoved back his blanket that he didn't remember covering with. Creeping over to the ladder, he squinted to see below him. A tiny sliver of moonlight shimmered through the open loft window, shedding very little light on the main level. He cocked his head, but he didn't hear anything. Maybe he was imagining things. He was just ready to go back to bed when he heard a muffled voice. Enoch crept back to his bunk, fumbling in the dark for his gun belt he'd slung on the edge of the bed. He gripped the Colt revolver and headed back to the ladder again.

The door to the barn was thrown open.

He hurried down the steps, wincing when his stocking foot connected with a sharp object.

"Who's there?" Jim's muffled voice came from above him.

Enoch ran outside. "Stop." He could barely see the outline of a man mounting a horse about a hundred yards from him. The moon slipped behind the clouds, making it difficult to see anything. The sound of hoofbeats thudded.

"Enoch?" Jim came up behind him. "What's going on?"

A light came on in the main house. The back door creaked open. "Jim? Enoch? What's happening?" The missus held a lantern high above her, her bare toes evident beneath her long night garment.

"I'm not sure. Woke to a noise. Best I can tell someone was poking around in the barn. I guess I scared him off."

"Did you get a look at them?" Jim pulled up his suspenders.

He shook his head, regretting the movement. "No. It was too dark. I think it was only one person though. Saw a single rider and horse."

"But why? Why would someone be searching in the barn?" Mrs. Williams folded her arms across her chest.

"I don't know, ma'am, but I will do whatever it takes to learn what's going on."

12

Gertrude yawned as she pulled the thread tight before snipping it. She stretched her weary back. The small stack of children's clothes, men's shirts, and pants testified to the many hours she'd spent when the shop was closed or not busy over the past few weeks. She bit back another yawn as she stood. If she didn't get to bed soon, it would be time to go down and open the shop.

One of the guinea pigs squealed once it heard her movement. She chuckled and walked over to the larger crate Josh had constructed so they'd have more room to roam. "I guess I really should name you two. Oh, my goodness." She rubbed her eyes and stared at the animals again. Four little furry miniature guinea pigs were huddled next to one of the original ones. "Where did you come from?" Her cheeks flamed. "I mean…I guess you are a mama and papa. I had no idea. You were quiet over here. I would've never known." She reached in and patted the mama. "Good job."

The guinea pig whistled. Her mate came over and butted his head into Gertrude's hand which he did whenever he wanted to be petted more.

She chuckled. "I see your four beautiful babies. Congratulations, Papa. Looks as if we need to come up with a name for all of you now." She smiled. "Maybe I can run a contest of sorts. Whenever someone makes a purchase, they get a chance to put a name in a jar."

The papa guinea pig squeaked his approval.

She rubbed the black stripe between his eyes. "What do you think of that idea? The first six names I draw will be what you'll be called."

He squeaked and whistled again.

She was tempted to pick up the babies but didn't know if the mama would like it. Instead, she patted the two adults again. "Rest up. I can't wait to introduce your family to my customers."

Sleep was slow in coming. Ideas for the contest whirled through her mind. An hour later she gave up trying to sleep and tiptoed over to the crate for another peek at the little furry family. Moonlight streamed through the window. The guinea pigs were all nestled together in the corner. She backed away so she wouldn't disturb them. Scooping up the clothes she'd finished sewing earlier, she crept down the stairs to her shop.

She didn't bother to light a lantern. The almost full moon gave enough illumination of its own. She arranged the newly sewn items on a table she'd cleared the day before. Now if only she could decide the best way to get the word out about the new items as well as the guinea pig naming contest. Maybe if she talked to Melissa Evans, Beatrice Smith, or Amelia Evans they'd spread the word. She chuckled. What was the likelihood she could get the three to share something good? Too bad the town didn't have a newspaper, or she'd advertise it there. She crossed to the window. A lone figure wandered the street.

Gertrude slipped into a darkened corner so she wouldn't be spotted. Her heart thudded beneath her nightgown. The man strolled through town, glancing over his shoulder multiple times as if someone was following him. She swallowed. When the man wasn't looking her way, she slipped over to the front door to make sure it was locked. Her pulse slowed. "Silly goose. You're worrying over nothing."

Maybe it was best to go upstairs and rest until daylight. Perhaps then her imagination wouldn't be running away and taking her captive.

~*~

Enoch had a sneaking suspicion someone followed behind him, stopping every time he did. Despite his trying to learn who had made a nighttime visit to the ranch weeks ago, he'd been unsuccessful. Typically, he'd be home in his bunk instead of wandering the streets in the dead of night, but Josh had asked him to take a late-night shift to see if they could discover what the Williams brothers were up to.

They had a knack for acting innocent whenever they knew they were being watched. The pair had been apologetic when confronted about the fight in the saloon. They said it was a miscommunication and were sorry Enoch got in the way of a minor disagreement. Minor indeed. He rubbed his temple, remembering.

Maybe God was trying to tell him He didn't want him to become a lawman, and he was just hardheaded and hadn't listened to Him. But peace had been elusive. His struggle to keep things going at the ranch while also being the best deputy he could be were weighing on him.

He stopped in the shadow of the general store. The footsteps behind him also halted. A sigh escaped before he could stop it. Whoever followed didn't want to be discovered. That much he knew. He wasn't as good of a lawman as Josh, but then, the man had been chasing criminals for many years before moving to Burrton Springs.

Guess I shouldn't be so hard on myself, Lord. He glanced at Gertrude's shop. Had he seen someone inside? He rubbed his eyes. Must be seeing things. Couldn't hurt to wander over there and make sure nothing was amiss. Maybe in the process he'd be able to either shake who was tailing him or at least see who it was. He crossed the street, whistling as if he had no care in the world.

No footsteps sounded as he made his way to Gertrude's shop. She'd yet to place a placard out front advertising her business. He pressed his face close to the glass window, peering inside. Everything appeared in order, but he couldn't ignore the prickles raising the hair on his arms. Something was off.

~*~

Gertrude shrank back. Could Enoch see her? In her haste to get away from his line of sight she bumped into a display of thread, knocking them to the floor. One rolled a few feet before bumping into the wall and stopping.

The doorknob jiggled.

Her pulse quickened. Could he hear her heart pounding as though she'd ran a mile without stopping?

"Gertrude? You in there?"

The doorknob jiggled again.

Was there any chance he'd give up and go away?

He was back at the front window again, shielding his eyes as he gazed in.

Cotton lined her mouth as she crept to the door, quietly unbolting the lock. She opened the door a sliver. "Enoch?"

He was there an instant later, not shoving his way in, just hovering outside the door. "Gertrude? Is something wrong?"

She grabbed one of the shawls she'd knitted and wrapped it around her shoulders before she slipped the door open another few inches. "I'm fine. Couldn't sleep, is all."

"You sure?" Concern laced his voice. The moon slipped behind a cloud, sending his face in shadows.

"I should ask you if something's wrong. Saw you stopping a number of times out there as though someone was following you."

He didn't answer right away, instead glancing over his shoulder. "You didn't happen to see anyone, did you?"

She shook her head and realized he probably couldn't see it. She cleared her throat. "No." Goosebumps raced up her arms. She drew the shawl tighter around her even though the air coming through the doorway was quite warm. "I'd ask you in but…"

"No, of course not." He shifted his Stetson. "Wouldn't be appropriate at this time of night." He took a step backward as the moon shone bright on the street again. "Good night, Gertrude."

A sense of loss swept over her. "B-be careful, Enoch."

He smiled. "I always am."

With a nod, he turned to leave.

"Enoch."

"Yes?" He hesitated.

"The guinea pigs. One of them gave birth a little bit ago."

A smile spread across his face. "Is that so?"

She smiled in return. "They had four little ones."

"Well, I'll be. Can't imagine what a baby guinea pig would look like." He dipped his hat. "Good night."

"Y-you could stop by in the morning and see them." She sounded desperate to be in his presence. "That is, if you'd like to. I plan on having a contest so folks can help me name them."

"What a great idea." He studied the barren street. "Sure hope it helps to bring folks in for you. I best be on my way now."

He turned away once more but glanced over his shoulder. "Don't forget to lock your door, Gertrude." He didn't wait for her to do so, instead sauntering in the direction he'd came from.

She watched him for a few minutes before she closed the door and locked it. Had he been avoiding her these past weeks? He hadn't been as friendly since she'd given in to listening to gossip after the saloon fight.

"Maybe he's just been busy." After all, Annie had mentioned Josh had a case he was working on and wanted to solve before he stepped down as sheriff. Likely Enoch had been helping with it. Had the two been regularly patrolling the streets so late at night?

Staying in the shadows, she situated herself where she could watch Enoch without being seen. A movement near the general store caught her attention. Should she warn him? Her heart pounded as she continued to watch. She glanced around her shop. What could she use as a weapon? Her gaze settled on the broom in the corner. She padded over to it while still keeping a watch over Enoch. Gertrude reached for the handle, wincing as a splinter pierced her fingertip. Ignoring it, she gripped the broom tight and crossed the room, unlocking the door.

She debated whether to call out to Enoch to warn him of whoever was following him.

There. She saw a movement again. There in the shadows. She crept after them, her heart pounding with each step. Surely, they'd hear her coming.

Enoch whistled as if he didn't have a care in the world.

Protect him, Lord.

Footsteps padded in front of her, in between her and Enoch. Didn't the man know he was walking into a trap? A low growl of sorts sounded.

"Enoch. Look out!" She ran forward, banishing her broom. She brought her weapon down on whomever was in front of her. An odd screech rang out in the humid night. Something streaked off to the side.

"Gertrude?"

"Quick, go after them." She held the broom to her chest with one hand and pointed in the direction the scoundrel had scurried off, down a shadowed alley.

He hesitated for a second before he took off at a run.

She pulled in a lungful of air, forcing her breathing to slow down. Her pulse skittered as she waited for Enoch to return.

At the sound of footsteps, she raised her broom ready to protect herself. The moon dipped behind clouds again.

"Don't come any closer. I have a weapon." Her voice shook. Hopefully the intruder wouldn't ask what type of weapon she had.

"It's just me, Gertrude."

"Y-you're all right? Nobody hurt you?"

The moon broke free of the clouds.

His brow wrinkled. "I didn't find anyone."

"Really? I saw someone or something following after you left my store."

"You did?"

Her limbs started trembling. She nodded.

"I thought for certain someone had been earlier, but I didn't see..."

"You're sure?"

He cleared his throat. "I didn't see anyone. Although I did see a cat scurrying away."

"A cat?" Heat sprang to her cheeks, and she felt herself swaying.

13

Enoch grabbed a hold of Gertrude's arm as she started to teeter. "Whoa there." She stumbled, falling towards his chest. His arms tightened around her as her curves brushed against him.

Her eyes widened.

His heart beat wildly and heat flared in his face like a fire stoked hot enough to sear the hide and brand a steer's hindquarters. He set her back on her feet, resting a hand on her shoulder to steady her. Best to keep her far enough away that she wouldn't have an idea how she affected him.

"I'm so sorry. That is…you sure there wasn't a person who got away instead of a cat?"

He bit back a chuckle. "There definitely was a cat." No use getting her caught in the middle of something. Besides, he hadn't seen anyone since he'd stopped by Gertrude's shop. Best to get her thoughts on something else. "Let me escort you back home."

She sucked in a noisy breath as she glanced down at her nightgown. Her shawl slipped.

He refrained from glancing at her form; instead he draped the garment around her shoulders.

She wrapped it tightly around her chest. And then threaded her fingers through the lacy design to secure it in place with a death grip from the looks of it.

Best if he got them on common ground. He searched for a topic. "I noticed you haven't placed a sign out front yet." He jutted his elbow, waiting for her to take hold of it.

She stared at his proffered arm, not saying anything.

He was about ready to pull it back toward his body, when her fingers slipped in the crook barely touching him.

"Haven't wanted to put forth the expense yet until the shop is making a profit." She stumbled.

Enoch tightened his grip on her arm. "I've got you." He inwardly groaned, hoping it didn't come across to her as wanting more than just a friendship. Clearing his throat, he loosened his hold on her. "You have a name picked yet?"

She nodded. "'Ruffles and Stitches' but now I'm thinking twice about it."

"Why?"

"Because originally it was to be a ladies dress shop only."

"And now?"

She sighed. "That's part of the reason I was still awake. I've been working on sewing clothes for the entire family – men, women, children, and babies. Ellie Lou and Annie gave me the idea. Don't know if it will take on or not, but I figured it's worth a shot."

He rubbed his chin. "Don't see why the name you picked won't work for having clothes for everyone. Your ruffles part of the sign implies things for womenfolk, and stitches can be for everyone else."

Gertrude chuckled.

Her laughter was one of the nicest things he'd heard in days. It was good to see she was able to find joy despite what the scoundrel had done to her.

"I suppose you're right. Maybe one day soon I'll be able to have a nice sign. Until then, I must come up with some ideas for my contest."

"Contest?" They were only a few steps from the shop. He wished it was a block or two away, so they had more time to talk. She had a way of putting a fella at ease.

Gertrude yawned. "Oh, sorry. I guess all the late-night hours sewing are catching up with me."

"No problem. I should let you go. Thank you for watching out for me." He dipped his Stetson and turned to go.

Her hand on his arm halted him.

"I hope you'll stop in to see me tomorrow, er, I mean the guinea pigs. I'm letting the customers name them through the contest."

She dropped her hand, and his arm suddenly felt chilled. Which made no sense since the night air was as warm as a cookstove on a winter's night.

"I think folks will flock in to see the critters. Can't wait to see them too." He hesitated. "Thanks again, Gertrude. Best go in now and lock the door tight."

"Good night, Enoch."

She slipped inside and a moment later he heard the lock sliding into place.

His heart pattered as he waited another minute. He needed to find someone who could woo Gertrude and soon. If he didn't, he'd be tempted to do so himself and after what he'd done, he knew well enough to forget matters of the heart and get back to doing penance for his misdeeds. The good Lord hopefully wouldn't mind him at least being friends with Gertrude.

He turned away. Only a couple more hours of night remained. Come sunup he'd welcome climbing in the saddle and heading back to the ranch. Maybe then he could get some shut eye and rid his thoughts of the beautiful shop owner. Perhaps while the hours passed, he could come up with some fella to court Gertrude.

Whistling as he walked, he mentally went through some of the men in town he'd encountered over the past weeks. None of them were good enough especially since she'd mentioned one time that none of the fellas in town had ever shown her any interest.

He shook his head. Couldn't they see what a wonderful woman Gertrude was? She had a sweet disposition. Her hair was like a cup of hot coffee in the morning. And those eyes of hers could draw a fella into them. As blue as the sky on a clear day with not a cloud in sight.

Some men would be hesitant to hitch their wagon with her since she had her own business. He could pitch it as showing her ability to figure things out by herself. She had the smarts to set up and run a business which could be helpful if the couple ever fell on hard times. Her ability to sew could keep her family clothed. Then there was her heart of compassion – wanting to help a friend in need. Being the one to volunteer and help at different church activities. She was a woman content to stay on the side instead of always pushing her way to the front. Willing to follow, but also lead when she had to.

Josh had told him how she'd worked with Annie when her spectacles had broken, and she'd needed someone to help her in the schoolroom. Gertrude had dropped everything to help her friend.

Yes sir. A woman like that would be an asset to any fella. But she was too good for just anyone. He needed to find someone who would treat her like the treasure she was. It just couldn't be him.

~*~

Gertrude's heart hadn't stopped it's thumping since she'd climbed the stairs. She tried to convince herself it had only occurred because she had thought a bandit was walking the streets and going after Enoch. It had nothing to do with their conversation, or just spending time in his presence. What was it about the man that caused her to relax and let down her guard? Maybe it was only because he was new to town and knew nothing about her. If he learned more, he'd be disappointed and no longer want to spend time with her, just like all the other men in Burrton Springs. Not even her overly zealous mother could convince any of the men to spend time with her. She snorted. Maybe their refusal of her had more to do with her overbearing mother than it had to do with Gertrude.

"Might as well keep telling myself that so I can avoid the simple truth that no man will ever find me of interest." She squared her shoulders. It was time to accept it and move on. Her business needed her attention if she ever hoped to get it off the ground. It would have to be enough.

She stopped and studied the guinea pig family. The parents and three of the babies were still snuggled into a corner. One baby had wandered over into the opposite corner of the cage. He squeaked. None of the others stirred.

"What's the matter, little fella? Did you lose your way?" She hesitated a moment before she scooped him up. Stroking his brown fur, she snuggled him close for a few seconds. "Welcome to the world, little one. I think if I chose a name for you, it would be Cocoa. You remind me of the cocoa powder Hiram Martin has for sale at the general store."

The guinea pig shivered.

"I won't hurt you." She gave him one last pat before settling him beside his mama. "There you go. Get some more rest." She watched them for another minute before she crossed to her bedroom.

Gertrude picked up the small watch she usually pinned to her dress. Fifteen minutes until five in the morning. If she tried to lie back down, she'd oversleep and miss opening the store on time. Might as well start her day. She folded the shawl, setting it on her bed. It didn't take long to dress and perform her morning ablutions.

Moments later she crept down the stairs again, quiet so the guinea pigs could sleep a little more. She wanted them well rested for their debut this morning. Crossing to the table in the middle of the room, she lit the lamp she kept there. Warm light filled the shop.

She pulled out a few sheets of paper, her ink well, and pen. Yawning as she walked to the back of her shop, she picked up one of the chairs and carried it to the table. If she hurried, she could make several posters and nail them up around town before the shop opened. Now if she could only decide the best way to entice people in.

Drumming her fingers on the tabletop, she contemplated the matter. She scooped up a pencil. Maybe she should use it and then go over it with the ink afterward. Across the top of the page, she wrote,

Naming Contest. Gertrude Miller is the proud owner of a family of guinea pigs.

She scratched out her name. Maybe it would be best if she left her name off the paper. There'd been enough gossip about her in the past weeks. Last thing she needed was more. Maybe if she included the name of the shop, it would draw people in.

She tried again.

Naming Contest. Ruffles and Stitches is the proud owner of a family of six guinea pigs. We need your help to name them. With any purchase, customers can enter a name in a drawing. Winners will be picked at the end of September.

She drew a sketch of the guinea pigs and added at the bottom of the page

Ruffles and Stitches – Clothes for the Entire Family.

Gertrude smiled. Hopefully, this was just what her shop needed to start making ends meet. *Please, Lord.*

She spent the next hour reproducing the poster until she had ten completed. She placed one in her shop window and one on the counter beside where she typically had the guinea pig cage. By the time she completed that, the sky was starting to lighten.

Her stomach gurgled as she pinned her hat in place. Food would have to wait until she distributed all the advertisements around town. She was halfway down the street when she remembered she had no way of hanging the posters. Maybe Josh had a hammer and some nails she could borrow. She diverted her direction to the jail. Sometimes he got there early. Hopefully, he had today.

She hesitated a moment before she knocked on the door to the jail. Somehow it didn't seem right to just barge in at this hour of the morning. Granted a lot of folks were early risers, but it didn't mean she was comfortable going in unannounced even if he was a friend.

The door creaked open.

Enoch.

She swallowed.

His hair stood on end. Had she wakened him?

"I'm sorry. I should've waited to come. I thought Josh would be here."

He ran a hand through his dark hair. "Josh won't be here for another hour or so. Is there something I can do for you?"

She caught her breath. "Hammer and nails. That is, I was hoping to post these around town and wanted to know if Josh had a hammer and nails I could borrow. I'll replace any nails I use."

"Come on inside, and I'll see what he has." Enoch opened the door wider.

She glanced over her shoulder. A few people were on the street already. "It might be best if I wait out here." Especially if someone had caught sight of her walking through town in her nightgown last night. The last thing she needed was folks to think she was following Enoch to try and tempt him to marry her. He didn't interest her in the least. Truly.

14

Enoch searched through the desk drawer. Nothing. He pulled out the other drawer. It yanked quicker than he'd counted on, slamming his knee in the process. He bit back a grunt, shoving aside old wanted posters and other paperwork. There in the bottom of the compartment he found a hammer and small sack of nails. He withdrew it and crossed the room, closing the door behind him. "I have another hour before Josh will be here. Figured I could help you hang your signs and do my rounds at the same time."

She reached for the hammer. "Nonsense. I've taken enough of your time already."

He pulled the tool toward him. "If you want to use the hammer, I'm going along to help."

She bristled like a porcupine. "I'm perfectly capable of swinging a hammer, Enoch."

He grinned. "I don't doubt it, but I'm still coming along."

"I grew up on a farm as an only child, which means I can manage things without a man's help." Her brows drew together.

He was surprised she hadn't fisted a hand on her hip as well. Just the thought caused mirth to well up in him. He choked it down, knowing she wouldn't appreciate it. Best to get them back on level ground instead of this slippery slope. Think. Think. What could he ask her about?

"You don't believe me, do you?"

Too bad she wasn't a mare. He knew how to settle one of those. She wouldn't take kindly to his patting the side of her face, but maybe he could gentle her with words. "I know you're a very competent woman, Gertrude. I've never doubted it for a moment."

She stared at him not saying anything.

He held his breath.

"Sorry. I guess a night without sleep has me a little testy." Her shoulders relaxed, and she motioned toward town. "I'd appreciate your help."

"Where's the first stop?"

"The general store. Folks tend to congregate there the most."

He nodded. "Makes sense. Can I see what you came up with?"

She held one of the posters so he could read it.

Enoch smiled when he saw her drawing of the guinea pig family. "I think folks will come just to see what they look like."

"I hope they do more than just stop by. I'm hoping it will help to increase my sales." She fanned herself with the stack of papers. "Mercy, it's hot already."

"I'll be praying folks take to the contest and purchase something so they can help name the critters. If anything, it should help to spread word about you having clothes for the entire family." He stopped in front of the general store. "You have anywhere specific you want it hung?"

She motioned. "Over here should work."

He pulled a nail from the sack and reached for a poster. His hand brushed against hers, sending a jolt up his arm. He almost dropped the hammer. He'd felt a woman's touch before, but it hadn't lingered like Gertrude's had.

"I thought we could go to the blacksmith next." She studied him. "Are you having trouble with the hammer?"

He swallowed. Good thing she hadn't been affected as he had. Best get to work or she'd wonder what was wrong with him. He nailed the poster to the banister.

At the next place, he made sure to concentrate on the task before him. As they walked to another business, he racked his brain trying to come up with something to talk to her about. The more he learned about her, the better chance he had of finding someone who would turn her head. He cleared his throat. "Josh mentioned something about a box lunch social coming up at church. I was on duty when they must've announced it. How do those things run?"

She sighed. "The women make up a basket of food and the fellas bid on it. The money raised usually goes to a good cause. The town is hoping to eventually have a separate schoolhouse, so the current one can just be the church."

"Sounds like a good idea. I've never been to one of those box suppers." He attached another poster, tucking the hammer under his arm when he'd finished. "Do all the ladies participate in it?"

"Most times. The younger women decorate their baskets and sometimes let their fella know how they look in advance, so the man knows which one to bid on. The married women usually participate too." She glanced at him. "They have a basket with enough food to feed their whole family."

"When will that be?" He already knew the answer, but he wanted to keep her talking.

"Saturday."

He sent her a sideways glance. "You planning on participating too?"

She shook her head. "I figured I'd just slip some money to Pastor Drew and let him know it's for the new school. No use setting myself up for an embarrassing situation where nobody bids on my basket."

"I'm sure that would never happen."

She just stared at him.

His gut churned. He hesitated. "It hasn't, has it?"

Color filled her cheeks. She gave a brief nod but didn't say anything else.

Aww. Poor thing. How blind were the fellas in Burrton Springs? He stared at his feet. "I reckon if you try again, you might have a different outcome this time."

"Not worth taking the chance. Besides, I'm sure I'll be tired after working in the store all day. I plan to spend a quiet evening at home reading a book."

"You can read a book any other time. I think it'd be good for you to go." He had to find a way to encourage her to attend. "If anything, it would let others see your support of the community, especially now that you're a business owner."

"I could bake a pie or something and give it to Pastor Montgomery. He mentioned about some of the ladies providing baked goods or food for those who can't bid on a basket."

"If I make sure someone bids on your basket, will you come?"

~*~

Gertrude's stomach churned. Why was Enoch pushing for her to not just attend the church activity but also to come up with a boxed supper? It made no sense. Hadn't she made it clear she didn't have any intention of getting close to the altar again? Besides, if she went to the event, she'd open herself up to folks poking around to discover what happened with George. So far, she'd managed to avoid answering pointed questions by using the tactics Ellie Lou had suggested.

Enoch cleared his throat, looking at her expectantly.

Had she ever answered his question?

"I'm sure I can find someone to choose your basket providing you tell me in advance how you'll decorate it. What do you say?"

I say to run away as fast as possible.

He smiled. A dimple flashed at the right side of his mouth.

She sucked in a noisy breath and glanced away.

The man was mighty handsome and likely didn't even know it. How many hearts had he broken in the past?

"Gertrude? Please?"

It took all her attention to keep herself from fleeing. "I don't think it's a good idea." Wait. If he was saying about someone else bidding on it, that meant he had no desire of doing so himself. She didn't know whether to be happy or sad about the realization.

He opened his mouth as if he meant to say something else but instead gave a short nod. "How many posters do you have left?"

Why did she feel disappointed that he'd given up on the topic so easily? She almost dropped the papers in her hand. She shoved aside her feelings. "Uh, looks like there's two left. I'm not sure where else to put them. Do you have any ideas?"

"How about the church?"

"You don't think it would be inappropriate?"

"We can always stop by and ask the preacher. Do you have time yet?"

She shifted her pin and checked the time. "I think so. But even if Pastor Drew agrees, that still leaves one yet to find a home."

"I can always post one outside the jail."

She bit her lip. "How often do people stop by there though?"

Color stained his tan cheeks. "Guess you're right about that. Not too many." He lifted his Stetson, running a hand through his hair before replacing the hat. "I think Josh mentioned someone in town who has rooms for let. Do you happen to know who it is?"

"Mrs. Walsh. I don't know that the town often has visitors, but I suppose it's worth placing a poster there providing she doesn't mind. We could split up. You could go to the church and ask Pastor Montgomery while I go to Mrs. Walsh. They're on different ends of town."

"How about we stick together for now. If you need to get going, I can always finish up for you."

"Well… I suppose so. I appreciate you helping me."

Enoch grinned. "I'm always happy to assist a pretty lady."

She bent her head. Nobody had ever told her that before. Her stomach fluttered. She should've eaten before heading out this morning. It had to be the reason for the reaction. Surely it had nothing to do with his words.

"Howdy, Gertrude. What're you and Enoch doin' so early in the mornin'?" Jules Montgomery waved as she headed towards them. "Didn't think I'd be seein' the two of you together." She waggled her eyebrows.

"Oh, no. We're not together." Heat sprang to her cheeks. "I mean, we're together only because he's helping me with these." She waved the posters. "Speaking of, do you think Pastor Drew would mind me hanging one outside of church?" She held it up for the woman to see.

"Well, isn't that somethin'. I've a hankerin' to see the baby critters myself." She rubbed her expanding belly. "Don't rightly need any clothes right now, but I might be able to come up with somethin' to purchase so I can help with the namin'." Jules patted Gertrude's arm. "Critters need a name that fits their temperament. It's why it took me a while to name my Pepper."

"Pepper?" Enoch's brows drew together.

"I reckon since you're new you don't rightly know about my dog."

"Ahh."

"I named her after one of my husband's sermons."

"I'm not sure I know that story, Jules." Gertrude smiled.

"Drew was talkin' about bein' seasoned with salt. My dog was just a puppy then and didn't look like salt since he's a mix of colors – brown, white, and black which is how I came up with Pepper." She glanced around. "He's a great dog. Usually he's with me." She shrugged her shoulders. "He does like to go explorin'. Likely where he is now."

"That's an interesting story." Enoch shifted the hammer.

"I can take a poster for you. I'm sure Drew won't mind. He'll want to help however he can."

"Thank you." Gertrude handed her the paper. "I appreciate it."

"You're welcome. Sure hope I see you both at the box supper. Should be a lot of fun." She waved. "I best get movin'."

Gertrude was thankful the woman hadn't pushed for a response to her invitation.

"See, I'm not the only one who'd like to see you attend." Enoch studied her. "What do you say?"

She fiddled with the last poster. "I say we'd better get this hung before I need to open the shop."

The thunder of hoofbeats drew both of their attention. A horse and rider drew to a halt in front of them.

"There you are, Enoch. I've been looking all over town for you." A slim man patted his horse's sweaty withers. "There's trouble at the ranch. We need you."

Enoch handed Gertrude the hammer and sack of nails. "I need to see what's happened."

"Go."

He sprinted back toward the jail.

"Enoch."

He halted and turned.

"Be careful, and let me know if Ellie Lou needs anything."

He nodded before running again.

The young cowboy tipped his hat. "Miss." He didn't wait for her to respond but instead turned his horse back toward the direction he'd came.

Help Ellie Lou, Lord. Gertrude ran her hand along her skirt. *Keep Enoch safe. I'd hate to see something happen to him. Or anyone, that is…*

15

Enoch's gaze settled on the room the boss had used as an office. Papers were strewn everywhere littering the floor. Drawers were left half open, the contents flung around the room. Books that had once lined a shelf were opened as if someone had been searching for something. The question was what?

Ellie Lou Williams rang her hands. Her lip quivered. "I-I don't understand who would do this."

"Any idea what they were hoping to find?"

She shook her head. "I can't imagine."

He rubbed his jaw. "I don't mean to pry—"

"Nonsense. You're a deputy now."

"Yes, ma'am. Did the boss own the ranch free and clear?" There had to be a reason for the continued mischief.

"He had, yes."

"Had? Meaning something's happened to change that?"

She fiddled with the edge of a book for a few minutes before she answered. "I'm sure you've noticed things have been tight as of late."

He nodded.

"My Charles was given this property from his grandpa, which I'm sure he told you. His cousins never got over the slight since they're older than my husband. They felt it was unfair and made it known whenever we got together."

"But why does that matter if you own it now?"

She fidgeted with the book again. "I had to take out a note to help pay the bills. I sold off as much of the herd as I could without fully depleting our chance of recouping our losses."

"What happens if you don't pay off the note on time?"

"I'll lose everything."

"How long before the note comes due?"

"The end of the year."

Not quite four months. "Does anyone else know about the note other than the banker?"

"I'm not aware of anyone."

"Where do you keep the deed?"

"Charles used to store it in his family Bible that's been passed down."

"We best make sure it's still there. Where is it?"

"In the sitting room, although you won't find the deed in it."

His gut clenched. "Someone took it?"

"I-I don't know. I just meant I stopped storing it there."

"We best make sure it's where you left it."

"You don't think someone would try and steal it, do you?"

"Not sure." He motioned her out of the room. "Why don't we check?"

Mrs. Williams didn't answer but moved into the sitting room, to where a smaller Bible was open on the fainting couch. Inside the back cover she withdrew a document. "I know the land meant so much to Charles." She fingered the edge of the paper before wiping a tear. "I don't have my husband anymore, but I wanted to have something he held dear close to me each day. It's why I put it in my Bible."

"I can't help but feel all these occurrences are intertwined. For now, you should keep the document somewhere safe." Enoch shifted his weight. "I have to ask…I assume there isn't any loophole in there that says you don't inherit, and the cousins do instead?"

She shook her head. "I made a point of asking Michael Browning after Charles died."

"Sorry, ma'am. Who is he?"

The missus smiled. "I keep forgetting you aren't as familiar with everyone in Burrton Springs. He's the bank president. Has been for years."

"Is he also the one you spoke to when you took out a note against the property?"

She nodded. "You don't think he's behind this, do you?"

He ran a hand along the tight muscles in his neck. "I don't think so, but I'll make a point of talking to him." And to Josh. He needed someone's help with this who had more experience than he did. Maybe it was the good Lord's way of showing him he wasn't equipped to take on the full role as sheriff of the town. Was God trying to tell him in many ways and he just wasn't getting it? He sighed, wishing the Lord would make it plainer. Couldn't He put up a sign or something? "I'll let the sheriff know what's going on here. For now, it might be best to make sure me or Jim know where you are always."

"Surely they won't come back." Her face paled.

"Might be a good chance of it if they haven't found what they were searching for." He swallowed. "I know the boss would want to know you're kept safe."

She laid her hand on his shoulder. "That's not your job, Enoch. The Lord will protect me."

Her words were like a sucker punch to his gut. Might as well say he couldn't handle the job.

"Look at me, Enoch." She squeezed his shoulder.

He dragged his gaze to meet hers.

"You are doing a fine job at being a deputy. I'm doing a lousy job trying to convey it. Only God is the One who truly protects us. My peace of mind can only be found in Him. Not that you and Jim haven't been here for me. You both have. Charles would be proud of how you've done your best to protect me. I know law enforcement serves a vital role in our community. I know you'll do great as either deputy or sheriff in Burrton Springs, whichever it is God's calling you to do. You care about folks, which is what people need. While I want to use sense and not do foolish things to invite someone taking advantage of me, I also want to learn to stand strong amid confrontation. I want to be like Shadrach, Meshach, and Abednego in the Old Testament. When they were faced with the decision to bow down and worship an idol, they refused even when the king threatened to throw them in a fiery furnace. They knew if God intervened and saved them from that fate, or even if He didn't, He was still God and worthy of praise. They refused to give in and dishonor God in the process." Her eyes lit up.

"I don't see how it compares."

Her face relaxed. "My life is in His hands to do with how He sees fit. I will do whatever I can to keep this ranch because it's what Charles would've wanted, but if it somehow gets taken away, I still must trust God has a plan even when I can't see it. I'll also be careful too. But Enoch, there will always be some things you can't control – either in your job or in your life. The question is, what will you do when things are beyond your control? Who or what will you look to?"

~*~

With each jangle of the bell above the door to Gertrude's shop, she hoped the person entering would be Enoch coming to see the guinea pigs. Not that he'd make a special trip to see her. Still, every time it failed to be him coming through the door, she bit back a sigh and pasted on a smile. A trio of boys entered the shop this time, two of them looking suspiciously like the ones who had ran from the store on the day Enoch had watched it when the guinea pigs had somehow gotten loose. He never had told her what had happened that day. With seeing the boys now, she couldn't help but wonder if they were part of the story.

They shoved each other in their haste to get to the cage first.

"Hello, boys. Is there something I can help you with today?"

One of the boys dug deep into a pocket and withdrew a coin. "Ma asked me to get a spool of black thread."

The taller boy elbowed the one who'd just spoken.

The first boy piped up again. "Since I'm making a purchase, do I get a chance to name the pigs?"

She smiled. "You certainly do. What about you other boys? Did your ma send you here to purchase something too?"

One hung his head and the taller one toed his scuffed shoe against the floorboards. They both shook their heads.

The trio was likely new to the area or at least she hadn't seen them earlier in the year when she'd helped in the schoolroom.

"Why don't you go pick out the thread over there," she motioned, "and I'll get a slip of paper for you to write your name on."

The boys ran over to the thread display. Several spools fell to the floor in the boy's haste to dig a black one from the basket.

Gertrude shook her head and chuckled. When she got close to the guinea pig enclosure, the proud papa started whistling. "Looks as though someone is interested in getting you named. Sure wish there were more."

The guinea pig nodded his head as if he understood and agreed.

A moment later the boys scurried to the counter, pushing, and shoving in their attempt to get closer to the cage. One put his finger by a wooden bar. "Will they bite?"

"Only if you're a carrot or some other type of vegetation." She smiled. "Although I still wouldn't put my finger there to tempt them, especially with the babies."

"Can I hold 'em?" The taller boy elbowed the smaller boy.

She shook her head. "Not right now."

His lower lip jutted. "Does Gideon get a chance to name all of 'em?"

"No, just one. One sale means one chance to provide a name." She handed the slip of paper and pencil to the boy who still gripped the thread. "As soon as you pay, you can write your choice of name down and drop it into the jar there." She indicated the large glass container she'd placed on the counter.

He handed her the thread and his coin.

She made change, handing him a few pennies in return. While he scratched his head, she dropped the thread into a paper sack and placed it in front of him. "Be sure to thank your mother for her business."

"What're you gonna call him?" The older boy pressed closer. "How about Killer or Rascal."

Good heavens. She never thought atrocious names would be entered. There had to be a way to discourage such an entry. "You could name them that, but I've always thought it a good idea to name someone according to their deeds. I bet your parents felt the same way, Gideon."

He ran a hand beneath his nose and wiped it on the side of his trousers.

Gertrude refused the urge to chastise him.

"What'ya mean? What's so special about my name?"

"Haven't you read about Gideon in the Bible?"

"Naw. My pa don't hold no account in it." He sniffled. "Ma don't say much either way."

"Well, there's a Gideon in the Bible. The name means mighty warrior."

The small boy puffed out his chest.

The tall boy chuckled and elbowed his cohort. "Imagine that. Gideon being a warrior. He's afraid of his own shadow."

Gideon's lip trembled followed by a scowl.

"Now boys…"

"I'll name one of them Gideon." The boy wrote the name on the paper and dropped it into the jar. "I bet the pig'll be a warrior one day too, like me."

The other two boys snickered.

She frowned at them and dropped her hand to Gideon's shoulder. "I have no doubt you'll be a warrior one day. Look to the Lord."

The boy nodded.

"Have a good day, boys."

The older two took off at a run, throwing the door open. Gideon hesitated.

"Was there something else you needed?"

He hesitated for a moment. "W-where in the Bible is the story of Gideon if I want to read it one day?"

She smiled. "Read Judges six to eight. My guess is your ma knew all about your namesake when she picked it for you."

He sucked in a breath. "How'd you know Ma named me?"

"I just had a feeling." She squeezed his shoulder. "Best not keep your ma waiting. I'm guessing she has need of that thread."

"Yes'm." He scooped up the package and took off at a run.

The door slammed open and shut. She turned back toward the counter with a chuckle.

"You did a great thing there."

Enoch.

Her pulse immediately spiked. "W-why's that?"

"Making a small boy realize he's more than what his friends think of him. That God made him for more." He leaned against the doorframe, crossing one leg over the other as if he had all the time in the world to talk to her.

"I merely told him what his name meant." She fiddled with straightening the stack of papers for the contest.

"No, Gertrude. You did much more than that. Shows the caliber of a woman you are."

It did?

16

Enoch's words of praise settled on her like melting butter on a baked potato, filling in all the nooks and crannies.

"Every boy longs to hear he has more in him than he thinks. Makes him strive to be better. To do more. To be more. To work harder."

He dipped his head but not before she caught sight of his sagging shoulders. What had he faced at the ranch? Would he answer if she asked him?

"I can't imagine you needed the encouragement as a child."

He grunted but didn't say anything more on the matter.

"How's Ellie Lou?" She kept a close eye on him.

Enoch flinched before schooling his expression. "She's a strong woman."

Didn't exactly answer her question. She narrowed her gaze. "I'll have to stop by and see her after work."

He was shaking his head. "That wouldn't be a good idea."

"I don't remember asking for your opinion."

Heat flared in his eyes. "As acting deputy, I'm recommending you don't go out to the ranch."

Gertrude thrust her hands on her hips. "You have no right telling me what I can and cannot do." She took a few paces closer to him. "Last I checked, Burrton Springs was a town where its people are free to go wherever they want without having to get special permission."

"Gertrude—"

"If there isn't anything else, Deputy Valentine, I'll bid you good day. I have a contest and a store to run." She didn't wait for his response. She stalked to the back and upstairs to her apartment. He wouldn't dare follow her there. She crossed to the window that looked out over the main street. Several minutes passed before she heard the door open and shut downstairs and caught a glimpse of Enoch staring up at her from the middle of the road. She sucked in a breath and took a step back so he couldn't see her.

She waited another five minutes before she headed back to the shop, not until after she'd peeked outside and watched Enoch mount his horse and head in the direction of Ellie Lou's ranch. He might try and stop her later, but she'd be sure to visit her friend to discover what was going on with her. The woman needed friends instead of an interfering cowboy, no matter how handsome that cowboy was.

The next hour passed without incident. Customers trickled in. By the end of the morning, she had a total of ten entries in her contest jar. It was a start, but still a long way toward making a steady profit. Her stomach churned. *It's hard to be at peace, Lord, when I don't know the first thing about being a successful business owner. But I want to learn – both how to do well with my business as well as experiencing Your peace. Can You please help me?*

Her prayer was interrupted by the bell above her door. She smiled and headed toward them, stalling when her mother stood in front of her.

"Your pa and I would like you to come for dinner tonight, providing you can pull yourself away from this ridiculous rodent naming contest long enough to spend time with your family."

"I don't know, Mama. I have a business to run."

"And you also have a responsibility to your family." Mama's lips pursed.

She groaned internally. "Not this—"

"I've invited Mrs. Williams. Thought maybe she could use some friends."

If Ellie Lou would be at her parents for supper, then Gertrude could discover how her friend was doing without having to worry about another confrontation with Enoch. Not that she wanted him to think he could boss her around.

"No wonder you can't get a man interested in you when you can't even carry on a conversation. Honestly, Gertrude. *Tsk. Tsk.* I know I taught you better than that." Gertrude bit her lip to refrain from saying something she'd later regret.

The bell above the door rang again.

She breathed a relieved sigh. "I must go, Mama. I'll see you later." Not waiting for her mother to respond, she scurried over to her customer. "How can I help you, young lady?"

"Howdy, Miss Miller. Ma sent me to get a couple yards of fabric for a dress for me." The girl's blue eyes sparkled. "She said I can pick it all by myself."

"Let's go take a look at what I have in stock."

Elizabeth Wheeler grinned and slipped her hand into Gertrude's.

"I expect you to be at the house no later than 5:30 PM, Gertrude." Mama strolled toward the door. "Don't make me send your father to come get you."

"Goodbye, Mama."

The air in the shop felt a good five degrees cooler after she left.

"Ooh, I like this one." The young girl pointed at a pink cotton bolt of fabric with small blue flowers.

Gertrude pulled it out and held it up to the girl. "It is pretty. Although I think something blue might look better with your beautiful eyes."

The ten-year-old grinned. "Pa told me I have pretty eyes too."

Gertrude couldn't hold back a smile. "What do you think of these two?" She placed the two bolts side by side for the girl to peruse. One had pink flowers and the other was a plaid with an assortment of colors running throughout the print.

"I like this one." The girl pointed to the fabric with flowers.

She'd figured it would be the one to draw the girl's attention. "Great choice. Will your ma be needing thread as well?"

The girl shook her head. "No, Ma said she has plenty. She just said to get the fabric I liked. I can't wait until she has it finished. Maybe I can wear it to the box supper at church."

Surely the child didn't plan to fix a box to bid on. She was far too young. Gertrude kept her opinion to herself as she cut the length of fabric.

"Ma will be fixing up a big basket for Pa to bid on. She said we should look our best for him since we're his gals, which is why she said about making me a new dress." The girl twirled around, her skirt flaring around her. "That and I've grown two inches this summer and Ma said my dresses are getting too short."

Gertrude led the way to the counter in the middle of the store. She cut the length of fabric, wrapping it in paper and tied it with twine, so it would hopefully stay clean on the journey back to Elizabeth's home in the country.

The girl watched the guinea pigs while Gertrude finished her task.

"You get a chance to name one of them because of your purchase today." She handed a slip of paper to the girl along with a pencil.

The papa squeaked and came over to investigate the newcomer.

Elizabeth giggled. "What are they? I've never seen any animals like them."

"Guinea pigs. That's the father."

The small rodent whistled again.

"I'll name him Squeakers since he makes that noise." She wrote the name on the paper and dropped it into the jar. "I better get home. The quicker I do; the faster Ma can start sewing my dress." She waved and ran out the door.

Gertrude stroked the papa through the wooden slats. "Seems like Squeakers would be an appropriate name for you."

The pig butted his head against her finger.

"You're blessed to have a family." She sighed. "Sure would be nice to have a little girl to sew clothes for." She shoved the thought aside. The store needed her attention instead of longing for something she'd be better off without. Best to keep her mind focused on the task at hand.

~*~

Enoch chaffed the entire trip back to the ranch. Why was Gertrude nice to him one minute and as prickly as a cactus the next? He shook his head as he dismounted Fee. No use trying to ponder about the pretty shop owner when he needed some shut eye. He glanced toward the main house. Maybe he should check in with the missus first. A moment later he knocked at the side door.

"Hello, Enoch. I thought you would've been sleeping by now." Mrs. Williams opened the door wider. "You're welcome to come in."

"I'm heading to bed but wanted to make sure you didn't need anything."

She shook her head. "No, I've been working on putting the house in order after…"

"Did you need some help?"

"No. You have enough to concern yourself with. Let me know when you talk to Mr. Browning."

"I tried a little bit ago, but he'd already left for the day. When I stopped by his house, his wife said he'd be out of town until Monday."

"Good heavens. I didn't think you'd question him today. Jim said you were on duty all last night. Please, get some rest. We can sort things out here after you've had some sleep. Don't you worry about me. As I said before, the good Lord will be watching over me."

Enoch would do whatever he could to help God too. Not that the Lord needed his help. But he'd made a promise to Mr. Williams to help watch over her. Enoch planned to do whatever he could to follow through. He refused to fail again. "Yes'm. Let me know if you need anything."

She waved. "Will do, although I'm sure I'll be fine."

He nodded and turned toward the barn, leading Fee. "C'mon girl." He yawned as he unbuckled the saddle, draping it over a rail.

It didn't take long to rub his mare down. He patted Fee before climbing the ladder to the loft. Not bothering to undress, he kicked off his boots and sank onto his bunk. He yawned again.

Sleep didn't claim him right away despite the tiredness dogging him. Gertrude filled his thoughts along with trying to narrow down suspects for the ranch disturbances. Josh hadn't had any ideas on the matter either. Maybe it wouldn't hurt to pay a visit to the Williams brothers again. They'd been less than forthcoming before but maybe he could find a way to get them to say something. He couldn't help but feel they were somehow involved in the problems plaguing the missus. They had the most to gain if something happened to her.

Keep the missus safe, Lord. Please give me direction as I try to unravel this snarl and learn who's responsible for it. He paused for a few minutes. *Could You be with Gertrude too? Something seems to be in her craw, and I sure can't tell what it is. One minute she's nice as pie to me and the next lashing out as if I'm her enemy. You sure created a mystery when You made women. I'm just glad I won't ever need to solve the mystery of them.* Enoch yawned once more. *Show me some fella who can woo Gertrude. She'll need a strong man who appreciates her.* The vision of her flashing eyes when he'd told her she couldn't come to the ranch made him smile. *She needs a fella who appreciates her fieriness and determination. Fine traits that can complement a man. Help her business to do well and for folks to start streaming in so she'll be successful. She deserves to be happy. Just can't be me who provides it for her.* He shook his head. *Don't get any ideas, Lord. You know I wouldn't make a good husband. I'm not even a good brother or son. Especially after—*

Enoch shoved the prayer from his mind. Best to forget his past and focus on the future. One that didn't have Gertrude Miller in it every day.

17

Gertrude's steps dragged as her parent's farm came into view. Mama would scold her for sure. A customer had come into the shop right when she was ready to flip her sign to say CLOSED, so she could lock up for the day. The gentleman had taken his time sorting through the shirts she'd stitched until he found one he liked. He hadn't wanted to name one of the guinea pigs though. By the time he left, it was almost a half hour after five.

She squared her shoulders for the upcoming onslaught that was sure to ensue. Her feet faltered when she saw a horse and buggy along with a team of horses harnessed to a wagon, all tied to the hitching post in front of the porch. Ma hadn't said anything about anyone coming other than Ellie Lou.

The door creaked open, and Papa stepped out. "Good, you're finally here. Your ma's about fit to be tied." He chuckled and gave her a hug. "I've missed you, my dear."

"Me, too, Papa." His hug gave her the extra measure of strength she needed to face her mother and whomever else she'd invited to supper. Was it too much to hope it was another couple from church?

Papa held the door for her.

The scent of fried chicken and some type of apple dessert filled her nose. Her stomach growled. She'd missed lunch since she'd had an influx of customers around that time and business had remained steady the remainder of the afternoon.

"It's about time." A frown marred her mother's face. "Another minute and dinner would be ruined."

"Sorry, Mama." Her words were softer than she'd intended. The woman always had a way of making Gertrude feel as though she was less than, not measuring up to any of the expectations her mother had for her.

"Never mind that now. I have someone I want you to meet."

Dread filled Gertrude like a visit to the doctor to have a tooth pulled. Oh, no. Who was Mama trying to fix her up with now? She didn't have long to find out.

A short man strolled into the sitting room. He was immaculately dressed in a black suit.

"Gertrude, I'd like you to meet John Alwood. He's been excited to make your acquaintance. He's the undertaker in Hutchinson."

An undertaker? Really? Had Ma had to stoop so low that only an undertaker showed an interest in Gertrude? She sighed. It looked to be a long evening.

Ellie Lou poked her head around the corner. "It's so good to see you, Gertrude."

She opened her mouth to respond when Enoch stepped into the room, his presence filling the doorway. Why was he invited? What exactly was her mother up to?

Mr. Alwood crossed the room to her. He clicked his heels together, dipped from the waist while reaching for her hand, bringing it to his lips. He planted a brief kiss on her knuckles.

The sensation brought to mind a cold, slimy fish. She couldn't hold back a shudder.

"Nice to meet you, Miss Miller. I've been looking forward to making your acquaintance ever since your mother shared your many fine qualities."

She couldn't state the same so what should she say? Gertrude glanced at Enoch as if he'd have an answer for her.

His face darkened, and his brows drew together. He left the room.

What was that all about?

Mama hurried over and wrapped her arm around Gertrude's shoulders. "I have you seated by Mr. Alwood." She sent a smile in the man's direction. "We've shared numerous conversations about you." Mama maneuvered her to the kitchen.

Why had her mother struck up a conversation with the undertaker to begin with?

Ellie Lou stepped in the way, pulling Gertrude in a hug. "Your dress is beautiful."

Mama dropped her arm and hurried over to the cookstove.

"Thank you." Gertrude whispered the words. "I heard you had a disturbance at the ranch."

Her friend nodded but didn't say anything else.

"Gertrude, get over here and assist me."

"Yes, Mama." She scurried to do her mother's bidding.

A few moments later the food was on the table, and they were all seated.

Papa said a prayer.

"Dear, why don't you tell Mr. Alwood about all the sewing you've been doing. Any man would be blessed to have a wife with your abilities." Mama outright stared at the man and then back at Gertrude.

She wanted the floor to open and swallow her whole. Anything to get away from her mother's blatant matchmaking scheme. She glanced at her pa.

He cleared his throat. "The chicken smells delicious. Can't wait to eat it." He picked up the platter and passed it to Enoch. "I hear you've been helping the sheriff and Mrs. Williams. Sounds like you've been mighty busy."

She breathed a sigh of relief as all gazes swung to the cowboy.

Enoch took the platter and placed two pieces of chicken on his plate before he passed it along. "With Jim helping at the ranch too, we're able to balance my being gone for part of the time."

"What was the cause of the upheaval this morning?" Gertrude smiled at him.

He glared and didn't answer.

"I'm sure it's nothing to worry about." Ellie Lou placed a hand on Enoch's sleeve for a moment before removing it. "Just someone trying to find something, and they disturbed some of my things. I'm sure it was a misunderstanding."

Gertrude's stomach churned, and it had nothing to do with being hungry. Enoch had reassured her he didn't have feelings for his boss, but maybe Ellie Lou had affections for him. And why wouldn't she? She was still young, and Enoch was a fine specimen of manhood.

He'd make any woman happy. He'd be a wonderful husband. Probably father too. Maybe he could give Ellie Lou the children she longed for. Gertrude should be happy for her friend. And for Enoch. They would make a fetching couple.

She suddenly had no desire for food and wished she could excuse herself from the dinner. Despite trying to avoid it, her gaze met his.

His brows rose as he studied her.

Lord, help me to be happy for them.

~*~

Enoch wished he knew what Gertrude was thinking. She'd been off ever since she'd entered her parent's place. Question was, who was making her nervous? The new fella? Surely she didn't care for a man like him, did she?

She fiddled with the cloth napkin beside her plate before finally spreading it in her lap. He didn't miss how her fingers trembled in the process.

"Having a woman who can sew for the family is a fine trait." The undertaker piped up.

Had the man missed the conversation that had happened in between? Or was he just trying to somehow soothe the uncomfortableness that had settled on the room? Enoch should be happy that the fella changed the topic from the mischief at the ranch but somehow it rankled.

"She can also cook and bake." Her ma passed a heaping bowl of mashed potatoes. "I made a couple apple pies for dessert but mine don't hold a candle to Gertrude's. It's a shame your time is taken up in town, dear or you could have made the pie for tonight. I'm sure Mr. Alwood would've enjoyed it."

The undertaker took a small spoonful of the potatoes and handed them to Gertrude. The man's hand grazed across hers.

Enoch flinched and did his best to look away, but his gaze kept dragging back to watch them as if his eyes had a mind of their own. He startled as the missus placed her hand on his sleeve again.

"Would you mind passing the gravy?" She smiled.

Had she asked him more than once? He fumbled with the bowl of gravy, nearly spilling it on the white tablecloth. What was wrong with him? He shook his head and handed the dish to Mrs. Williams, realizing afterward that he failed to pour some on his potatoes.

"You know I'm too busy with my shop." Gertrude's shoulders were hunched. She didn't make eye contact with anyone.

"Pish, posh." Her ma waved her hand as if dismissing the topic.

"I heard lots of folks talking about your shop today. You came up with a great idea with the naming contest." He willed her to look at him. "Heard you had a lot of entries."

Finally, her gaze sought his for a moment before she stared at her lap again. "I don't know that I had a lot, but at least I had some sales."

"What are you selling, Miss Miller?" The undertaker butted into the conversation again.

"She has a clothing shop for the entire family. Everything made to order." Enoch narrowed his gaze at her ma. The woman had the decency to keep her mouth closed on the topic.

"I've heard several women express interest in having you sew a dress for them." Ellie Lou took a bite of her food.

"Really? That would help business." Gertrude sat up a little taller.

"What? You own your own establishment?" Mr. Alwood's face paled. "Your mother hadn't told me that. I'm afraid... That is…I never understood why a woman wanted to make her own place in the world when the good Lord made women to serve men."

"While I agree as a woman of faith that I can serve others, it doesn't mean I need a man in my life. I have no desire to marry." Heat flew into her cheeks.

"Gertrude!" Her ma's hand flew to her chest.

Her pa's mouth gaped open.

Enoch chuckled. That was the Gertrude he knew. He smiled.

~*~

Gertrude bit down on her tongue hard enough to draw blood.

She wished the dinner was over, and she was back home where she could hide her face. Her mother would never let her hear the end of this. She closed her eyes, imagining the whole meal had just been a bad dream. One she would wake up from and find relief in knowing it was only a nightmare.

She kept one eye closed and opened the other one a slit. No. No dream. She puffed out a breath and studied each person around the table. Mama was seething. Papa's brows rose as if questioning her sanity. Ellie Lou had a hand over her mouth as if holding back laughter. Mr. Alwood's expression was as if he'd tasted something sour. Enoch was the only one smiling…almost as if he was proud of her. It made no sense.

The dinner went steadily downhill after her outburst.

The undertaker scurried out the door as soon as he'd eaten his last bite of chicken, refusing the apple pie.

Soon afterwards, Ellie Lou and Enoch said their goodbyes.

A moment later Gertrude gathered her reticule. She should probably stay and help Mama with the dishes, but she didn't have the energy for another battle.

"I'll see you home, dear." Papa squeezed her shoulder. "Why don't you come to the barn while I hitch up the wagon?"

She didn't need to be asked twice. Papa had offered her a lifeline, and she planned to grab ahold of it. "Bye, Mama." She waved and slipped out the door before her mother could say anything.

A moment later she breathed in the familiar scent of hay. The cow mooed from the back stall. She strolled toward her, stroking the cow's head for a moment.

Papa didn't say anything as he hitched the wagon. He helped her onto the high seat and clicked for the horses to get moving.

Dusk settled over the countryside. An owl hooted.

A tear trickled down Gertrude's cheek. Would she forever be a disappointment to her parents?

"She means well." Papa's words broke through the silence.

She sighed.

He stretched across the seat and gripped her hand. "She loves you and just wants what is best for you."

"Oh, Papa. I've never been good enough for her."

There was just enough light to see him shaking his head. "That's not true. She's always been proud of you, Gertrude. She's just not good at letting it be known. It's why she touts your abilities to everyone she encounters."

"She just wants to see me married off." To the highest bidder, no doubt.

Papa halted the wagon. "You're right in that she wants you to find a husband, but it's not so she can get rid of you. Deep down she's proud of you for opening your own shop."

She shook her head. "No, she thinks it's a hindrance to my getting married one day." She blinked away another tear. "I…I would love to marry someday but after—"

He gripped her hand tighter. "Not every man is a scoundrel. One day you'll find one who will turn your head."

"No, Papa."

"I know it don't seem like it now, but just wait, one day you'll feel differently. Until then, throw your all into this shop of yours. But promise me you won't close yourself off to love when it comes knocking at your door."

"It won't find me, Papa."

He patted her hand and started the wagon again. "Promise me."

She sighed. What would it hurt to agree? She knew it wouldn't ever happen, especially when she had no plan to be looking for love. If anything, she'd be running from it. No use hurting him in the process. "I promise, Papa."

"That's a good girl. Now don't you worry about your ma. I'll smooth things over with her. For now, you work at making the best business you can while also keeping a watch out for that fella to sweep you off your feet."

She chuckled. If she could help it, there would be no sweeping off her feet. The only sweeping she'd be doing was the floor of her shop, but Papa didn't need to know that for now.

18

Enoch worked to rid his thoughts of last night's dinner – more so how Gertrude and the others had reacted after her outburst, and how quickly the undertaker scurried away. Good riddance to the man. The fella wasn't at all what she needed. Question was, what qualities should Enoch search for when finding a man to woo her? The thought plagued him throughout his morning chores at the ranch, and he still hadn't come up with a list of things to search for by the time he finished.

Jim sauntered into the barn. "I rode the fence line again. Didn't see any problems."

"Hmm?" He glanced up from checking the tack. "What did you say about the fencing?"

The younger ranch hand chuckled. "What's snagged your focus today?"

"Just something I'm trying to solve."

"Like who keeps causing trouble around here?" Jim pulled off his leather gloves and tucked them in his back pocket.

"That's part of it." Enoch finished with the tack and hung it on a hook.

"What's the other part?"

Enoch didn't answer but instead studied the cowhand. The man was close in age to Gertrude. He was a hard worker. Didn't drink or play cards like some fellas were prone to. And most importantly he always spoke about faith in God. He made sure the missus was taken care of too. Enoch rubbed his chin. Would Jim be a good candidate to woo Gertrude? Enoch cleared his throat. "You have a gal you're interested in?"

The man's brows quirked. "Why the sudden interest?"

He busied himself by grabbing a pitchfork. "Just realized we hadn't had much time to jaw lately." Enoch forked some straw into a stall. One he'd already placed clean bedding in.

"Nobody in particular. Don't seem to be many available women at the church in Hutchinson." Jim shifted his Stetson, wiping the sweat from his forehead. "What about in Burrton Springs? Any unmarried women there?"

"There's quite a few. Maybe you want to go to church with me one Sunday." He got another forkful of straw and tossed it. "Don't know if you'd be interested or not, but there's a box supper on Saturday."

"What's that?" The younger man leaned against a post.

"I guess all the women cook and make up a box for the menfolk to bid on. They're trying to get enough money for a new school."

"Sounds like a good cause. I've been saving my money for a spread of my own, but I guess it wouldn't hurt to give a little toward the school." The ranch hand grinned. "Sure would be nice to eat supper with a pretty lady."

Good. Now, how to get him to bid on Gertrude's basket, providing Enoch could convince her to participate. After her outburst last night, she'd sure as shooting dig her heels in more than she had before when he talked to her about it. "Heard tell the new owner of the clothing shop in town might have a basket too."

Jim stared at him.

Enoch's mouth went dry. What he wouldn't do for a swig of water.

"What's so special about the shopkeeper?"

Everything. Best not appear too eager to sing about Gertrude's fine qualities or Jim might get suspicious. Enoch hesitated. What should he say about her? "She's not looking for a fella right now so she would be a safe person to eat with." That didn't sound good. "She's real pretty though. I mean, you could eat with her and still get a feel for how the other gals are by watching them and seeing how they act with the fellas they're paired with. Ma always said the best way to learn how someone is, you have to observe them when they don't know anyone's watching."

"Huh?" Jim rubbed his stubbled chin. "You aren't making any

sense. Wouldn't they know they were being watched when they're eating with the fella?"

"Uh..."

"If this shopkeeper's so pretty, why aren't you bidding on her basket? Besides, I'd rather take my chances with one of the other ladies if that shopkeeper isn't interested in finding a fella. I'd rather spend time with a gal who wants to eat together and maybe see what happens."

This wasn't going at all the way he wanted it to.

"Makes more sense for you to eat with the shopkeeper gal. She sounds like a safe person for you to be with, since you both have the same inclinations of not getting hitched." Jim waggled his eyebrows.

He shook his head. Might as well change the subject. "Have you seen the missus?"

"You going to ask her to pack one of those baskets for you to bid on?"

"What? No. What made you think something like that?"

"That's right, you're probably holding out on the shopkeeper gal."

Enoch's head hurt.

"The missus went to town. Said she had some things to get for Saturday." Jim shrugged his shoulders and moseyed out of the barn.

Why had she gone off on her own? Enoch followed after Jim. "She go to Hutchinson? Say when she'd get back?"

Jim's brow furrowed.

"Just trying to keep an eye on her since all the trouble we've been having here."

"Makes sense. She said she was going to Burrton Springs. Left about a half hour ago."

"Maybe I'll head into town early. I'm not due at the jail until this afternoon but it couldn't hurt to make sure the missus doesn't have any problems." He whistled and Fee trotted over to him in the corral. He opened the gate and the horse trailed after.

His sister's words rose to haunt him. "Fee follows you like a dog."

He shoved the memory back in the far recesses of his brain where it belonged–locked behind a closed door and double bolted.

It didn't take him long to saddle Fee and swing onto her back. He set off at a gallop wishing he could as easily run away from the memories of his greatest failure.

~*~

Weariness tugged at Gertrude's frame and refused to let go. After the disastrous meal at her parents' last night, she had been unable to sleep, making it two nights in a row without rest. She yawned, every muscle protesting as she knelt again to pin the hem of the dress Ellie Lou had selected.

"I shouldn't purchase anything right now with how poorly things have been going at the ranch, but I couldn't resist." Her friend smoothed the fabric of the burgundy skirt.

Gertrude's stomach churned. While she appreciated the sale, she didn't want Ellie Lou to suffer because of it. She withdrew the pins from between her lips, shoving them into the small cushion strapped to her wrist. "While the color does wonders for your complexion, maybe it would be better if you wait to purchase it when things turn around at the ranch. I don't want to be the cause of you having even more problems than you already do. I can always set aside the dress until things get on more even ground." She sat back on her heels and studied her friend.

Ellie Lou sighed. "I really wanted to do something to make your day but perhaps you're right. I thought it would be fun to wear a new dress to the box supper on Saturday."

Gertrude's gut tightened remembering the couple times she'd witnessed Ellie Lou touching Enoch's arm last night. "Why don't we still figure out the hem length so I can have it ready when you do have the money to purchase it?"

"I don't know. Someone else might come in and decide they want to buy it. It would be better if we don't. I wouldn't want you to miss out on a sale on account of me." She shifted away. "I'll just change back into my old dress."

"Wait. At least let me finish putting in the last pins since we were almost finished." Gertrude started the task again before Ellie Lou could protest. It only took another minute to complete pinning the hem. "There, why don't you go get changed now?"

Ellie Lou had no sooner gone into the tiny changing room on the side of the shop when the bell above the door chimed.

Enoch.

"Howdy." He glanced around.

"Is there something I can help you with?" *Please, Lord, don't let him mention anything about last night.*

"I was wondering if you happened to see Mrs. Williams today. Jim said something about her coming to town. Thought maybe she'd stop by to see you." He removed his Stetson.

At least Ellie Lou had someone interested in her. Enough. *Time to accept the fact you'll remain single. At least you have the shop.*

"Gertrude?"

How long had she been woolgathering? "Um, she's getting changed. She should be finished any minute now." Gertrude untied the pin cushion at her wrist and set it on the counter.

Enoch strolled to the guinea pig enclosure. "I never did get to see the little critters the other day." He stooped over. As always, the papa let out a squeal and came over to investigate. "Do you mind if I hold him?"

She shook her head. "He's the friendliest right now. I think it's because the mama is busy with her babies."

He opened the small door and scooped up the father. "You definitely are getting a little herd there, aren't you?"

"Could you imagine a ranch with a herd of guinea pigs?"

Enoch chuckled, the sound filling the room like a soft blanket. "Sure would be hard to protect them from all the varmints who'd try to attack them."

She smiled. "But it would make for an interesting ranch."

"That it would."

"What're you two talking about?" Ellie Lou joined them. She stepped close to Enoch, petting the guinea pig in his large hands.

"Gertrude was saying about a ranch for guinea pigs." The corner of Enoch's eyes crinkled as he smiled at his boss. He placed the animal back in its cage.

Gertrude swallowed, forcing herself to glance away from the couple. *Let the shop be enough, Lord.*

"It would make for some interesting stories having a ranch with only guinea pigs." Ellie Lou laughed. "It would be the talk of the town."

Gertrude busied herself with straightening her small stack of receipts from the day. She had no desire to be the talk of the town, having a hard enough time avoiding questions that still cropped up from time to time about George.

"If they're like rabbits, there would be more than you knew what to do with in a short time." Enoch laughed again. "At least you wouldn't have to worry about keeping the grass trimmed. They'd do the job for you."

Ellie Lou touched Gertrude's arm. "Gertrude, are you feeling poorly?"

"What? No." Her gaze darted to Enoch despite telling herself not to do so.

"You sure?" His brows rose. "You haven't been yourself—"

He didn't finish his sentence. Didn't need to either. She hadn't been herself last night when she'd spurted all over them like a gully washer following a torrential downpour. Wasn't herself now either. Her hand trembled, and she started to sway.

"Gertrude? Quick, Enoch."

Her friend's words buzzed like an insistent fly by her ear.

A moment later she felt herself being lifted into his arms and cradled close to a warm body. A solid, masculine chest no less. She couldn't stop herself from snuggling her head against his shoulder. Might as well enjoy being in a man's arms for a minute before reality clicked into her brain.

Heat coursed up her neck and face as Enoch tromped up the steps and settled Gertrude onto her bed. Good heavens. She'd thought she'd imagined the whole thing. But no, the blue quilt she'd stitched while she dreamed about who she might marry, brushed against her fingertips as he eased her shoulders onto the pillow. Her twelve-year-old self believed in the dream back then.

Ellie Lou motioned for him to step aside. She laid a hand on Gertrude's brow. "You don't feel feverish. Are you feeling peaked? What can I do for you?"

Enoch rested his shoulder against the doorframe, filling the room.

She tried to swallow but couldn't.

He stepped forward and poured water from the pitcher into the glass she kept on the table by her bed. "Here." He pressed it into her hands, his fingers brushing against hers. She could feel the callous on his finger.

She needed to get him out of here so she could think straight. Her heart pounded as she took a swallow.

"Maybe you should run and fetch the doc, Enoch." Ellie Lou settled on the bed beside her. "I don't like how flushed she's gotten all of a sudden."

"No." Her voice came out in a squeak. Did she sound like the guinea pig he'd just held? "I'm fine, really. Just haven't slept for a couple nights."

"I don't know…" Ellie Lou glanced at Enoch.

She needed to get them both out of here so she could think straight. Taking a big gulp of the water she tried to settle her thoughts. "I don't want to keep either of you from your responsibilities."

"I probably should get to the jail."

"I can stay with you until you're feeling better. If you'd like, I can watch the store while you take a nap."

"No!" She sat up and placed the empty glass on the table. "That water did the trick. I'm feeling much better now. You two go on now. I'm sure you have other things demanding your attention."

Enoch waved and clomped down the stairs.

"Something seems to be bothering you still." Her friend frowned. "You know I'll help you any way I can."

"I appreciate it." She stood, thankful that the room didn't sway in the process. "If I think of something, I'll let you know."

Ellie Lou just nodded and slipped down the steps.

Gertrude breathed a sigh. Her friend couldn't help her, but Gertrude could do something to help Ellie Lou. She'd do anything she could to make sure her friend was happy. Even if it meant giving up her own happiness.

19

Gertrude didn't have a lull in customers during the next two and a half days. It seemed everyone wanted to have something new to wear to the box supper. By lunch time on the day of the event, the store stood empty. She glanced out the front window. Not a soul walking the streets either. More than likely the women were working on their meals for their baskets. She hurried upstairs and placed the pie she'd prepared earlier into the oven. When it was finished, she'd deliver it to Jules before running her other errand.

Back downstairs, she folded the burgundy dress Ellie Lou had tried on earlier in the week and wrapped it in paper, tying it with a string. She glanced at the clock on the wall. The festivities at church started in a few hours. It should give her enough time for the pie to bake and take care of her other delivery before folks started arriving in town. She planned to spend the evening reading the copy of Louisa May Alcott's *Rose in Bloom* she'd picked up at the general store yesterday.

The bell above the door jangled. Elizabeth Wheeler smiled when she saw her.

"Hello, Elizabeth. What can I help you with today? I thought you'd be busy helping your ma get your basket ready."

"Ma said I could come and get some ribbons to help decorate our basket. She said maybe I could find some that match my new dress." The girl smiled.

"I'm surprised you aren't wearing it." Gertrude smiled too.

"I didn't want to take a chance of it getting dirty." The girl slipped her hand into Gertrude's.

Gertrude's throat tightened and tears pricked her eyes. She cleared her throat. "Let me see, you picked this fabric, right?" She grabbed the bolt.

"You remembered." A grin spread across Elizabeth's face.

"Of course. I always remember my best customers."

The girl gave her a hug.

Gertrude patted her small back. "Now, let's see which ribbons will look the best." She took the bolt to the small table where various ribbons and laces were stored. Sorting through the assortment, she picked a few different ones. "What do you think of these?"

"Ooh. They're pretty." The girl handed her a coin. "This is how much Ma gave me."

"I think you have enough for both the pink and blue. Both will go well with your dress. What do you say?" Gertrude spread the two across the bolt of fabric.

She beamed. "Won't Pa be surprised when he sees the ribbons match my dress?"

"I'm sure he'll see what a beautiful young lady you're turning into."

The girl stood up a little taller. "You think so?"

She bit back a laugh. "I'm sure of it." She set the fabric down, took the spools of ribbon to the counter, cut two separate lengths, and placed them in a small sack. "With your purchase today, it means you get another chance to name my guinea pigs."

The girl's eyes shone. "I've been thinking about them. I came up with another name too."

Gertrude handed the girl a slip of paper and pencil again. "What name did you come up with this time?"

"Fluffy on account of the mama looking real soft." She nibbled on her lip as she started to write the name on the paper. "How do you spell it?"

"F-l-u-f-f-y."

"Thank you, Miss Miller." Elizabeth dropped the paper in the jar. "You're sure getting lots of names in there."

She nodded. The jar was half full of slips of paper.

"When're you picking the winning names?"

"I'll draw the winners on September twenty-ninth."

Elizabeth leaned over the cage. "I can't wait to see if my names are picked. I'll be sure to bring Ma and Pa. Will you have anything special that day?"

"Hmm. That's a great idea, Elizabeth. I hadn't even thought that far ahead yet. It's a good thing you came in here today." Gertrude snipped off an extra length of pink ribbon. "Maybe you can help me come up with ideas the next time you're in town."

Elizabeth's blue eyes twinkled. "I'd like that, Miss Miller. I best get home now so Ma don't worry about me."

"Before you go, here's an extra length of ribbon. Maybe your ma can put it in your hair for tonight."

The little girl hugged her tight. "Oh, thank you, Miss Miller. You're the best. I can't wait to show you my dress and ribbons tonight. See you."

She was out the door before Gertrude could tell her she wouldn't be attending the festivities. She sighed as she placed the ribbon spools and the bolt of fabric back where they belonged.

The next hour she spent straightening the shop even though it didn't need any attention. It helped to keep her mind on something other than the box supper. The scent of apples wafted down from her apartment. Gertrude hurried upstairs and removed the pie from the oven, setting it in a wooden crate. It would hopefully be enjoyed by a few people tonight. She'd pick up her empty dish after church services tomorrow. Lifting the curtain, she studied the street. Still empty. It wouldn't hurt to close the shop a couple hours early and make her deliveries.

Decision made, she pinned her hat in place and picked up the crate. A moment later, she was on her way to the parsonage.

She knocked on the door. It swung open.

"Howdy, Gertrude. What's this?" Jules rubbed her bulging stomach.

Her twins toddled over. Elliot tugged on his mother's skirt. Emily plopped down and started to cry.

"I can see you're busy. I wanted to drop this off for tonight. Thought you might need some extra desserts." Gertrude handed her the crate. "I won't keep you. It looks as if you have your hands full. Good day." She turned to leave.

"Aren't you comin' tonight?" Jules called after her.

"Not this time."

Not ever if she could help it, at least not for an outing that paired men and women.

~*~

"I don't think it's a good idea." Enoch rubbed a hand across the tight muscles in his neck.

"Why not? We haven't had any trouble the past couple of days." Mrs. Williams frowned at him. "I think it would be good for all of us to go to the festivities." She placed a cherry pie in the basket. "Jim's been looking forward to it."

"He can escort you into town, and I can stay here and keep an eye on things to make sure nobody breaks into the house or barn again." He folded his arms across his chest.

"Nonsense. If you're to take the sheriff position in Burrton Springs, people need to see you at community events. Even if you decide to remain as the deputy, folks need to start putting your face with your name. Only way to do so is to show up at various doings in town." She picked up a knit wrap. As warm as it was, she wouldn't be needing it.

"I still don't think I should go."

"If it'll make you feel better, I'll lock the house before we leave." The missus planted her hands on her hips. From the looks of it, she wasn't budging.

A knock sounded at the side door. He stepped out of the way.

The missus opened it. "Gertrude. What a nice surprise. I wasn't expecting you. Come in. We were just about ready to head to the box supper. You can ride with us."

She stepped into the room and glanced at him and the missus. "I'm sorry, I didn't mean to interrupt." She thrust a wrapped package in the boss's wife's hands. "Here, I wanted you to have this."

"For me?" Mrs. Williams's head cocked.

"Open it." Gertrude smiled.

The wrappings fell away and the missus lifted a red dress, holding it up to her. "Oh, Gertrude, I can't accept this. It's far too expensive."

"I wanted to do something special for you." She gripped the missus' shoulder. "I know it's been hard for you since your husband died. You haven't been to many activities since then. So, when I knew you were going to the box supper tonight, I wanted you to have a special dress to wear. Please put it on."

"Well, I…I don't know what to say." A tear streaked down the missus' face.

"Don't say anything." Gertrude gave her a quick hug. "Go get changed and let me see how it looks before I get going."

"I'll be right back." The missus swiped the tear away and left the room.

"That was right nice of you." Enoch shifted his feet. "I'm glad you decided to go to the box supper."

"Oh, I'm not going. I just stopped by for a minute, and I'll be heading home."

How could he convince her to go when he didn't plan to attend either? He'd only agree to go if she did. He rubbed his jaw. Maybe it was best if he stayed home. No sense in placing Gertrude in a situation where she might get hurt again. He'd do anything to make sure that didn't happen.

The sound of rustling fabric pulled him from his thoughts.

The missus ran her hand along the front of the red dress. "It's beautiful, Gertrude. I'll be sure to let everyone know who made it."

Bright pink filled Gertrude's cheeks. "No need to do that. I'm happy it fits. Well, I'd better be going."

"Wait, we'll ride together. Here, Enoch, will you place my basket in the wagon for me?"

"Yes'm." He gripped the handles of the basket. "Make sure all the doors are locked."

"I already did." She removed a key from her pocket. "Just this last door to see to."

The ride to town was uneventful. The women chatted while he drove the team and Jim followed on his horse. He soon pulled up alongside the church.

Buggies, wagons, and horses were already tied to the hitching posts and trees around the edge of the building. Children were laughing and chasing each other on the grass while parents kept an eye on them. A gaggle of young women were standing to the side. A group of fellas stood beneath a copse of trees, casting glances at the women.

Jim quickly dismounted, tied off his horse, and joined the men.

Enoch jumped from the wagon seat and made quick work of tying off the team. Once that was accomplished, he helped the missus down, and then Gertrude. Her hand trembled in his.

"I better head home now." She glanced at her feet.

The missus grabbed a hold of Gertrude's arm. "No. Please stay. I want to have someone I can talk to tonight."

"But you have Enoch and…" She studied the basket he was holding. "I'd just get in the way of your time together."

What was she talking about?

"Please, Gertrude. I only accepted the dress so that we could spend the evening together."

From the looks of her face, she was trying to figure a way to get away without hurting her friend's feelings. "You mean you aren't…" She bit her lip and turned a brighter shade of red.

"Please?"

Gertrude puffed out a breath. "All right. I'll stay—for a little while."

"Oh, good." The missus tugged the basket from Enoch's hands. "Gertrude, would you mind taking this inside?"

She fumbled with the handles. "Uh, of course."

"Thank you, dear. I'll see you in a minute."

Gertrude started up the steps, stopping partway and glancing over her shoulder before she disappeared into the church.

The missus smiled and placed her hand on his arm. "Enoch, I have a favor to ask of you."

"Anything, Mrs. Williams. What can I do for you?" He started to lead her inside the building, but she pulled him to a stop.

"I need you to bid on the basket I made up."

"Why sure, ma'am." It was only fitting that she wouldn't be alone or have some fella taking up with her when she was still mourning her husband.

"Good, because I made it up so you can share it with Gertrude."

20

Gertrude fidgeted with edge of the tablecloth. She shouldn't have stayed. The church building was filling up. She glanced at the doorway. Why had she promised Ellie Lou? It was a mistake.

"Sorry it took me so long." Her friend squeezed behind the table to join her. "Looks like a great turnout."

She nodded. "I can't promise—"

"Hello, dear." Mary Scott interrupted her. She stood across the table laden with baskets and desserts. She smiled. "Betty and I thought this would be a great way to get to know everyone."

Gertrude introduced Ellie Lou to the older woman.

"Are you getting settled at Mrs. Walsh's?" Gertrude racked her brain, trying to remember all the woman had told her when she and her niece first visited her shop.

"We are, at least for now. We're still trying to find a permanent place." The older woman studied the room. "I haven't been to a box supper in ages. I'd forgotten how much fun they are. Betty wasn't so sure about coming since she has a beau back in New York. Betty is my niece, Mrs. Williams."

Ellie Lou nodded.

Gertrude searched the room. "Is Betty here? I don't think I've seen her?"

Mary chuckled. "If I know that girl, she's outside with the young men buzzing around her like bees to a flower. She knows how to turn heads." The woman patted her gray hair. "She didn't get that from me, which is why I'm an old maid. Of course, it probably didn't help that all my life I made it known I didn't need a man to make me happy." Her eyes twinkled. "My mother had a conniption over that one. But the good Lord has been my constant companion. Now, Betty is different than me. She thinks she needs a man to make her complete."

Gertrude wasn't sure how to respond to the woman's assessment. Mary's openness reminded her a little bit of Jules's brusque honesty.

"Did you pack a basket, Miss Scott?" Ellie Lou studied the long line of packaged meals.

"Please, call me Mary." The older woman reached into her reticule, pulled out and flicked a fan open, and set it in motion. "Mercy, it's hot here. I packed a basket, yes, but I don't plan to have it put up to be bid on. I'm fine eating by myself."

"I'm sure Betty wouldn't mind you eating with her and whoever bids on her basket." Ellie Lou adjusted the desserts to make room for a cake that had just been dropped off.

"I'd be happy to eat with you, Mary." Gertrude smiled. "I didn't bring a basket and hadn't planned on staying." She glanced at Ellie Lou who frowned at her. "That is, I hadn't planned on staying long."

"Ladies and Gentlemen, if I can have your attention," Pastor Montgomery called in a loud voice. "Thank you all for coming and showing your support as we work to raise money for a new school. Let's pray and we'll get started.

"Dear God, thank You for this opportunity to support the education of the young ones You've placed in our care. Bless the food provided to nourish our bodies. May we always have a desire to live for and follow You with our whole heart. In Jesus's name, amen. Let's get started, folks." He held up a basket decorated with blue and pink ribbons.

Elizabeth Wheeler grinned. "That's the one to bid on, Pa."

Chuckles filled the room.

After the basket was sold, Elizabeth came forward with her parents. She waved to Gertrude. "Hi Miss Miller. See my new dress?" She twirled a few times. Her blonde braids tied with matching ribbons flailed around her shoulders as she spun.

"It's beautiful."

The girl waved before she took her pa's hand.

The next basket was displayed.

Pastor Montgomery opened the lid and took a big whiff. "Mmm. Looks like fried chicken, potatoes, gravy, and I'm not sure what else is in there, but you won't be disappointed fellas." He started the bidding process again.

"Ooh, that's Betty's." Mary whispered. "See, she decorated it like her dress."

Sure enough. The same frills and lace were on both the basket and her dress. The young woman primped as the amount for the basket grew with each man who bid on it.

"Sold for five dollars."

A collective gasp could be heard throughout the room.

"Such a large amount for a basket," Ellie Lou whispered. "At least it's for a good cause."

Betty pranced forward to collect her basket. A teenage boy reached in his pocket for the payment. A frown marred Betty's face.

"Here's another winner." The pastor held the basket up. "Who will be the first to bid?"

Enoch named a price.

Gertrude glanced at the basket. It was Ellie Lou's. Her stomach lurched.

The bidding went back and forth between Enoch and one of the Williams brothers.

"Oh, dear, I pray he doesn't get it." Her friend glanced at the side of the room where Charlie and George sat.

Enoch increased the bid.

"One dollar going once. Twice. Sold to our new deputy."

Gertrude searched for an escape, but Ellie Lou had her blocked behind the table. As soon as the couple left the building, she'd slip away and return home. They wouldn't even notice she'd left. It was better that way. They could spend time together and not have to worry about her. She should be happy for her friend. Instead, tears blurred Gertrude's eyes. She blinked them away. Any crying would have to wait until she was home. Alone. Where she belonged.

Enoch picked up the basket. His gaze met hers.

She needed to get out of here. Deciding not to wait, she started to push past Ellie Lou. "Excuse me."

"Not so fast, Gertrude." Her friend grabbed a hold of her arm. "I fixed this basket—"

"I know, so you could have some time alone with Enoch. I understand. I'm happy for both of you. Really." She pasted on what she hoped would come across as a smile.

"No, Gertrude. I fixed the basket so *you* could spend time with Enoch." Ellie Lou beamed. "Go have fun, you two."

She what?

~*~

Enoch watched as a series of emotions flowed across Gertrude's face. She didn't appear too eager to eat the basket supper with him. Was she afraid of gossip circulating because of their spending time together? Just why had the boss's wife decided to pull such a stunt? Not that he minded spending time with Gertrude. He just didn't want her to get the wrong impression.

The room buzzed with conversations as he led her outside. He welcomed the quiet once they stepped into the sunshine.

"I don't know what would possess Ellie Lou to do such a thing, especially after—" She sawed off the rest of the sentence, her cheeks flaming with color.

"No need to worry about that." He patted her arm.

He didn't think it possible, but her face bloomed even more. This wasn't getting off to a good start. "I'm guessing you're as surprised as I was. Why don't we just make the most of it? I know you don't have any intentions of getting hitched and neither do I. There's no reason why we can't just eat the meal as friends."

"Except it isn't how other people will view it." She glanced back at the church.

"You don't have to stay if you don't want to." But he hoped she would.

She sighed. "No, we'd better otherwise Ellie Lou won't let either one of us hear the end of it. Might as well get it over with."

As if that didn't prick a fella's pride.

"I'm sorry. I didn't mean that like it sounded." Her cheeks flushed again. "This is why I've never been good at having someone interested in me. I always manage to say the wrong thing."

"Let's put the whole topic aside, what do you say?" He motioned to a spot beneath the trees. "Should we sit here?"

"Looks good."

He set the basket down and started withdrawing the food the missus had packed. "There's plenty here. Should've asked the missus to join us."

"Although, I doubt she would've." She sat down, smoothing her skirt.

He chuckled. "Probably not." He handed her a thick roast beef sandwich.

"Thank you." She took a small nibble of it. "So tell me about you and your family."

His gut churned. It wasn't a topic he liked discussing. "What did you want to know?"

"Where did you grow up?"

"Grew up on a small farm in Illinois." He took a big bite of his sandwich hoping it would dissuade her from asking more questions.

"What made you move to Kansas?"

He closed his eyes for a moment wishing he could get away from the memory. Maybe it was best to only share part of the story. He finished his bite and swallowed. "I always had a hankering to own a ranch with a couple hundred head of cattle on it. Spent a lot of years driving herds to Abilene and Ellsworth."

"How did you end up here?"

"Met the boss one time at a sale in Ellsworth. He was needing some hands at his ranch. I'd always planned on herding doggies, but when he mentioned a horse ranch, I thought I'd try something different." By then he'd heard from home that he wasn't welcome to return. He'd needed a change, something demanding his attention to help him forget what he was missing out on. Something to help him forget what he'd done.

"Do you have family still in Illinois?" She set down her sandwich. "When's the last time you were home?"

Enoch hefted a sigh.

"If it's too personal, you don't need to tell me." Her lips pinched together.

Part of him longed to spill his story, but if he did, would it change how she looked at him? Not that she'd ever expressed an interest in him. At least not a romantic interest–only a friendly one. He didn't answer right away, instead finishing his sandwich. He pulled a small jar of pickles from the basket and opened it. Vinegar and garlic assaulted his senses. He tipped the jar toward her.

The juice sloshed from the container, dripping on her skirt.

"Oh!" She jumped up.

"I'm so sorry." He withdrew a handkerchief from his pocket and handed it to her.

She sat back down. "No harm done." She took the fabric and dabbed it on her dress.

The scent of vinegar permeated the air.

Great. Nothing like dousing a woman in vinegar. She'd remember their time together as the time he was a clumsy oaf and spilled pickle juice all over her.

Should he tell her about his family or let it be? Why make the outing worse than he'd already done? He slanted his gaze toward her.

She still was soaking up the moisture from her dress.

More and more folks had joined them outside as the box suppers were paired with the men and women. He was just getting his courage up to tell her more when the general store owner hurried over to them.

"Sorry to interrupt you two lovebirds."

"We're just friends." Gertrude shifted farther away from him.

While it was true, her words still bothered him.

The man fished an envelope from his pocket. "This came in on the stagecoach this afternoon." He handed it to Enoch. "Didn't know if it was something important. Thought maybe I should give it to you now instead of waiting."

He recognized the handwriting. His gut clenched at his name scrawled on the front of the envelope.

"Well, I best get going so you two can get back to enjoying your time together." The man smiled and waved before heading in the direction of the church.

He debated whether he should shove the note into his pocket and read it later or excuse himself.

"Please don't let me stop you from reading it." Gertrude motioned at it and brushed the crumbs from her lap. "I can just head on home."

He had the feeling he could use her moral support. "No, please stay." His hands trembled as he ripped open the envelope and withdrew the single sheet of paper.

Enoch,

I'm only writing to you because your sister insisted I do so. Your pa and I wanted you to know Anna died two weeks ago. Don't bother coming home. You aren't welcome.

21

Gertrude started to stand until she witnessed the color draining from Enoch's face. There was no doubt his news hadn't been good. She settled her hand on his very muscular forearm. A bolt of something unfamiliar surged through her. She didn't stop to consider what it could be. "Enoch? Are you ill?"

He blinked but didn't say anything.

She tightened her grip on his arm.

Still, he stared at the paper before crumpling it into a ball and shoving it in his pocket.

Something was dreadfully wrong. She'd never seen him like this before. Packing the remainder of the meal back in the basket, she positioned the handles of the container over one arm. She tugged his hand. "Come on. Let's find somewhere a little more private so we can talk." What would Mama say if she'd heard Gertrude's words?

Shoving the thought aside, she led him away from the church and back toward town. The likelihood of them being followed was slim. She looped her arm through his, not pushing him to talk. She prayed her presence would be a comfort to him. That he'd open up and talk to her, but she refused to pressure him. He'd been there when the bottom fell out of her life. The least she could do was return the favor.

As they passed by her shop, she dropped the basket by the front door. Enoch hadn't even seemed to notice their slight detour. Gertrude continued to hold onto his arm as they walked. Before long they'd meandered through town and entered the countryside. The dry grass crinkled beneath their feet, grasshoppers jumping out of their way with each step.

The tall cowboy stayed quiet.

Dear God, be with Enoch. I don't know what kind of news he's had, but

You do. Be with him. Give me wisdom how to be a good friend for him. I have a feeling he really needs one. Guide my speech. Give him peace in the middle of whatever storm he's in right now. Help me to know what to say to him and when.

A bird swooped ahead of them, snatching one of the grasshoppers mid jump.

Enoch halted and glanced around. "Gertrude? How did we get here?"

"I thought you could use time away from people after…" She didn't know if she should bring up the correspondence or not.

"I'm sorry. I can see you home now." He turned them back toward town.

She ran her teeth across her lower lip. Was he ready to talk about whatever had upset him? "We wouldn't need to go back just yet." Maybe he'd accept the lifeline and talk about what was bothering him.

He sighed, shoving his hands deep in his pockets.

"I'm here if you need or want to talk." She laid her hand on his sleeve. "But if you aren't ready to, I respect that."

Enoch's gaze swung to hers. "You're an unusual woman, Gertrude."

She didn't know if she should be affronted by his remark or not.

"Don't get me wrong. I happen to appreciate that about you. Most womenfolk feel the need to fill a silence when it spreads too long." He studied her. "You aren't like them."

She opened her mouth to respond before snapping it shut. Maybe this was one of those times when it was best to remain silent.

He didn't say anything else for several minutes.

A sparrow landed a few feet away from them, pecking at the dirt.

"M-my sister died."

"Oh, Enoch. I'm so sorry." She gripped his arm again. Would it be inappropriate to give him a hug? Before she could talk herself out of it, she leaned into him, wrapping her arms around him.

His muscles stiffened for a moment before, his arms circled her waist, drawing her to him. She could hear his heart thrumming beneath her ear.

Comfort him, Lord as only You can. I've never lost someone, so I don't even have words to know how to soothe his hurt. But You do. Tears streamed down her cheeks, dampening his broadcloth shirt.

"I…I won't ever see her again." Enoch's voice was thick.

Was he crying too? She didn't pull away to see, but instead ran a hand along his muscular back. "Did she know the Lord?"

He sniffed. His chin dipped against the top of her head. "She did."

"Then you'll see her one day in heaven."

His fingers stroked her shoulder blades.

She sucked in a noisy breath and pulled back a fraction of an inch to gaze at his face.

Moisture lined his cheeks.

Her heart felt as if it would break in two. She lifted a hand to touch his cheek.

He closed his eyes and leaned into her hand.

Her pulse quickened. If only she could think of some way to comfort him. Before she had time to think about it, she rose on tiptoe and kissed each of his cheeks where the tears had halted their path.

His arms drew her closer, and his mouth dipped to hers. Warmth spread through her all the way down to her toes. A fluttering stirred in her chest. She pressed her lips to his, delighting in the sensation swirling through her, one she'd never experienced before. Her heart swelled to near bursting.

~*~

Enoch pulled Gertrude so close not even a piece of paper could fit between them. He deepened the kiss, his heart racing with each passing second.

She pushed against his chest with her hand, breaking the contact with his lips. Color sprang to her face. Her fingers brushed across her lips…where his had just been. She took another step backward, breaking his hold on her.

His pulse jumped as he tried unsuccessfully to calm his heart and his thoughts. What had come over him? "I'm sorry." No, that wasn't true, at least not fully. "That is, thank you for being here for me."

Enoch puffed out a breath and took a step backward. He couldn't think straight with her so close to him. Even with the distance now separating them, his heart still was racing. It had to be because of the news from Ma. He'd only latched on to the person closest to him when he'd heard the crushing news. Once he had time away from Gertrude, and time to grieve his sister's passing, he'd see that the seamstress had only cared about comforting him in his time of need and nothing beyond that. Right? His head whirled with all the confusing thoughts. He rested his hand against his temple as if it would help to somehow halt the swirling.

"Enoch? Are you hurting?" A second later, her fingers pressed against his temple. "What can I do for you?"

Heaven help him. He removed her hand from his temple, keeping a loose hold of it. Somehow, he still needed the connection with someone to help ease his pain. "Why don't we sit for a few minutes?"

She stared at him, her big blue eyes not blinking. A slight breeze tugged at her hair, a wisp escaping the tight bun at the nape of her neck. The hair pranced across her forehead. She nodded and sat on the grass.

Enoch settled beside her, still gripping her very feminine hand. He rubbed his fingers across her fingertips. Rough skin was prominent on several. Maybe where a needle had pricked it from all her sewing? The coarseness reminded him of the last time he'd seen his sister. He continued to hold Gertrude's hand, but his mind was on the past.

"W-what was she like?" Her words brought him back to the present.

He pictured Anna the last time he'd seen her five years ago. "Full of energy and sass."

"Is, I mean, was she close in age to you?"

He shook his head. "No, I was fourteen when she was born. Ma always said Anna was an unexpected surprise. She brought joy to the whole family. Pa used to say God knew we needed her…" His throat constricted.

Gertrude's hand tightened in his. He clung to it as if it could somehow strengthen him.

"She couldn't have been very old then."

He sniffed. "Just turned twelve about a month ago."

"Oh, my. That's so young to die. Had she been sick?" Gertrude's thumb rubbed across the back of his hand.

Did he really want to tell her the sordid tale? He sighed and plucked a blade of grass, rubbing it back and forth between his fingers.

"If it's too painful to talk about…" She left her sentence hanging.

He could let it go but somehow, he couldn't get past the thought she'd be disappointed in him if he didn't share more about his sister. Enoch sighed, gathering his courage as if it was a shield he could use to protect himself.

"Anna was three when she fell off a horse."

Tears filled Gertrude's blue eyes.

He glanced away, knowing he didn't deserve her compassion. "S-she wasn't ever able to walk again after that."

"No." She grabbed ahold of his arm and squeezed.

Tempted to shake off her comfort, he shifted away. "It was my fault." His voice came out flat. "I looked away for just a few minutes. A young girl from school stopped by to see me and my attention was on her. I knew better. My concentration should've been on my sister. Pa had told me Anna was too young to be on the back of a horse, but she'd begged me to let her ride Fee."

"Fee?"

Heat rose in his neck. He'd never told anyone how his horse had been named. The unusual nickname had caused an inordinate amount of ribbing through the years when he'd ridden the cattle trail as other cowpokes speculated on the origin.

"How did your horse get such an odd name?"

He rubbed his jaw. "Anna named her when my mare was born. My sister was only two at the time. When she felt the soft coat, she called her Fluffy."

She chuckled. "And you didn't want to call her Fluffy, so you shortened it to Fee?"

He nodded. "Anna always could get me to do almost anything."

"So what happened?" Gertrude's words were soft.

Puffing out a breath, he continued. "I turned my head to see the gal from school. Anna must've decided she wanted Fee to go faster and kicked her little legs. Fee took off at a gallop. By the time I got to Anna, she was crumpled on the ground." He could still see the scene in his mind. "T-the doctor said she broke her spine in the fall. Said she'd never walk again."

"Aww, Enoch. How old were you?" She flicked a tear away.

"Seventeen."

"I can't imagine. Surely your parents knew it was an accident."

He shook his head. "They blamed me, and they were right. I knew they didn't want me to have her on a horse. I knew to keep an eye on her, but I got distracted by a pretty gal." He wiped a tear with the back of his hand. "Before it happened, I planned to become a preacher."

"And after that?"

"I knew I'd never be fit enough to be in God's service after what I did."

"Oh, Enoch." She wrapped her arm around his waist.

He didn't deserve her sympathy. "I left home the next day."

Her lips pinched together. Now she could see the truth of what he really was.

A coward.

"Did you not ever see her or your parents again?"

"Twice. I stopped to see her when she was five and seven. I sneaked in her bedroom window both times."

"Your parents must have forgiven you after all this time."

His throat thickened again. Enoch blinked his eyes and shook his head. He reached in his pocket and withdrew the envelope, handing it to her.

The envelope was addressed to him with several names of towns crossed out in different handwriting. Obviously, the stage company had worked to get the letter to the right person. The paper crinkled as she removed the short note. As she read it, tears streamed down her cheeks.

He glanced away, not willing to see her disapproval of him. It was enough that his parents felt that way. He couldn't handle seeing it mirrored in Gertrude's eyes too. Enoch shoved to his feet and away from her. He strolled a few yards away, staring at the horizon. "She was like you…Anna…she wanted to grow up and be a seamstress. Hoped to have a dress shop."

Her arms wrapped around his waist again. "She sounds as if she was a sweet girl."

He nodded, not trusting his voice.

"Sounds too as though she didn't blame you for the accident."

He knew better.

"Enoch. Look at me."

He dragged his gaze toward hers for a second before glancing away.

Gertrude placed her hands on either side of his face, forcing him to look at her. Her face was wet with tears she'd shed. "I don't know why your parents never forgave you, Enoch, but I know God does. He doesn't blame you for an accident that wasn't your fault. Should you have obeyed your parents? Yes, but I know God forgives you despite that. I don't understand why God allowed the accident to happen, but He did. You may never know why He called her home and didn't allow her to live to see her dreams, but I must trust He knows what's best even when we can't see why He did something. Tell me, when you visited Anna, what did she say to you each time?"

The memories rolled over him as if it was yesterday. She'd squealed and reached out for him to hold her. He'd had to remind her to be quiet so Ma and Pa wouldn't come to investigate. They would've kicked him out if they'd caught him.

"That she loved me. Missed me. Wanted me to come home. Said Ma and Pa would one day forgive me. Wanted to know how she could write to me."

"And did you write to her?"

He nodded. "I couldn't deny her that. Don't know if my parents ever let her read them. Although knowing Anna, she probably found a way to convince them to do what she wanted. She wasn't a spoiled child, but she did have a way of making you want to do what you could to make her happy." He swallowed. "Could be because the doctor didn't think she'd live long after the accident."

"She sounds as if she was a very special little girl."

"She was." Too bad he hadn't been able to be with her through the years. Now he'd never get to see her on this earth again.

22

Gertrude longed to comfort Enoch, to somehow take his pain away from him, or at least bear it with him. She couldn't imagine having a sibling die and not being able to be there for the funeral, or to be comforted by her family. She may not always appreciate her mother, but she'd be lost without her. "I wish I'd had the chance to meet Anna."

"She would've liked you." His words were whispered against her hair as he held her in his arms.

She could get used to having this, except he only had his arms around her because he needed someone physically to hold him up, support him, and comfort him in his time of loss. There was no way he'd ever be interested in her beyond this moment. She was a friend. Nothing more. And she'd learn to accept that…once she was back in her apartment and thinking straight. Later tonight she could remember the kiss they'd shared…and relive it in her mind. He probably wouldn't even remember it. But she would. For the rest of her days.

"I should get you back home." He pulled away.

She immediately sensed the loss. A chill ran through her despite the warmth of the evening.

He guided her back to town, keeping a distance between them as they walked side by side. Probably didn't want anyone to get any misconception of their relationship if they were seen together.

Outside her shop, she picked up the basket and handed it to him. "Please thank Ellie Lou for me."

He lifted the lid and glanced inside. "Are you sure you don't want to eat the rest of the food?"

She shook her head. "No, I'm sure you're hungry. Maybe you could eat some on your way home."

He opened his mouth as if he would say something. Instead, he dipped his Stetson toward her and turned away.

Her heart broke as she watched him stroll down the street toward the church. He didn't turn to look at her again. Once he was no longer visible, she sighed and unlocked the door to her shop.

Papa guinea pig squealed as soon as he saw her. It was still light enough to see them clearly. She opened the cage, and he scurried over to her. Lifting him, she snuggled him beneath her chin. "I should be happy having the shop. It's what I've always wanted."

The small critter butted his head against her chin as if he could sense her mood.

"At least I have you and your little family." She petted his soft fur. "It will have to be enough." A tear ran down her cheek. "One day it will be enough."

The babies came over to investigate. She placed the papa back inside and closed the door to the cage before they could escape. "Maybe sometime I'll be known as the seller of guinea pigs too." She chuckled. "Who wouldn't want to have one of you as a pet?" Although she'd be hard-pressed to let any of them go. At least they could keep her company as the many years of long evenings alone stretched before her.

Gertrude shoved the thought aside. "No use feeling sorry for myself." She squared her shoulders and headed upstairs. "For now, God's called me to be the best seamstress I can be. And shop owner. Somehow it would have to be enough. I'll learn to be content with what You've provided, Lord."

That decided, Gertrude stepped into in her small living room. She took off her boots and sat with her feet propped up on the little stool by her comfortable chair. Something crinkled in her pocket. She withdrew the letter Enoch's parents had written to him. She reread the missive. Tomorrow, she'd make a point of delivering the letter to the ranch when he was in town. She wouldn't embarrass them both by seeing him after the tender moment they'd shared. Chances were he wouldn't remember it anyway, and she'd be uncomfortable and hurt by his not remembering. For now, it was best if she didn't see Enoch. Didn't call attention to his hurt and pain.

She'd do anything she could to help him heal.

Lord, what would You have me do to ease his pain without making him think I'm interested in him? Is there something I can do to help him? Will You show me how to be a... good friend to him? What she wouldn't do to be more than that. She shoved the thought aside...again.

She glanced at her Bible sitting on a small table beside the chair. Lifting it onto her lap, she tried to remember the verse Ellie Lou had told her about. John 14:27. She flipped the pages until she found it. 'Peace I leave with you, my peace I give unto you: not as the world giveth, give I unto you. Let not your heart be troubled, neither let it be afraid'.

She ran her fingers over the words as she read them again. Maybe there was something she could do. Decision made, she pushed to her feet and crossed to her bedroom. She searched until she found a small stack of paper. Not bothering to put her shoes back on, she crept down the steps to the counter in the middle of the store. There was just enough light to find her bottle of ink and a pen. She scooped them up and carried them upstairs.

In her kitchen, she shifted a lantern to her small table. She lifted the glass globe, lit a match, igniting the wick. Sliding the globe back in place, she blew out the match and set it aside. Gertrude pulled out a chair and sat, perched on the edge. She thought for a moment before she started her letter.

~*~

By the time Enoch returned to the church, most of the people were packing up and preparing to leave. Some folks shot him strange looks.

He steeled himself as Gertrude's ma caught sight of him and made a beeline for him. Now what?

"Where have you been, and where is Gertrude?" She planted her hands on her wide hips. "I knew you couldn't be trusted."

"Now, Mrs. Miller, there's no reason to get riled." Pastor Montgomery came up behind them, clapping a hand on Enoch's shoulder.

"That's easy for you to say. He didn't cart your daughter away from the festivities and return without her."

"She's fine, ma'am." He tipped his hat. What were the chances he could leave it at that?

"I don't trust you." She wagged her finger in his face.

The feeling was mutual. The woman had yet to prove she cared about her daughter other than marrying her off to any man who came along. It's no wonder Gertrude had taken to find a man on her own without her mother's approval. Couldn't say he blamed her.

"What's going on here, dear?" Gertrude's pa shuffled over to them. He placed a restraining hand on his wife's arm.

She frowned. "I saw the two of them leave at least an hour ago. He just got back but not our daughter. How do we know he didn't do something awful to her?"

"Now, dear, let's not jump to conclusions."

The older man studied him. "Do you know where Gertrude got to?"

He nodded. "Dropped her off at her shop a few minutes ago."

"You see—" Pastor Montgomery interjected "—there's nothing to worry about. I'm sure you can stop to check on Gertrude on your way home."

"I still say I don't trust him." Mrs. Miller folded her arms across her chest.

He didn't need this right now. Didn't need it ever, in fact. *Lord, hasn't it been enough that I got news of Anna's passing?*

Mrs. Miller turned and huffed off.

Mr. Miller hesitated. "Sorry, son. She tends to overreact when it comes to Gertrude." The man didn't say anymore, instead he trailed after his wife.

The pastor clapped him on the back. "Enoch? Is there something I can do for you?"

He really didn't want to get into the death of his sister right now. He needed time to process it. As much as he'd love to go home to his parents, he wouldn't be welcome. Someday he'd make a point of returning to see his sister's grave, but for now it was out of the question. "Not at the moment."

The man reached out a hand, gripped Enoch's, and stared him in the eye. "If ever you need to talk, my door is open to you."

Enoch shifted his Stetson a little lower. "Appreciate it." Best to get away.

"Enoch?" The missus' face was flushed. "I've been searching all over for you and Gertrude. Did she leave already?"

"Saw her home a little bit ago."

"Good." A smile spread across her face. "Hope you two had a nice time together."

The pastor waved and left them.

"Guess I should get you home." He glanced around. "Did Jim head out yet?"

She nodded. "He was seeing one of the young ladies home, and said not to wait for him." She reached for the basket and frowned, lifting the lid. "There's so much food left. I hope Gertrude didn't leave you stranded. Oh, I guess not, you said you saw her home."

"That's right, ma'am." Best to leave it at that. "If you'll excuse me, I'll go get the team." He didn't wait for her response.

On the ride home, neither of them spoke. Enoch was thankful the missus didn't ply him with more questions. It was dark by the time they reached the ranch. He set the brake and helped her down from the wagon.

"Thank you, Enoch." She handed him the basket. "I imagine you're hungry yet. I'm in no hurry for this back."

"I appreciate it, ma'am."

She loosened the strings of her reticule, withdrawing a key and handing it to him. He slipped it in, unlocking the door before he gave it back to her.

"Did you want me to make sure nothing's been disturbed?"

She shook her head. "I know where to find you if need be."

"Yes, ma'am. Good night."

He waited until she closed the door behind her before leading the team to the barn. Enoch tied them to a fence. He'd take care of them once he checked on the herd.

Fee nickered as he got closer.

He stopped to scratch between her ears. "Hello, girl. Any trouble while we were away?"

Fee nodded her head up and down.

Enoch chuckled. "Folks will think I'm loco talking to you."

His mare whinnied, following him along the fence line as he squinted to count the mares in the corral. The moon broke free from the clouds, making it easier to see each of them.

He breathed a sigh of relief. All of them were where they should be. From the looks of it, nobody had created trouble while they were away from the ranch. He'd know for sure in the morning when he rode the fence line to check there weren't any cuts or breaks in it again.

Thank You, Lord.

"Looks as if things were calm, Fee." He glanced toward the house. A light shone from within. The missus would've come out by now if there'd been trouble.

The tightness in his chest eased. Maybe whoever had been causing mischief had decided to stop. He walked back to the team and grabbed hold of the bridle of the lead horse. Five feet from the barn doors he halted them, sliding the board, and pulling the doors open.

Immediately the acrid smell of sulfur caused his nose to wrinkle. He bit back a gag. Fishing his handkerchief from his pocket, Enoch tied the material over his nose and mouth. He fumbled as he found the tin of matches and lit a lantern. Lifting the light high, broken eggs shells were tossed about the main area, their contents dripping down the wall, spilling on the wooden floorboards and rails.

Who would do such a thing?

23

Enoch shoved his hand through his hair. "Got any ideas?" He'd waited until Monday to ask his boss, not wanting to disturb the man and his wife after the basket supper.

Josh tapped his fingers on the desk for a few minutes. "It's unlikely the Williams brothers were the culprits. You said you didn't see anyone on the ranch when you left. I witnessed them arrive a good half hour before you did, so there's no way they could have egged the barn and got here before you."

"Then who would have a reason to do such a thing?" He shoved to his feet, pacing the tiny enclosure, staring at the jail cell wishing the troublemaker was already behind bars.

"Always thought the Williams brothers had the most to gain if they scare Ellie Lou away from the ranch." Josh rubbed his chin. "Maybe we're looking at this all wrong. Could be it's just some kids causing mischief."

"But wouldn't they cause trouble at different homes instead of just on the ranch?" Enoch stopped his pacing to study the sheriff's reaction.

"Now you're thinking like a lawman." Josh beamed. "I knew you had the makings of a good one in you."

"You think?"

"Yes. I figured with your experience on the ranch, you have the ability to focus on details. Something always needed in an investigation. Sometimes just the smallest thing can help solve a case. You ready to give me an answer yet?"

Was he? After the note from Ma, he wouldn't be welcome back in Illinois. Not that he wanted to live there again. Unless things changed at the ranch, the missus couldn't afford to keep both him and Jim on the payroll. The other man needed the job since he didn't have any offers anywhere else. The Lord hadn't told Enoch no concerning the position. Maybe it was His way of saying Enoch should take the sheriff job. Besides, it'd be a while before he made enough money for his own spread. "You sure I can handle it?"

"I know you will. Besides, I don't plan to leave town. My wife and I will still be here. Any time you have a question, I'll be here for you. What'd'ya say?"

"As long as you keep giving me pointers...and don't plan to leave town anytime soon." He chuckled and thrust out his hand. "If you'll have me, yes, I'll be the sheriff. After we solve this case, that is."

Josh shook his hand. "Annie will be glad to hear it. So will Doc. He's been wanting to retire for a while now. Think he'd rather be fishing."

"I can attest to that since it's where I found him on the day your wife was travailing."

"You said Michael Browning hadn't told anyone about the note Ellie Lou took out on the property?"

Enoch shook his head. "No. Said he handled the matter himself. Didn't even have his secretary write it up."

"So there's no reason to believe someone saw it by accident." Josh started pacing. "Did he file the paperwork right away? Any chance he left it sitting on his desk, and someone saw it?"

"Not according to what he told me. Said he made a point of filing it himself since Mrs. Williams came in at end of day and everyone else had left. Says he tries to always make sure his desk is cleared off at the close of business so he can start fresh each morning." Enoch leaned against the desk.

"I'm fresh out of ideas." Josh came to a halt. "Don't worry. We'll come up with the answer before long of who's causing all the trouble."

Enoch just hoped it wouldn't be too late and someone got hurt in the process, especially if they interrupted the troublemakers during their next act of vandalism. While he hoped it wouldn't happen again, Enoch had the feeling it was just a matter of time until it did. "Just thought of something, did the Williams brothers ever say who they were scrapping with when they knocked me out cold?"

"No. Couldn't get them to say who it was, and the saloon owner said he'd never seen him before. I've stopped in there from time to time since then, and apparently he hasn't been back in the area either." Josh grabbed his hat from the hook by the door. "Knowing the Williams brothers, they tend to get in a disagreement with almost anyone. Jules said one time she got in a scuffle with them at the general store."

"Really? Don't think I ever heard that story before." Enoch grabbed his Stetson too.

"Jules made mention of it once. Never did get a full answer from her about what occurred." Josh opened the door. "I'll see you later. Promised Doc I'd help in his office this afternoon. Let me know if you learn something or need my help."

"I will." He waved. Might as well make rounds in town. He'd have to give the missus a heads up that he'd soon be leaving the ranch. Speaking of which, he needed to find a place to live.

A few minutes later, he opened the door to the bank. Several folks were in line. Mr. Browning, the bank president, sat behind his desk at the side of the room. Enoch strolled over to him. "Howdy. Do you have a few minutes?"

The man finished writing on a paper before placing it in a wire basket. "What can I do for you, today?"

"Was wondering if you know of any property for sale in the area." He probably couldn't afford a place of his own yet but maybe one day.

"As a matter of fact, the asking price for the Zeller farm just got reduced this morning. Would you be interested in seeing it?"

His pulse quickened. No use getting worked up. More than likely it was way out of his price range. "How much?"

The man quoted a price.

He could definitely afford that. There had to be a catch. "What's wrong with the place that it's going for so low?"

"The buildings are a bit run down. The owners are in a hurry to sell."

"Can you tell me where it's located?" Best to check into it without the banker in tow.

The man gave a brief description of how to find the property. "Let me know if I can do anything else for you." He went back to his paperwork.

Enoch hurried through his rounds anxious to see the place.

What would Gertrude say when she learned he was putting down roots in the area? Would she be pleased?

~*~

Gertrude delayed opening her shop for a few hours so she could pick up a few necessities at the general store. By the time she closed each evening, the general store also had shut down for the day. She couldn't delay any longer, or she'd have nothing to eat. Hurrying down the busy street, she scurried into the store. The bell above the door chimed.

"Howdy, Gertrude. Let me know if you need help with anything." Hiram Martin, the storekeeper, waved and went back to sweeping.

"Will do." She shifted the basket she'd brought along with her. It didn't take her long to fill it with canned goods and a few other odds and ends she needed. Checking her list against everything in her basket, she headed to the front of the store to check out.

"Did you see the fancy dresses there in the back?" Hiram swept near her, sending up a cloud of dirt.

She coughed.

"Oh, sorry about that." He chuckled. "Guess I need to sweep a little more often."

"What dresses?" She thought she'd remembered to retrieve all of the dresses she'd stitched that the storekeeper had agreed to sell before she'd opened her own shop. Had she forgotten some?

"That new gal asked me to sell them until she finds a place to set up her own shop."

Her mouth went dry. No. This couldn't be happening.

"Mighty fine work she does. The women have been oohing and aahing whenever they see them." He rested his chin on the top of the broom handle. "Thought you'd want to check out your competition."

Gertrude's stomach tightened. "W-where did you say they are?"

"There in the corner where I used to have yours." He motioned to the back section of the store.

Her heart was in her throat as she plodded to the place indicated. Thankfully he hadn't followed her, and the store was currently empty except for the two of them.

Four dresses hung from a hook. She walked over and touched each one. All the garments were made from the finest material she'd ever seen. She lifted the skirt of one of them to examine the hem and seam. Beautiful, tiny stitches near invisible. Gertrude dropped the fabric back in place and reached for the tiny tag pinned to the sleeve. She covered her mouth with her palm.

The shopkeeper shuffled up behind her. "Thought the same thing, but Miss Hadler insisted at the price."

"I-it's so expensive."

"It's what I told her. Said folks around here wouldn't be able to afford it." He ran a hand across his whiskered face. "Or at least most. Although she's sold two already. If you ask me, I don't see what all the fuss is. Your frocks are more serviceable."

She closed her eyes refusing the temptation to ask him if anyone had mentioned anything in comparison to her work but there was no sense in pushing him to gossip, something the man often was prone to do. No, best to see what she could do to promote her shop being practical for the whole family.

"Gertrude? You feeling sick?" Hiram's brows rose.

"Yes…I mean no." She shifted the basket on her arm. "I think I have everything on my list."

"You sure?" His gaze felt as if he were pitying her.

She squared her shoulders, standing taller. "I'm ready."

He gave a brief nod, setting the broom aside as he walked to the counter with her. "Let's get you checked out so you can be on your way."

A few moments later she was back on the street. Heat hit her like a cookstove. She put her head down and scurried toward her shop, hoping nobody would stop her to chat.

Next thing she knew, she collided with a solid chest. A very masculine, solid chest. Heat flew to her face as she drew back. "I'm so sorry."

"My fault." Enoch grinned at her. "Wasn't watching where I was heading."

She chuckled. "Me, either."

The memory of their kiss galloped through her mind. She swallowed and cleared her throat. What were the chances he was thinking about the same thing?

"I'm surprised you aren't in your shop." He glanced in that direction.

Apparently, the kiss hadn't meant anything to him. Nor should it. Why did she have to keep reminding herself of that? "On my way there now. Just had to pick up a few things." She pointed to the basket on her arm.

"I can carry it for you." He reached for it.

She pulled her arm back. "No, thank you. Looks as if you're going a different direction."

"I am, but I can make a detour for my favorite seamstress."

Tears sprang to her eyes at the reference. Her throat constricted.

"Whoa there. What's going on?" He tipped her chin, forcing her to look him in the eyes.

She couldn't halt a tear from trickling down her cheek. Reaching up, she brushed it away. "Nothing."

"Never heard nothing making someone cry."

"I'm not crying." She blinked her eyes rapidly, willing them to stop producing moisture.

A muscle in his jaw flickered. Did he plan to contradict her statement? Oh, who was she kidding?

Enoch took the basket from her arm and steered her in the direction of her shop. "Let's get you home, and you can tell me all about it."

Except she didn't want to talk about it. Didn't want Enoch near. It was easier to deny her growing feelings for him when she couldn't smell whatever he'd placed on his face after shaving. She swallowed, needing to get away from him so she could think straight.

"I'm fine." She tugged the basket, but he refused to release it.

"What's gotten into you?" His dark brows rose under his black Stetson.

"Nothing." She scurried the last few feet to her shop.

Mama turned toward her. "Where have you been? How can you run a successful business when you're off galivanting with him again?"

24

Enoch groaned. Gertrude's ma sure had a habit of showing up at the worst possible time. He plastered on what he hoped was a welcoming grin. "Howdy, Mrs. Miller. How're you this fine day?"

She scowled at him. "Keep away from my daughter."

"Mama!"

"What? He has no business sniffing around you. Can't you see he's only after you for your money? Now take Mr. Alwood—"

"Mama, please." She unlocked the door to her shop and turned to him. "Thank you, Enoch. I can take that from you now." She reached for the basket.

He lifted his chin. Wouldn't hurt to delay checking on the Zeller farm. Best to see if she needed his assistance first. "I might as well take it inside for you."

Gertrude darted a glance at her ma before she gave a brief nod. "You can place it on the counter, and I'll deal with it later."

"Nonsense. No use you toting all these canned goods upstairs by yourself when I can do it." He glared at her ma, daring her to stop him.

"Honestly, Gertrude. I taught you better than allowing a man in your living quarters. What's come over you since you moved away from your pa's protection?" Mrs. Miller shook her head from side to side.

"It's not like I haven't seen a sitting room and kitchen before." Enoch waggled his eyebrows.

Gertrude snickered and then clamped her lips shut after seeing the angry look on her ma's face.

"I'm not staying, ma'am, just carrying a heavy basket of groceries upstairs, so your daughter doesn't have to. My ma called it being a gentleman." He headed toward the back of the store and upstairs before he said something to anger her ma even more.

His temper calmed by the time he set the basket on the table in her kitchen. He didn't linger or else her ma would have more to say against him. Enoch figured he'd poked the bear enough for the day. He smiled at the thought.

Back downstairs, he probably should listen to reason and leave, but he couldn't help thinking about Gertrude's tears. Something had set her off. Problem was, he wouldn't be able to find out what it was with her ma hovering.

"You need to give up this fairytale of running a business. What you need is a husband and children."

"Mama." Dark circles were beneath her eyes. Had she not been sleeping?

"I put everything on your kitchen table." He glanced back and forth between them.

Her ma lifted her chin and looked down her nose at him.

"Thank you, Enoch." Gertrude lifted her hand as if to touch him. She halted, dropping it against her side again.

"You're welcome." He moseyed over to where a stack of men's shirts were on a table.

The ladies were quiet for a moment.

Her ma was probably trying to bore a hole in his back with her eyes. Ignoring them, he rifled through the stack as if searching for a certain color.

"You realize it's just a matter of time until you fail." Her ma's words cut through his trying to concentrate on what he was doing.

Gertrude didn't respond.

He glanced at her.

Her chin trembled.

It took everything in him not to go over there and put his arm around her.

Her gaze caught his for a split second before she stared at her feet.

"If you were at the general store just now, I'm sure you saw the dresses sewn by Miss Hadler. You've always had a way with a needle, Gertrude, but clearly you can see she's more gifted than you are." Her ma gripped her hand. "I'm not trying to hurt you, child. I just want you to wake up and see what's important. A woman wasn't made to have her own business. It's not what I or your pa want for you."

She sniffed.

He fisted his hand. *Come on, Gertrude. Where's that fire I know you have inside you? Don't let her keep talking to you like that.*

"Miss Hadler is only selling dresses for women and expensive ones at that." Gertrude folded her arms across her slim waist.

He smiled.

"I have a shop for the entire family." She stood a little taller.

That was the Gertrude he loved.

His thoughts faltered.

Loved?

No… not loved.

Cared about. Deeply.

Like a brother or sister. Like how he'd cared for Anna.

"Most women sew the clothes for their family." Her ma kept pecking at Gertrude like a woodpecker.

"True, but there are some who are too busy to do so because they're helping their husband."

He felt as proud as a rooster strutting around the barnyard.

Her ma shook her head. "I don't think it'll ever take on, Gertrude. I'm just trying to protect you. It's why I've been trying to find you a suitable mate."

Gertrude strolled over to the cage that housed the guinea pig family. Immediately one of them started whistling.

He smiled. Seemed like they wanted to come to her rescue too. Enoch couldn't blame them.

"Now, if you're finished, Mama, I have a store to run."

The woman's lips pinched together as though she'd taken a bite of something sour. She shook her head. "Very well, I'll let it rest for now, but mark my words, you won't ever get this business off the ground because you don't have what it takes. Besides, who would want to keep shopping here when you don't even have a placard out front? Your lack of faith in yourself is on display each time someone wanders by the shop and can't tell what's inside since you don't have a sign." She turned on her heel and left.

Good riddance.

"I'm sorry you had to hear all that." Pink colored her cheeks.

"I'm sorry she doesn't treat you like the treasure you are." He tossed one of the shirts on the counter.

Other than telling him the price and making change, Gertrude said nothing more other than handing him a slip of paper to pick a name for the guinea pig naming contest.

He glanced back at her before leaving.

Her back was already turned away from him.

Enoch knew what he could do to make a difference.

~*~

Gertrude couldn't resist digging through the jar of names after Enoch left, to find the one he'd written an entry on.

Ruffles–after the shop name and like her owner who isn't easily ruffled in the face of opposition.

She smiled. *Well, Lord, I may not be able to sew fine dresses like Betty, but it doesn't mean I can't still be who You made me to be. Right?*

She sighed. But what would happen if Mama was correct, and she couldn't make a go of the shop. What then? Would she have to move back home? Could she handle years of Mama pecking at her about finding a man?

Lord, please don't let that be all You have for me.

Other than the contest, what else could she do to bring business into the shop? She walked around the area straightening piles of clothes and refolding items that didn't need her attention.

The bell above the door rang out. She turned towards the door.

Ellie Lou hurried toward her. "I thought you might need a friend today."

"How did you know?" Gertrude hugged her friend. "You always seem to know."

Ellie Lou laughed. "No, I just try and follow through when God prompts me to do something."

"You're such a godly example." She looped her arm through her friend's and led her to the back of the store. "I hope you have a few moments to talk."

"Don't go putting me on a stump, or I'm liable to fall off it." Ellie Lou's brown eyes twinkled. "Believe me, there's plenty of times I fail or don't do what I feel God's telling me to do. Or times I delay doing what He's asked me to do."

They both sat on the chairs.

"You make it sound so simple to know what God's saying." Gertrude glanced around her shop. "How do you hear His voice in the midst of all the chaos around you?" Her cheeks warmed. "Not that I'm saying you live a chaotic life."

Laughter filled the shop. "I would say we each have tumultuous times in our lives. Some last longer than others."

"I still haven't figured how to be at peace when turmoil strikes." Gertrude ran a fingernail along the seam in the front of her skirt. "Every time I think I'm making progress, something else happens to throw me off track. Just when I feel I've gained some headway, I'm blown several steps backward."

Ellie Lou reached over and squeezed her hand. "That's where trust comes in."

"Trust? What do you mean?"

"I've told you before that God promises us His peace, right?"

"Yes. So where does trust come in?"

"Do you remember the verse from the Gospel of John I told you about?"

Gertrude nodded. "Yes, I read it the other night. But it didn't say anything about trust in it."

"We find our peace by looking to Him and trusting He's working even when we can't see it. I can't tell you how many times I've prayed a prayer like, 'Lord, You promised me Your peace. I can't feel it right now because of what's going on in my life, but I choose to trust You. I choose to trust You're working. I trust You have my good in mind.' The more I've gone through, I see the correlation between peace and trust. We have peace when we trust in Him. When we trust in Him, He gives us peace."

She thought about it for a moment. "Can you have one without the other?"

Ellie Lou shook her head. "No, dear, I don't think you can."

"But what if He allows something awful in my life?" As soon as the words were out of Gertrude's mouth, she wished she could snatch them back. "I'm so sorry, Ellie Lou, I wasn't thinking…"

"Even in the painful trials, God is still trustworthy. Amid heartache, He provides peace."

Gertrude glanced at her shop before smiling at her friend. "How did you get to be such a wise woman?"

Her friend laughed. "Charles would've enjoyed that. I wasn't when we were married. In fact, I was foolhardy, often going off halfcocked. He…and the ranch taught me to seek the Lord in all things. Believe me, there are times the old me comes back, and I have to beat it into submission again. I can only do so with the Lord's help. You can't rely on your own strength. You'll fail every time. I know I do when I try it on my own."

Gertrude sighed. "I keep seeming to fail."

Ellie Lou squeezed her hands again. "That's the beauty of each day; each moment can be made new again. Each time we have the opportunity to ask Him to help us. To make us more like Him. To ask for His peace. To ask Him to help us to trust Him. Another one of my favorite verses is from Proverbs. It talks about trusting God with all our hearts and not looking to our own understanding. When we do this, and acknowledge Him, He promises to direct our paths. I don't know about you, but I'm counting on that promise."

"Thank you, Ellie Lou. I'm blessed to have you in my life." She hugged her friend, choking back tears.

"And I you." She stood. "Now, let's see what we can do to bring in more customers for you."

"Before you do, would you mind praying with me? I'm ashamed I haven't spent a lot of time praying about the shop and how I can use it for Him."

"There's no time like the present." Ellie Lou sat back down. "Let's pray together, shall we?"

25

Over the next two and a half weeks, Enoch kept thinking about Gertrude's exchange with her ma at her shop. Their paths didn't cross during that time other than glimpsing her across the room at church each Sunday. He'd been kept busy taking on more and more responsibility as sheriff without officially having the title yet. Josh spent most of his days at Doc's instead of the jail. There hadn't been any more trouble at the ranch. Enoch liked to think whoever had caused the disturbances had either moved on somewhere else or had given up trying to intimidate the widow. His gut told him otherwise. It wouldn't do to let his guard down.

As he entered town, the sky was filled with pinks and purples as the sun crested the horizon. Temperatures had finally started cooling. Bird calls broke the silence of the morning.

Lord, help Gertrude to have a lot of people show up for the close of the guinea pig naming contest this morning. Help them to purchase something while they are there too. He patted Fee's neck. *And don't let her ma stir up trouble.*

A few minutes later, he tied Fee to the hitching post in front of the jail. He should have just enough time to complete his mission before Gertrude opened her shop. Pocketing a handful of nails, he balanced the hammer and the surprise he had for her.

He dipped his head in greeting as he passed folks on the street. Hopefully seeing more people than normal meant they planned to come to the clothing shop.

Outside Gertrude's, he set down the oversized board, studying the wall beside her large store window. Finding the perfect spot, he pulled out a few nails and started hammering.

A minute later the door to the shop opened. Gertrude poked her head outside. "Enoch? What're you doing here so early?"

He didn't answer, finishing the task he'd started.

She stepped out and stood beside him. "Enoch?" Gertrude gasped.

He glanced at her and then the placard. *Ruffles and Stitches.* He'd wanted to have it say Gertrude's Ruffles and Stitches but knew her well enough to figure she wouldn't want to call attention to herself.

She sniffed.

Did that mean she liked it or didn't?

Her arms wrapped around his waist for a fraction of a second before she stepped back. Her slight touch had him longing for more.

"Thank you, Enoch. And you even made it in the shape of a spool of thread." She smiled, her eyes twinkling.

She'd never looked more beautiful than that moment.

He sucked in a breath and cleared his thick throat. "You're welcome. Figured it was high time you had a sign out front, especially with the end of the contest today."

"You remembered." She took a step closer to him.

Would she hug him again? "Course. Couldn't forget something as important as a guinea pig naming contest." He grinned at her.

"It makes it more permanent now."

That was a good thing, right? Wasn't it what she'd been wanting all this time?

She beamed. "Thanks again, Enoch." She squeezed his elbow. "You have no idea how much it means to me. I don't think anyone has ever done a kinder thing for me."

"Yes, well…" She'd think him a simpleton with his lack of words.

"I best get back to my preparations." She gave a little wave. "I do hope you'll stop by when the shop opens, and the winners are announced."

He wouldn't miss it. "Is there anything I can help with?"

Gertrude shook her head. "I want it to be a surprise."

For him or the town in general? He dipped his head for a second. What had gotten into him? He was acting like a lovesick fool. Hadn't she told him numerous times she had no interest in getting married?

She glanced back at him.

"I'll be there."

She nodded and disappeared back into the shop. The sound of the lock slid in place.

He picked up the hammer and went towards the jail. If he hurried, he'd have enough time to drop it off and do a brief check of the town before heading to Gertrude's shop. He planned to be there as soon as she opened at eight o'clock.

The minutes crept by as he strolled through town. By the time he went in the direction of the clothing shop, folks were lined up outside and down the street.

He grinned. Gertrude would be pleased to see the community coming out to support her. The buttons strained on the shirt she'd made. He couldn't be prouder of her. He got in line.

It took at least a quarter of an hour for all of them to file into the shop. Folks lined the aisles, filling every nook and cranny. The scent of fresh baked muffins wafted in the air making his stomach grumble in complaint. He'd left the ranch this morning without eating anything.

A group of children stood near the guinea pig cage. He recognized the boy Gertrude had encouraged weeks ago. A slip of a girl stood with her parents, bouncing on her toes in excitement.

Gertrude started to speak but folks were too busy talking to each other.

He gave a shrill whistle to get their attention.

Chatter halted and all gazes swung to Gertrude.

Pink tinged her cheeks. "Thank you all for coming to Ruffles and Stitches. I can't tell you how much your support has meant to me over this past month or so. I hope you'll continue to find your clothing needs here. If there's something you don't see, please make me aware so I can remedy that." She smiled and glanced around the room. "It does my heart good to see you all here today. Please help yourself to refreshments." She motioned to a table laden with an assortment of baked goods.

"When're you gonna pull the names?" One of the boys piped up.

Chuckles filled the room.

Gertrude grinned. "I guess that means it's time to get started." She reached inside the cage and withdrew one of the babies. The tan, white, and black guinea pig nestled in her hand. She held it close to her chest and reached into the big glass jar with her other hand. "The first name is…Ruffles."

His heart quickened. Did she know it was the name he'd picked?

~*~

Gertrude's pulse jumped as she met Enoch's gaze.

"When will you pick the next name?" One of the young boys interrupted her.

She settled the guinea pig back in the cage and withdrew the mother. Reaching in the jar, she drew the next name. "Fluffy."

Elizabeth Wheeler let out a squeal. "That's one of the names I picked."

Her parents smiled and hugged the girl.

"Congratulations, Elizabeth." She set the pig back in the cage. "Let's see, next we have the black and white baby." She held it up for everyone to see.

The group of boys pushed closer to the cage.

"Checkers is our next name."

Someone in the back of the room waved their hand. "That's my pick."

Gertrude replaced the guinea pig, swapping it for another baby. This one was a mix of black, white, brown, and tan. She dug deep into the jar. "Our next baby will be called Gideon."

"That's mine." Young Gideon was grinning from ear to ear. His buddies elbowed him with excitement.

"Now, for our last baby." She held up a small brown pig. "And her name will be… Cocoa." She nuzzled the brown guinea pig with a white stripe down her face and belly. "How appropriate."

"And last but not least…" She replaced the baby with the father. As always, he let out a loud squeak.

The crowd laughed.

"His name is Squeakers."

The guinea pig whistled his approval.

"That's the name I picked too." Elizabeth beamed.

One of the boys frowned. "That's not fair she got to pick two of the names."

Murmurs filled the shop.

Gertrude held up her hand to silence them. "On the contrary. The rules of the contest stated each purchase provided a chance to name the guinea pigs." She motioned to the girl. "This young lady made a couple purchases. Thank you for coming out today. Don't forget to help yourself to refreshments but before you do that, I have one more announcement. Whoever picked the name for the first guinea pig wins either a dress or shirt made to their specifications. Please see me afterwards to identify yourself as the one who wrote 'Ruffles' for a name." She willed herself not to glance in Enoch's direction. "I hope you'll consider shopping here in the future as I will continue to have special contests from time to time. Again, thank you all for coming to show your support of me and your interest in naming my little family." She motioned to the guinea pig enclosure.

The next couple hours were a blur as people continued to mingle, enjoying the food she'd spent hours preparing. She lost count of the number of purchases made. At times she wished she had an assistant to help her. Maybe one day she could afford one. Several women said they'd come back next week for her to take measurements for dresses they wished her to sew.

Her heart welled with each purchase, each word of encouragement, each show of a sign of supporting her new endeavor.

As the store slowly emptied, Enoch remained on the fringes, just watching her. When the last person left except for him, he made his way over to her. Her heart pounded in her ears. She prayed he couldn't hear it. "What can I help you with?"

He tightened his grip on the brim of his Stetson.

Was he nervous?

He cleared his throat. "I'm the one who named the little gal Ruffles." He ran a hand along one of his dark sideburns. "I won't be needing a dress."

She chuckled. "No, I don't suppose you would." Gertrude studied his shirt, the one he'd purchased from her recently. "Looks like your shirt is a little tight on you. I could either alter that one or sew a brand new one for you." She licked her lips. "Or I could do both. It's the least I can do after all you've done for me." She picked up the cloth tape measure. "I could take your measurements now unless you have somewhere to go."

His brown eyes studied her.

She swallowed.

"I don't have anywhere else to be at the moment."

Gertrude fumbled with the pencil. It slipped from her fingers.

Enoch stooped over and picked it up. His fingers brushed hers as he handed it back.

Good heavens. Had the room grown warmer or was it just her? She resisted the urge to fan herself. "If you can turn around…"

He did so.

She blew out a breath and measured from shoulder to shoulder and notated the figure. Next, she measured from his neck to his trim waist, careful not to touch his middle. Then she stretched the tape to notate the length of his arm from the top of his shoulder to his wrist.

A bead of moisture rolled down her backbone. She circled around him. "I uh, need to measure your neck…and um…chest." She willed the warmth to subside from her cheeks.

He stretched his neck so she could perform the task.

Her head pulsed with each beat of her thudding heart. She wrapped her arms around his chest toward his back, pulling the tape taut as she measured. Her fingers trembled as she stared at the markings on the tape measure.

"Did you figure the calculation, or did you need some help?" His deep voice drew her from her trance.

"I uh…"

His head dipped towards hers.

Would he kiss her?

She closed her eyes and rose on tiptoe to meet him.

"Gertrude Miller! What are you doing?" Mama's voice rang out.

26

Gertrude yawned as she headed downstairs a few minutes before the shop opened. The excitement from the contest on Saturday had carried over to church yesterday. Numerous ladies had made a point of talking to her stating they would come to see her over the next couple weeks. She'd been unable to push the thoughts aside and welcome sleep. Also, her mind kept drifting to what would have happened with Enoch if her mother hadn't interrupted them.

As soon as her foot hit the bottom step, Squeakers made his presence known. She chuckled and scurried over to the cage.

"Good morning. I bet you all are hungry. Give me a minute, and I'll fetch your breakfast." She reached through the wooden slats and rubbed Squeakers. "I know I shouldn't have favorites but…"

He whistled and bobbed his head.

"I get the idea. You're wanting food. I'll be right back." Gertrude gave him one last pat before going to the back door. Once outside, she took a deep breath of the morning air. The weather had turned cooler overnight. She welcomed the change. Hurrying over to a thick patch of grass, she stooped and grabbed two big handfuls.

When she came back inside, young Gideon had his nose pressed against the glass window. As soon as he saw her, he waved, his little arm swinging like a flag on the breeze. Gertrude dropped the food into the guinea pig cage and went over to unlock the front door.

"Howdy, Miss Miller." The blond-haired boy glanced at the cage on the counter. "Would you mind if I look at Gideon?"

She smiled, refraining from touching the boy's shoulder. "I think it's a good idea for him to get acquainted with his namesake."

His forehead wrinkled. "Does that mean I can or can't?"

Gertrude chuckled. "It means you can."

"Thank you, Miss Miller." His slim arms wrapped around her

waist in a quick hug before running over to the cage.

She shook her head.

He stood on tiptoe to look into the enclosure. One side of his shirt was tucked while the other hung free. His hair was tousled as though he'd recently gotten out of bed, thrown his clothes on, and scurried to town. Had he let his mother know where he was?

"Excuse me, Gertrude. Do you have a few minutes that you could help me pick material for a new dress?" Sarah Brown stood by the bolts of fabric. "David and I will be celebrating our anniversary, and I wanted to have something new to wear." She shifted baby Joel on her hip. The youngster stuck a finger in his mouth, drool soaking his shirt.

She crossed the room, stretching her arms out. "Why don't I hold him so you have your hands free to see if you can find something special?"

Sarah glanced from her child to Gertrude. "Are you sure you wouldn't mind? He's been fussy lately since he's cutting more teeth."

"Give him to me." She took him in her arms, surprised at his weight. Taking a handkerchief from her pocket, she wiped his face. "There, isn't that better?"

His big eyes studied her, and his lower lip quivered.

Oh, no. She jiggled him and made a funny face.

Joel's lip stilled, tears glistening in his eyes.

She lifted him high and made a noise as she settled him back on her hip.

He giggled.

Sarah glanced up from searching through the stack. "You'll make a wonderful mother one day, Gertrude."

"I'm afraid that won't ever happen." Her throat tightened. "Did you find something?" She prayed the child's mother would be distracted and not say anything more on the subject.

"We all can see how you're taken with the new deputy." Sarah stopped searching, a smile spreading across her face.

She held the toddler in front of her line of vision hoping it would deter his mother, while she made some more silly sounds.

"It's obvious he cares for you too."

It was? Had he said something to someone? Hadn't they agreed to be friends…and nothing more?

Gertrude cleared her throat. "How about that blue cotton with the pink and yellow flowers? With your coloring and eyes, I think it would make a beautiful dress for your special occasion."

Sarah's eyebrows waggled. "You obviously don't want to talk about it, but one day your feelings will catch up with you."

What did that mean?

The young woman held the fabric up across her chest. "You really think this is the one?"

She cocked her head. "Most definitely. Would you like me to cut you a length? And will you be needing any thread?" She situated Joel on her hip.

"I'd love for you to make it for me, but I wasn't sure how expensive it would be."

Gertrude quoted a price. It was a little lower than she normally would charge, but she wanted to help the young mother. Sarah obviously had her hands full with Joel.

"Oh, I think I'll let you do it." She glanced around the shop and leaned closer. "Could you make sure the skirt has extra fabric?"

Did she mean…?

Sarah nodded. "I'm expecting again. I plan to tell David on our anniversary, so please don't tell anyone."

"Of course not. Your secret is safe with me. If you'll place the fabric on the counter there, we can go into one of the fitting rooms, and I'll take your measurements."

She started to hand the now fidgety Joel back to his mother.

"Help, Miss Miller!"

Gertrude glanced toward the center of the room. She'd almost forgotten about Gideon.

He ran over to her, tears streaking down his cheeks.

"What is it? What's happened?"

"I-I'm so sorry…I just wanted to hold Gideon, so I could talk to him better." His lower lip trembled. "I should've asked you first. He got scared and nibbled on my finger. I dropped him."

Oh, no. Please don't let him be injured, Lord. "Is he…?" she couldn't finish the question.

"H-he's somewhere in the store. When I tried to close the door to the cage, Gideon's papa got out too."

Not Squeakers.

The bell chimed as the door swung open.

"Close it, quick!" Her words came out louder and harsher than she intended.

~*~

Enoch reined Fee. Had that been Gertrude's raised voice? Best to check on her and make sure things were under control. His pulse quickened with the thought of seeing her again. He dismounted and looped the reins over the hitching post.

He opened the door to her shop.

"Close it. Oh, no, they didn't get out, did they?" Gertrude stood with a toddler on her hip, her hair disheveled.

Enoch secured the door. He could get used to the image of her with a child in tow. What would it be like to be his child? He shoved the thoughts aside. "What's going on?"

She handed the child off to one of the women in the shop. "Squeakers and Gideon got loose." She glanced at the boy. "The guinea pig baby might be injured."

At her words, the boy's lip quivered, and a tear ran down his cheek. "I didn't mean for it to happen, Miss Miller."

"I know." She squeezed the boy's shoulder. "Let's work together to find them."

"Yes'm." He wiped his nose with his sleeve before dropping to the floor and crawling around on all fours.

"Why don't we each get a section of the store to search." He motioned to the boy. "Gideon, take the back there."

"Yes, sir." The child scurried to his position.

Enoch prayed the boy wouldn't squish one of the guinea pigs in his haste to help.

The mother went to the front corner while Gertrude picked the other corner. The other woman stood in the middle of the store.

"I'll help Gideon. Each of you slowly search your area and work toward the center. Miss, if you can stay in the middle and keep a watch for the critters, we'll hopefully herd them in your direction." He didn't wait for them to answer, instead moving into position and watching each step he took. Once he got there, his gaze caught Gertrude's.

Tears filled her eyes.

"We'll find them." *Please, Lord.*

She nodded and stooped low to check underneath displays. "Come here, Squeakers. Come on, Gideon."

After a half hour of searching, it was clear the critters weren't in the shop. The doors to the back hallway and Gertrude's quarters had been closed, so there was no chance they'd escaped that way.

He sighed, shoving his hand through his hair. Time to face the facts; the critters had somehow escaped outside.

A tear trickled down Gertrude's face, dripping off her chin. Enoch reached over and wiped the moisture away. "We'll find them."

"B-but the chances of finding them before…"

"Let's go, folks. Tell anyone you see to be on the lookout for them." He held the door open and flipped the sign to say CLOSED before taking Gertrude's arm. "We probably should split up."

She nodded.

He watched her for a second and glanced around the town. *Where would a guinea pig go, Lord?*

Fee's ears perked. The horse snorted and pulled on the reins, backing away from the hitching post.

"Whoa, girl." He patted her, reaching for the reins.

She shook her head.

What had gotten into her? He didn't need a contrary mare on his hands too.

The horse backed up again, her ears swiveling back and forth.

This wasn't like her. Something was up.

Enoch glanced at the town. Every person he saw was calling for the guinea pigs, looking behind crates, and under bushes.

Fee trotted down the street.

"Whoa. Come back." He scurried after her.

The horse stopped for a second, her ears twitching again. She shifted directions, increasing her gait.

Don't I have enough to deal with, Lord?

He hefted a sigh, trekking after his horse, all the while keeping an eye out for the guinea pigs. Every time he got close enough to almost grab the reins, the mare shifted direction. She'd never been so ornery.

She whinnied and shook her head.

Stop. Start.

Stop. Start.

They played the strange game all the way through town. Each time Fee halted as if waiting for him to catch up. Then she'd lead the way again.

The longer he chased his horse, the more exasperated he became. *I don't have time for this, Lord. Can You make my crazy mare stop so I can get back to helping Gertrude look for her critters?*

The mare charged into the livery.

He scurried after her before she got into trouble. She'd never had her stomach drive her like this before.

"Fee, where are you?" It took a moment for his eyes to adjust to the darkened interior of the building. His horse stood at the edge of the first stall, glancing back at him.

A strange whistle came from the walled area.

He cocked his head. That almost sounded like…

The sound came again.

Enoch eased past his horse and stared at the straw filled area. A bale of hay was broken open on the side of the stall and in the middle of it stood two guinea pigs chewing away. He chuckled and patted Fee's neck. "I guess you're not so crazy after all." He scooped up the critters, securing them in his hands. "Come on, Fee."

The horse snorted and bobbed her head up and down.

"Guess I owe you an apology, girl."

She nodded again, and he chuckled.

Back out in the bright sunshine, he squinted. Giving a shrill whistle, folks glanced in his direction. "Found them." He kept his voice even so he wouldn't startle the critters.

A minute later, Gertrude ran towards him, her skirt lifted. Tears streaked her cheeks. "Squeakers, Gideon. Are they…?"

"Just fine." He handed her the adult guinea pig.

"How did you find them?" She rubbed her cheek against the small animal.

He chuckled. "I didn't. Fee did." He nodded towards the mare that trailed behind him.

"Fee? How?"

The critter butted against Gertrude's face.

"Don't know for sure. I'm guessing she somehow heard them. They were in the livery eating hay."

"Thank God. I was so afraid something happened to them." She rested her cheek on Squeakers again.

He couldn't help wishing it was him she was snuggling instead of the guinea pig.

27

Gertrude checked the cage, reassuring herself that all the guinea pigs were where they were supposed to be. She released a breath after she counted them again. Two days had passed since the incident and still she hadn't been able to relax. Her brain kept going back to the look Enoch had given her as she snuggled Squeakers after the guinea pig and his baby had been found. She hadn't been able to read Enoch's expression. Sarah's words kept flowing through her thoughts, and it was getting harder to thrust them aside.

She was thankful for the chime of the bell at her front door, welcoming the chance to shove her musings back into the far recesses of her brain. Gertrude pasted on a smile as Beatrice Smith and Amelia Evans pranced in. "Hello, ladies. What can I help you with this afternoon?"

They whispered to each other and glanced at her.

She held back a sigh. "I'll be over here if you need me."

Beatrice came closer and twirled in a circle, her skirt flaring. "Do you like my new dress?"

Gertrude studied the form-fitting bodice that accentuated the girl's figure. The upper part of the dress had two blue tones, complimenting each other. The skirt hugged her hips before flaring into a series of ruffles and lace at her feet. It was stunning. "It's lovely, Beatrice." She wasn't sure she wanted to know where the girl had purchased it.

Amelia touched the sleeve of her friend's dress. "We're so thankful we finally have a real seamstress in town. One who has exceptional abilities instead of mediocre ones like…" She dipped her head.

The girl didn't need to finish her statement.

Gertrude knew her skills were lacking compared to this.

"Ma said she'll purchase a new dress for me as soon as Miss Hadler's shop opens on Saturday. Beatrice managed to convince her to sew a dress in advance as a way of advertisement. In fact, Miss Hadler hired her to be a model for a few hours at the opening." Amelia lifted her head. "I'm sure the community will come out to support an exclusive lady's dress shop. Miss Hadler said her designs are taken from fashion plates from Paris. Can you imagine?"

Her chest constricted. She couldn't imagine. "W-where will her shop be?"

Beatrice smiled. "Just two doors down from you."

She hadn't heard anything about this. Hadn't even known the building was available. Paper had covered the shop windows for years. When she'd inquired about it, the banker had said the owner wasn't willing to sell. What had changed the owner's mind?

"It will be so nice to shop in a place where the proprietor is professional." Amelia sniffed. "One who doesn't have rodents in the middle of her business." She glanced at the guinea pig enclosure. "You may have gotten people interested in coming in so they could name them," she motioned, "but you don't have anything that will keep ladies returning."

"We'd better be going." Beatrice looped her arm through her friend's.

Gertrude spent the next hour sewing, ripping out, and resewing the seam of the dress Sarah Brown had ordered. She set the garment aside. If she kept working on it and had to rip her work out again, she'd weaken the fabric and would have to cut a new length of material and start all over. She couldn't afford a costly mistake, not when another shop would soon woo customers away from her.

The bell chimed, and she breathed a sigh of relief when Ellie Lou entered. Her friend had a knack for showing up when she needed her the most. Gertrude crossed the room to hug Ellie Lou. "I'm so glad to see you. What can I do for you this morning?"

"I wish I could purchase something from you today…" She glanced around the room. "One day, hopefully. When things get better."

"Are you sure there isn't a way I could help you?" Gertrude

motioned to the back of the shop. "Would you like me to make us a cup of tea?"

"I'd like that if you can spare a few minutes." Ellie Lou sunk onto a chair.

"I'll be back in a moment. I started the water a little bit ago." Gertrude hurried upstairs. She quickly prepared the hot beverage and carried two mugs downstairs. One day she would love to own some fine dishes like Ellie Lou had used to serve her tea when she'd visited the ranch. "Here you are." She handed the mug to her friend. "Now, what's going on?"

"It's one of those days when I'm struggling to find peace." Ellie Lou chuckled. "I know, I've been preaching to you about it—"

"I wouldn't call it preaching." Gertrude squeezed her friend's hand. "You've been sharing your wisdom and insight on the subject. Something I'm trying to learn and am not always doing the best at executing." *Especially today.*

"Join the crowd." Ellie Lou took a sip of tea. "Mmm. This is good. Thank you. It's hard not to worry sometimes." She huffed out a breath. "I only have less than three months until I might lose the ranch."

"What? How can that be?" Gertrude set her mug on the small table beside her.

"Things have been tight since Charles died." Her brown eyes filled with tears. "I had to sell off most of the stock, and I'm still having a hard time making ends meet. The man who had a contract with Charles to buy our mares for the military didn't want to work with a woman so he cancelled it."

"He can't do that. Surely you can fight it." Gertrude hugged her friend's shoulders.

"Not from the sounds of it. I guess there's some kind of clause included that stated if Charles died, the military was under no obligation to continue the contract." She took a sip of tea. "I'm saving some money since Enoch isn't with us anymore, but I'm afraid it still won't be enough to make up what I owe the bank."

Wait. What? Enoch left and hadn't said goodbye?

~*~

Enoch breathed deep of the morning air. Land spread out all around him. His land. Well, it would be his once he made all the payments to the bank. He stooped and scooped up a handful of dirt, letting it sift through his fingers. It would take a lot of work to turn the farm into a working cattle ranch, but he was up to the task. The hardest thing would be balancing his soon to be sheriff duties with his newly purchased property. He glanced at the house. It needed repairs and a good whitewashing. What would Gertrude think of it? It was the same question he'd asked himself too many times to count over the past couple weeks.

He'd moved his few belongings into the house a few days ago. The Zellers had left behind a few pieces of furniture they hadn't been able to fit into their wagon – a rope bed, dresser, kitchen table and a couple chairs along with the cookstove and dry sink. It wasn't much, but it was enough for his current needs.

It had been hard to say goodbye to the missus and Jim. Not that he wouldn't still see them around town, but it wouldn't be daily. After he'd committed to the sheriff position as well as setting down roots with the land purchase, he'd felt God's peace descend on him. Sometimes God was like that – providing peace after a decision was made and other times during a storm.

Thank You, Lord, for this place. Guide me as I move forward. I want to be in the center of Your will. If that includes Gertrude, I'd be mighty happy. He stood. *I know I wanted to find someone to woo her. Didn't stop to think that I want to be the one to woo her. That is, if she'll have me. Somehow, I think it will take some convincing to let her know what a special woman she is. Guide me, Lord.*

The sound of hoofbeats drew his attention to the dirt road in front of his house. He waved when he recognized Pastor Montgomery and strolled in his direction. "Howdy. How're you doing today? Were you needing me?"

The man dismounted and patted his horse. "Doing well. Just was exercising Champ here. I'm afraid he doesn't get as much riding as I'd like. Between visits to my parishioners, the twins, preaching, and keeping up with Jules, I don't get time away like I used to." He chuckled. "Not that I mind. I wouldn't trade it for the world." He glanced around. "So, you're the one who bought the Zeller place. Heard it was sold but didn't hear who'd bought it. Glad you decided to settle down in the area. Guess that means you'll be taking the sheriff job?"

Enoch shifted his Stetson. "I'm surprised your brother-in-law didn't tell you."

"With him taking over for Doc, we haven't seen a lot of him. Annie may be wishing he'd kept his position since he seems to be keeping longer hours as a doctor then he did as sheriff." He shifted the reins. "Do you mind if I water Champ in your stream?"

"Not at all." He motioned. "Go on ahead."

Drew clapped him on the back. "I'm happy for you, Enoch. I think for the most part you'll find not much happens around town that'll need your attention. You'll want to put time in improving this place, I imagine. Do you have any plans for the land?"

"Always wanted my own ranch with head of cattle on it. The Zellers only used part of the farm for crops. The banker told me Zeller always wanted to expand, but with only having daughters, he didn't get as much of the land cleared as he would've liked to. Ends up working in my favor. Figured I can have a nice sized garden next spring with the spot he used for crops and leave the rest of the grassland for cattle, when I can afford to get some."

They meandered across the field toward the stream that ran close to the house. The sound of hoofbeats was all that could be heard for a few minutes.

"You plan on looking for a wife?" The pastor stared at him over his horse's back.

He swallowed. "Still seeking the Lord on that one."

Drew studied him for a moment, not saying anything.

Enoch refrained from shifting his feet. Should he say something about Gertrude?

"I'll join you in that prayer then."

"Thank you, Pastor."

"Again, call me Drew or Pastor Drew." He smiled. "Well, I'd best be on my way. Jules is due any day now. I don't like being away from her for too long. Thank you for the use of your stream." He mounted his horse. "See you on Sunday if not sooner." He waved and headed back in the direction of town.

Enoch watched until he could no longer see the man, and then he went inside. Removing his hat, he chucked it on the table. A piece of paper blew and fluttered to the floor. What was that? He didn't remember seeing it there before. Stooping down, he picked it up. Scrawled across the slip were the words–*Mind your own business.*

What on earth? What was that in reference to? He scratched his head. Enoch was sure it hadn't been there when he'd purchased the place. Question was, who would've slipped in and put it there and, what did it have to do with?

He heard a sound outside. "I guess Pastor Drew forgot something." He chuckled and stepped out into the bright sunshine. "What did you need, Pastor?"

A sound came again, and he turned in that direction. Blinding pain seared through his head as something hard connected with it. His vision dimmed. He struggled to stay conscious. Another blow came, driving him to his knees. "Help." The world went black and the last thing he knew was his face hitting the dirt.

28

Gertrude's heart constricted. How could Enoch have left Burrton Springs without saying goodbye? Whatever happened to his being the town deputy while helping Ellie Lou at her ranch? Didn't he care about sticking to the commitments he'd made? Maybe he wasn't the man she thought he was. Tears sprang into her eyes. She willed them away. She would not cry for a man who clearly had no regard for her.

"...and then pigs can fly."

"What? Why are you talking about pigs?" Gertrude stared at a smiling Ellie Lou.

"Was wondering when you would catch on to the conversation. It's apparent your mind has been somewhere else the past few minutes." She touched her shoulder. "What's going on?"

"I'm sorry. I didn't mean to ignore you when you were sharing about your financial troubles. I wish I could do something to help you, but now with another shop opening..."

"Shop? What shop? Having another business open in town should be a good thing, right? Why's it troubling you?"

She puffed out a breath. "I was just told Betty Hadler is opening an exclusive dress shop in three days."

Ellie Lou frowned. "That shouldn't hurt your business too much, should it? Especially since you've branched out into carrying clothes for the entire family."

"Except most of my sales are from women coming in for either material or dresses. I've had only a few men stop by so far, and I still haven't sold clothes for children or babies yet. Perhaps in time, but..." She wrung her hands. "I want to help you, Ellie Lou, and it pains me that I may soon be in a similar financial situation. Amelia Evans and Beatrice Smith stopped by before you came in. I think they wanted to make a point of showing off Beatrice's new dress Betty had made. It's stunning. I've never made anything so beautiful before in my life."

"Doesn't mean you can't."

"You don't understand. It's beyond my abilities."

Ellie Lou thrust her hand on her hips. "Who says?"

"Anyone can see it." She flung her hand out to encompass the shop. "As you can witness."

"Nonsense. Beatrice and Amelia don't get to define who you are. Neither can your ma. The only one who can do that is Jesus Christ."

"Yes, but—"

"No buts. Don't fall into comparing yourself to others, Gertrude. God never does that. He never looks at you and finds you lacking. He loves you. He created you. He has a purpose for your life. The important thing is to discover it and rest in it. Be who He wants you to be and not someone else." Ellie Lou shoved to her feet. "Look at all you've created here. You should be proud of it. I know I'm proud of you. You remind me of the need to trust God with my circumstances."

"I do? But how? I'm always failing it seems, and I'm in need of your advice and wisdom." Gertrude stood beside her friend.

"It's why I came in to speak with you. I knew that talking to you would help calm my spirit. Knew it would help tether me to the necessity of giving my concerns to my Heavenly Father. Sometimes a friend helps to carry our troubles, but I also have to remind myself to look to the Lord for His wisdom and direction for my future. I need to trust Him even if I don't know what the next steps look like."

"I wished I had your faith…"

Ellie Lou held up her hand. "Don't say that. We aren't to envy each other or wish for what they have. God gives us what we have need of, and when we need it. I guess I should take my own advice. Faith comes by trusting God through the trials in life. It comes by looking to Him. Releasing ourselves to Him – giving our lives fully to Him. I don't know why He's allowing my struggles or yours either, but I pray we both can trust Him with whatever He has in store for us."

Gertrude sighed. "You're right, as always."

Her friend chuckled. "Believe me, I'm wrong many times.

Charles could attest to that. Now, what were you thinking about when I was talking about pigs flying?"

Heat flared in her cheeks.

"I'm guessing it was something more than just a new dress shop opening." Her brows lifted. "So what was it?"

Gertrude picked up her mug and took a long drink to stall for time.

"Yes?"

She glanced at her friend.

Ellie Lou wouldn't drop the matter.

Gertrude puffed out a breath. "I…that is…you said Enoch left…I would've thought he'd at least say goodbye."

Ellie Lou's forehead wrinkled. "Why would he do that?"

Did she need to spell it out? She'd come to care for him. That is, he'd become a part of her life. One she'd miss. She should've told him sooner how much she appreciated him. Appreciated his calm manner, his care, his concern, his…

"Gertrude?"

Tears welled. "I don't know…that is…it will be different around here without him."

"I think there's some sort of miscommunication here." Ellie Lou gripped her shoulder. "He only left the ranch. Not the area. He's taking the position as sheriff here. In fact, he bought a place of his own just outside of town."

"He did?" Her heart sped up.

"Oh, girl. Have you told him how you feel?"

"W-what do you mean?" She licked her lips.

Ellie Lou laughed. "It's clear you care for him."

"Of course. He's been a good friend."

"Gertrude, look at me."

She dragged her gaze to Ellie Lou.

"He's more than a friend to you. Everyone can see that. I'm surprised *you* haven't seen it before now. But I guess that's how love is sometimes. It sneaks up on you, and you move from just being friends to longing for more. I love when God does that."

"But what if he doesn't feel the same way?" Her throat tightened and tears welled.

~*~

Gertrude shifted in the saddle. It had been a while since she'd ridden. After her discussion with Ellie Lou, she'd sensed an urgency to see Enoch. She'd closed the shop early and searched all over town to no avail, even stopping and asking folks if they'd seen him. Nobody had. She'd even dragged Josh away from a patient so she could ask him when he'd last seen Enoch.

Josh hadn't been too happy about the interruption. "You're making a mountain out of an ant hill."

She shoved the thoughts aside. Worry nibbled at her brain. *Lord, help me find him.*

The outskirts of town gave way to the countryside. Fields stretched on either side of the dirt road. Her tenseness eased. While she'd gotten used to living in town, there was nothing like being closer to God's creation. Did Enoch feel that way too? She'd have to ask him sometime.

It took a few minutes for the old Zeller farm to come into view. She could see Fee in a pasture nibbling grass. Odd that Enoch hadn't been in town today especially since he'd taken over as sheriff. She rode the borrowed horse up to the barn. Dismounting, she tied the mare to the hitching post in front of the building.

She shielded her eyes from the sun, perusing the fields but didn't see him anywhere. Butterflies fluttered in her stomach. She should have thought this through. Her mother would never let her hear the end of it if she discovered Gertrude had visited Enoch alone without a proper chaperone. Not that it mattered as much at her age.

Stuffing her concerns aside, she headed in the direction of the house. Paint peeled on the clapboard home. "Enoch? Where are you?"

No response.

She rounded the corner and saw him lying face down in the dirt. Her heart slammed in her throat as she lifted her skirts and ran. *Dear God help him.*

The acrid scent of blood assaulted her nostrils. Dark red stained the back of his head and the ground. "Enoch, can you hear me?" She stooped beside him, gently shaking him. *Please let him be alive, Lord.*

Not a muscle moved. He lay still.

Too still.

Her fingers fumbled to find a pulse at his wrist. There. Slow but steady. *Thank you, God.* She patted his back. "I'll be back. You hang on, you hear?"

She didn't wait for a response, instead running for her horse. The reins tangled and her fingers shook as she untied the knot. A moment later she swung onto the mare's back, kicking her into motion. "Come on, girl."

The ride back was a blur and seemed to take way too long. Her heart thudded in her throat as she prayed for Enoch. She breathed a little easier when she stopped at the doctor's office. Gertrude prayed Josh was here and not on a call somewhere else. She swung down from the horse and ran into the building. "Josh! You've got to come quick."

"Gertrude?" He poked his head out of one of the rooms down the hallway. "What's going on?"

She glanced at the folks in the waiting room. "It's Enoch. Someone knocked him out cold. He's bleeding."

"Give me a second to get my bag."

An eternity passed in the time it took for Josh to get his medical bag and his horse. "Where is he?"

"The Zeller farm." She didn't wait for his response but kicked her horse's side. "Hyah."

"Gertrude, wait."

There was no way she was hesitating when the man she loved lay bleeding. The ground beneath her horse's hooves flew by as she urged the mare to run faster. She sawed on the reins as she reached the farm, almost flying over the mare's head when she stopped quick, her sides heaving. Gertrude jumped to the ground and ran to Enoch.

He hadn't moved.

Josh came up alongside her a moment later, immediately stooping in the dirt and checking the back of Enoch's head.

She stood back, wringing her hands, and praying.

Josh felt Enoch's limbs. "Nothing appears to be broken. Run inside and see if you can find a container and get some fresh water from the stream."

Thankful to have a way to assist, she rushed to the house, pushing the door open. She glanced around the kitchen and found a bucket. Grabbing the rope handle, she scurried to the stream. Gertrude hefted the bucket to her hip and hurried over to Josh, setting the bucket down beside him. "Here. What else can I do to help?"

"See if you can find a clean towel inside."

She ran to do his bidding. Back inside she scanned the kitchen but didn't see anything. Two of the rooms were empty. The last one held a bed. Her cheeks flushed as she stepped across the threshold. There on a shelf was a small stack of towels. She grabbed a couple of them and ran outside. "What next?"

Josh dipped one of the towels in the bucket and took his time cleaning the wound, putting pressure on it for a while to stop the bleeding. "He'll need some stitches. Good thing he's out cold. I'd prefer to do it inside, but with his dead weight I don't think we can manage him ourselves."

Dead weight. *Oh, please, God, don't let him die.* She gripped Enoch's calloused hand.

"Hold tight to him while I stitch his head." Josh searched in his bag and withdrew a needle and some sort of thread along with a bottle of something. Using the clean towel, he soaked it with the liquid in the bottle and dabbed it on the wound. When the needle pinched the skin, Enoch flinched and moaned.

"Shh. You'll be fine. Lie still now." She rubbed her thumb against the back of his hand.

He settled down and didn't make another sound.

Josh soon finished the task, placing items back in his bag.

"Who would do this to him," she whispered.

29

Enoch moaned.

A hand probed the back of his throbbing head.

"Have pity." Cotton lined his mouth preventing him from saying more. He didn't remember his new bed being so hard. Groaning again, he forced his eyelids open. Sunlight seared, forcing him to squint. Why was everything sideways, and why was he so close to the dirt? Scratch that. Why was he lying in the dirt?

"Enoch? How're you feeling?" A deep rumble came beside him.

"Josh? What're you doing here?" He started to roll over when hands stopped him.

"Hold up there. I just stitched and bandaged your head. Careful you don't get dirt in the area." Josh stooped down beside him. "Do you think you can push up with your arms, or do you need help?"

He could handle a simple push up. Enoch shifted his hands and strained for all he was worth. His limbs trembled with the effort. He managed to ease to his haunches. Sweat poured down his back, and his vision dimmed.

Josh's hand fell on his shoulder. "Sit for a minute until you get your bearings."

"Will his head mend?"

A long skirt flashed before his vision. Gertrude? When had she gotten here? When did Josh arrive? He didn't recall either of them visiting him.

"Give him a minute." Josh squatted in front of him. "Follow my finger with your eyes."

He did his best to follow the simple instruction despite the woodpecker hammering at the back of his head.

"Good. How many fingers am I holding up?"

"I can see fine, Josh. You've got four fingers in front of me."

"Have to be sure, especially with you having a head wound again. Let me know when you're ready, and Gertrude and I will help you to your feet."

Enoch figured it was a waste of breath to refuse them. He waited a minute longer for his vision to return to normal. "I'm ready."

Gertrude shifted to one side. Josh went to his other side and helped him to stand. He felt weaker than a newborn colt. Was he wobbling as much as one? He wasn't sure.

The scent of flowers distracted from his throbbing head. He breathed deep. She sure smelled good. As much as he liked having her by his side, he needed to get her out of here as soon as possible. If she got caught in the middle of whatever was going on, she wouldn't be safe. He'd do almost anything to make sure nothing happened to her.

By the time they sat him in one of his kitchen chairs, he was sweating profusely.

"I still say you should lie down for a while." Gertrude's lip jutted out.

He glanced away from it. "I'm fine here. You'd best get back to the shop now."

She looked at him as if he'd slapped her. Lifting her head up a notch, she folded her arms across her chest. Spoiling for a fight or protecting herself?

Enoch shifted his gaze to Josh. "Appreciate your help. I'll be fine now. I'm sure you both are needed back in town. I won't hold you any longer."

"I'm not leaving until you tell me what's going on." Gertrude's toes tapped against the wooden floor.

"Same with me. How did you get hit on the back of your head?" Josh leaned against the dry sink.

"I'll tell you all about it but not until Gertrude heads back to town."

"And I said I'm not leaving." Her blue eyes flashed.

"Then I'm not saying anything." He could be stubborn too.

Josh's gaze flitted back and forth between them. "Gertrude, can I speak to you outside for a moment?"

She bit on her lip but nodded.

Enoch breathed a sigh as they left the room. He folded his arms on the table, letting his pounding head relax on them.

A good ten minutes passed before Josh entered the kitchen again. Alone. "You've got one angry woman on your hands."

He sat up. "If you ask me, you're the one with the angry woman since you were the last one to speak to her."

Josh chuckled. "You aren't getting off that easy. For now, I got her to agree to let me handle things with you. Said it would be best if you told her what happened when you were up to it. I convinced her you needed to rest for now, but I'm guessing you won't be listening to your doctor's orders?"

"Can't."

His friend stared at him for a moment before nodding. "Out with it. Who hit you on the head? Did you happen to see anything?"

He shook his head, wincing at the motion. "No. Pastor Drew stopped by and chatted for a few minutes. After he left, I came back inside and found this." He withdrew the paper from his pocket, handing it to Josh.

"Definitely sounds like a threat. Don't suppose you saw who left it?" Josh sank into the chair across from him.

"No. I'd just read the note when I heard a noise outside. I figured the pastor had forgotten to tell me something and had come back. I went to see and next thing I knew, someone knocked me on the back of the head."

"You don't remember anything else?"

"No."

"Looks as if I stepped down from the position as sheriff too soon." Josh rubbed a hand along his jaw. "Not that I'm saying you can't handle the job. I just had hoped since there hadn't been any more trouble for a while that whoever had done it had moved on somewhere else. Guess not."

"Do you think the note and my being hit on the head are connected to the mischief at the Williams's ranch, or could it be something more than that?"

Josh stared at the table as if he weren't really seeing it. "Seems more likely they're related. Unless someone else was trying to purchase the Zeller farm and you swooped in and purchased it first. Although it doesn't seem as feasible since it's been for sale for a little while."

Enoch scrubbed a hand across his forehead. "My gut says they're connected."

Josh nodded. "Mine does too. I'm guessing that's why you didn't want Gertrude to hear about it."

"I don't want her to get in the mix of this. Couldn't ever forgive myself if something happened to her on account of me."

~*~

Gertrude fumed all the way back to town. Couldn't Enoch see she cared about him? What made him think he could get rid of her? Didn't he know she loved him? She pulled back on the reins.

Love?

Whoa. When had she begun to think of Enoch in those terms? It wasn't true, was it?

She should head back, return the mare, and open her shop but her heart wasn't in it. Instead, she kneed the mare into motion. It had been far too long since she'd visited Annie. She shifted directions.

A few minutes later she pulled the horse to a halt in front of Annie's home. The white picket fence stretched around the house. She smiled when Wolf, Josh's shaggy dog came around the corner of the house, his tail wagging. "Hello, fella." She dismounted, looping the reins through a slat in the fence before patting the dog.

The front door opened, and Annie stepped on the porch, Eve in her arms. "I thought you might be Josh, but you're a welcome surprise. I hope you have time to visit for a little while."

"I have as long as you'll have me." She opened the picket gate, closing it behind her. Walking up the steps, Gertrude hugged her friend careful not to hurt the baby sandwiched between them. "Do you mind if I hold her?"

Annie handed her the baby.

She kissed Eve's soft cheek. "Hello, little one. My, you're

growing. Mama must be feeding you well."

Annie's cheeks colored. "Come inside. I'm not sure when Josh will be home."

"I don't know." Should she say more? "That is, last I saw him he was at the old Zeller farm with Enoch."

Annie's eyebrow quirked. "Sounds as though there's more to the story than what you're sharing."

She filled her friend in on what had transpired. "I don't know why Enoch was so insistent on my leaving." She shifted the baby on her shoulder, patting the small back.

"It's obvious if you ask me." Annie motioned to a chair. "Have a seat. Can I get you something to eat?"

"No, I'm fine. What do you mean? What's obvious?"

She chuckled. "You can't tell?"

Gertrude shook her head.

"He cares about you."

"I don't know how you get that idea. He didn't want me around and was upset I was there. Insisted I leave, in fact." She jiggled Eve when she started fussing.

"Probably because he didn't want you to get hurt." Annie reached for the baby when Gertrude couldn't quiet her. Her friend lifted her blouse and settled the baby at her breast.

Her throat tightened. Such a simple act–a mother feeding her child. Would she ever have the pleasure of having a child at her breast? It didn't look as if that would happen with Enoch's rejection. "I don't know, Annie. I've been overlooked most of my life."

"Just because the men in this town haven't realized the treasure you are, doesn't mean Enoch doesn't see it."

Gertrude shrugged, running her fingertip along a groove in the table.

"He's paid special attention to you ever since he took the position as deputy." Annie shifted Eve to her shoulder, rubbing her back.

The baby burped.

Gertrude smiled as Annie shifted the child to her other breast. "I imagine the children are missing not having you in the classroom anymore. Have you heard if Mr. Sanson has found a replacement yet?"

Her friend nodded. "I miss being with the children, but I wouldn't exchange it for my time with little Eve." She leaned over and kissed her daughter. "I heard the new teacher will be arriving on the stagecoach on Saturday."

"She'll get here in time for the church picnic then."

"They'll be starting school later than last year, but she'll hopefully be able to get the children up to where they should be." Annie placed the child in her lap and tucked in her blouse before patting Eve's back again.

"Did you hear what her name is or where she's coming from?"

"No, I guess we'll learn more about her in a few days."

Annie's cat wandered into the room. She rubbed against Gertrude's legs before jumping into her lap. She chuckled. "I missed you too, Bella."

The cat meowed and turned in a circle before curling into a ball. A moment later, purring rumbled in her small body. Gertrude stroked the cat's head.

The door opened. Josh strode inside, stopping short when he saw her. "Howdy. Didn't realize you'd be here, Gertrude. Was wondering whose horse was out front." He crossed the room and kissed his wife and daughter. "I planned to head back to the office but wanted to check on you two."

"We're fine." Annie pushed up her spectacles and smiled at her husband.

Gertrude glanced down at the cat again. Maybe she should leave. No. While she had him here, maybe she could get some answers. "How's Enoch doing?"

His gaze flitted to hers before dropping. "Headache, but that's to be expected."

"Did he tell you what happened? Who hit him?"

A muscle in his jaw flickered. "He doesn't know who hit him."

Why did she get the feeling he was withholding information from her? She scowled at him. "What aren't you telling me, Josh?"

He squirmed. "Now, Gertrude, you know I can't tell you about an active investigation."

"Investigation?" Annie frowned. "I thought Enoch took over as sheriff. You aren't helping are you, dear?"

Josh fidgeted with the brim of his Stetson. "There's something I need to see through before I officially hang up my hat and spurs."

"And what might that be?" Gertrude pressed.

"I'll see you later, ladies." He kissed his wife again. "There's nothing for either of you to worry about." He exited as if he were being chased.

Annie stared at the door, not saying anything. She stood, crossed the room, and placed Eve in a cradle beside the fireplace. "I've found that whenever he says there's nothing to worry about, it's the opposite."

That's exactly what Gertrude thought.

What were the men hiding?

30

Enoch's head throbbed with each clop of Fee's hooves.

If Josh had his way, he would've kept Enoch house-bound for a couple days, but they both knew delaying wasn't an option. Josh was tied up with having to see patients.

Time for Enoch to do the job the town had hired him to do. He wasn't sure he had an answer on how to do that though. He bit back a moan as he dismounted in front of the saloon.

Josh had said the Williams brothers had taken residence in the rooms above the establishment.

Enoch tied Fee to the hitching post. He wrinkled his nose as the scent of alcohol wafted as he entered the room. A few men sat at a table. Cards were spread in front of them. Behind the counter, a man stood wiping a glass with a rag. Enoch strode over to him. "Can you tell me if the Williams brothers are in?"

The man placed the glass on a shelf behind him and turned back around. "What did those two do now?"

"Didn't say they did anything. Just wanted to talk to them."

The saloon owner grunted. "If I had a nickel for each time those two got into trouble, I'd be a rich man." He motioned to the stairs. "Haven't seen them come down yet today. They have the first two rooms on the left."

If it was true, it meant they couldn't have been the ones to knock him out earlier. But he couldn't just go by what the man said. "Thank you." He clomped up the steps, knocking on the first door he came to. "It's the sheriff. Open up."

He heard scuffles behind the door before the door swung inward.

Charlie Williams grinned at him. "Sheriff? Last I heard you were just a deputy. Looks as if you've been promoted. C'mon downstairs, and we'll celebrate."

"Stay right there." Enoch walked a few paces away and knocked on the next door repeating the same instructions.

The door cracked open, and George Williams squinted at him. "That you, Deputy? What're you doing here?"

"Come with me." He motioned towards the other room. "Let's have a little chat in your brother's room." He waited until the two were seated. Snagging a chair, he flipped it around, sitting so he could keep an eye on both of them. The scent of urine and alcohol infiltrated the room. "Where were you two this morning?"

They glanced at each other, not responding.

"You can either answer my questions here, or I can take you to the jail. Which would you rather have?"

George scrubbed a hand across his whiskered chin. "No reason to get testy, Sheriff. I know you're new to town, but whatever you think my brother and I did, we're innocent."

Charlie kicked his brother's boot. "We were right here, Sheriff. In fact, you just woke me. From the looks of it, you woke George too."

The brothers nodded.

"I'm sure Jeb can vouch for us." George's eyes narrowed.

"And who's Jeb?" Enoch leaned forward.

"Jeb. You don't know Jeb?" George glanced at Charlie.

Charlie shrugged.

"He's the owner of this fine establishment." George scratched his oily hair.

Fine. Right. There was nothing *fine* about it.

"How did you get the knock on the head, Sheriff? Did you fall?" Charlie studied him.

"We're not talking about me." He shifted on his chair.

"Whewee. He's mighty touchy, isn't he, Charlie?" George grinned at his brother. "Bet that hurt." He got up and shifted closer. "You even needed stitches."

"I imagine the former sheriff came to your rescue," Charlie said.

He didn't like the direction the conversation was going. Maybe it was better to change tactics. "When was the last time either of you were at the Williams's ranch?"

"You mean the ranch that's rightfully ours?" George glared. "The one our cousin stole from us?"

"Now, George, you know Grandpa gave it to him." Charlie exchanged a look with his brother. "We haven't been there in years, have we, George?"

"No, we haven't. We know when we're not wanted, although if Ellie Lou finds herself desiring help, especially with you leaving her, I guess we could offer our services. Wouldn't want the land to fall into disrepair. She doesn't have enough men to make a go of the ranch since you left her high and dry, so you could become a lawman. I'm sure it wouldn't take much to turn it back into a farm again." George rose to his feet. "If there's nothing else, Sheriff, you might as well be on your way since we haven't left our rooms until you came."

"I'll check into your story." He didn't like being dismissed by the two. Enoch still had a feeling the two were up to something. What, he wasn't sure.

Back downstairs, he had to wait while Jeb filled an order for someone Enoch hadn't seen before.

"Were you wanting a drink?" Jeb eyed him. "Thought most lawmen didn't drink on the job, but I guess there's always a first time. Although the doc might tell you it's best not to drink with a head wound like that. Me, on the other hand–it helps to dull the pain." He took a swig of an amber liquid. "Some of us need to dull the pain. One way or another."

"About Charlie and George. When was the last time they left their rooms?"

"Can't be too sure. I don't keep regular tabs on them." He squinted. "Yesterday? Maybe the day before. As I said, I don't keep an eye out for their coming and going. But if you wanted to pay me, I could maybe keep watch on them for you." Jeb scratched his chin. "I'd give you a special since you're the new sheriff now. And from the looks of your head, you can use all the help you can get."

"How about you do it anyway as a law-abiding citizen and let me know if they're up to something."

"Sure. Sure, Sheriff." Jeb smiled. "Have a good day."

Enoch stared at the man. There was something about the man he didn't trust. Charlie and George Williams weren't trustworthy, either.

~*~

Fee had turned cantankerous refusing to go in the direction Enoch wanted the mare to go. "What has gotten into you today?" He tried again to get her to head back home. She turned back around and trotted into the livery.

"Whoa there." A grizzled man with gray whiskers and a balding head put his hand up to halt the horse. "I can board her if you need me to, Sheriff, but most times I like some sort of agreement up front."

He swung down. "I don't know what's gotten into her. She knows better than to barge in somewhere I haven't directed her."

The man chuckled and leaned on the handle of a pitchfork. "Well, in my experience a horse is pretty smart. Never saw one do something without a reason. Trick is figuring what that reason is. Why do you think she'd want in here?"

Enoch patted Fee's neck. "Don't know for sure. The only other time she came in your livery was when she found the guinea pigs that had gotten loose."

"Heard about it from some of the townsfolks. I was exercising some of the horses at the time. Maybe she's wanting to see them again." He pitched some fresh straw into a stall. "You could always take her over to Miss Miller's shop. Maybe she'd let you bring one of the critters outside so your mare can see them."

That wouldn't do. He wanted to avoid Gertrude until he discovered who had knocked him on the head. She was safer if he kept his distance. When things simmered down and he had the culprit in jail, then he could consider what was next with their relationship. Until then, it had to wait.

"Well, you can take my advice or not. If your mare's like most females, once they get something in their craw, they won't let it go until they accomplish their goal."

Enoch hefted a sigh. The last thing he needed was a horse with a mind of her own. One who didn't take his instructions.

The man held up his hand. "I won't keep you, Sheriff. Best of luck with the little lady."

He managed to get Fee backed out of the livery and back on the road again. His chest eased. He kicked the mare into motion as they started to ride past Gertrude's shop except once again Fee had ideas of her own. She stopped in front of the big window, her head bobbing up and down. "Come on, girl. You're killing me here."

He shifted on the reins for her to turn, but she refused. Enock kicked her side. Still she refused to move. He pinched his lips together and swung down from the saddle. "Come on, Fee."

She bobbed her head again.

Using the reins, he put his weight into trying to pull her in the right direction. She shifted her weight to counteract him.

By then, folks were starting to laugh and point.

His ears burned.

"Horse trouble?" A chuckle came from behind him.

He glanced at Josh. "It's not funny. She won't listen to me."

A twinkle flashed in the man's eyes. "And here I thought you used to have a job on a ranch and knew a thing or two about horses."

"You would think." He crossed his arms and scowled at his horse.

"Maybe she wants to see Gertrude."

"No. It's not that."

Merriment filled the man's eyes again. "You sure about that?"

He bit back a groan. "The livery owner thinks she wants to see the guinea pigs."

Josh slapped his knee. "Isn't that funny? Never heard of a horse and guinea pigs becoming friends, but then I never even heard of a guinea pig until that swindler brought them for Gertrude."

"Give a fella a break here. Do you have any ideas to get her moving since she's refused taking orders from me?" He tugged on the reins again.

"They always say you can catch more flies with honey. Not sure if that applies to horses, but maybe a treat will get her heading in the direction you want to go." Josh grinned. "Do you want me to go get some sugar cubes from Hiram before he closes the general store for the day?"

Fee snorted and shook her head.

Enoch adjusted his Stetson. What could be more embarrassing?

He nodded. "I'd appreciate it. And not a word of this to anyone?"

Josh motioned towards the street. "Too late for that."

He bit back a groan. Had everyone come out of their homes or businesses to see his horse problems? At this rate, he wouldn't be taken serious as sheriff of the town. *Lord, couldn't You show me a little mercy here? Make this crazy horse start obeying instead of making me stand here like a fool.*

Movement at the window caught his attention.

He closed his eyes.

Please, Lord, not that. Isn't it enough the townsfolks have seen this, but Gertrude too? She'll just think I'm ignoring her. His ears burned. *You're right, I am ignoring her, but You know I have a good reason to. All I want is for her to be safe. Can't she see that?*

He caught a glimpse of tears streaming down her cheeks before she turned her back and walked away from the window.

31

The remainder of Gertrude's week had gone from bad to worse. The worst had been watching Enoch and Fee outside her shop when the horse had refused to obey his master. From the exchange, it was clear she'd misread Enoch's intentions toward her. After the occurrence, several people had come into the shop talking about the sheriff and his misbehaving horse. Folks were beginning to wonder if he was the right man for the job. They speculated whether his lack of ability with his horse after working on a ranch correlated to how he'd do as a lawman. She'd refused to get involved in the conversations.

She shoved aside the memories, wishing it would be a better day, but with the opening of the new dress shop today, the likelihood of things improving was minimal at best. Gertrude welcomed the bell chiming above her door.

"Howdy, Miss Miller." Elizabeth Wheeler skipped up to her. "Ma said we can go see the new dress shop even though we prob'ly can't buy anything."

Gertrude glanced behind the child but didn't see anyone else. "Where's your ma?"

"Oh, she had to stop by the general store first. Said I could come here and see the guinea pigs until she's ready." Elizabeth leaned close and whispered, "I think she wanted me out of the way for a bit since I have trouble standing still waiting on her while she shops."

She chuckled. "Waiting can be difficult."

"It's harder than a peppermint stick." The girl hugged her before strolling over to the guinea pig cage. "Hi Squeakers and Fluffy."

Squeakers made himself known.

Funny. He usually only did that for her. Maybe he knew the girl had named him.

Elizabeth sighed. "I sure wish I could have one of them."

Hmm. Would other townspeople be interested in purchasing a guinea pig if she decided to breed them? Couldn't hurt to supplement her income any way she could especially with another shop in competition with her. Wouldn't hurt to investigate the matter. Maybe Josh would be willing to build smaller cages providing the doctor's office didn't keep him too busy.

A knock sounded at the front window.

"That's Ma. Guess I'd better go. See you, Miss Miller." The girl hugged her before running towards the front door. "I still think your shop is the best one in town. Bye."

The girl was gone before she had the opportunity to respond. Gertrude chuckled and wandered to the front window. Ladies were beginning to line up along the boardwalk, chatting to themselves. Her gut churned.

Lord, I know it's not You who says I'm not enough. She took out a rag and rubbed a spot on the window. *But it's hard not to feel that way at times. Especially when my skills are lacking compared to someone else's.*

Several of the ladies turned in her direction. She smiled and waved.

Ellie Lou keeps talking about peace. It's been elusive. Between this new dress shop opening and whatever is going on with Enoch…I don't know where I fit. Don't know that I ever have. Ellie Lou says it all boils down to trust. I want to trust You, Lord. I want to be in the center of Your will. She paced away from the window, tears pricking at the corner of her eyes. *But I guess I don't know how. I want to let go and trust You. Please show me the way. I'm not as strong in my faith as Ellie Lou. I'm ashamed to admit it. I know she said not to compare. I want to be different. Please help me, Lord.*

Squeakers whistled, standing on his back legs, his front paws resting against the rungs of the cage.

"What is it, buddy?" She crossed the room.

His small body continued to make shrill sounds.

She opened the cage and lifted him out. "I don't know how you always know when I could use some encouragement." She stroked the length of his soft body. "What do you think, boy? How does one go about learning to trust God more?"

If Squeakers had an answer, he didn't share it.

Gertrude placed him back in the cage with his family. "How about some grass?"

He whistled his approval.

She chuckled. "I'll be right back." As if the animals were going anywhere.

Outside, she breathed deep of the morning air. She was tempted to close the shop and run away for the day. The likelihood of people coming in was slim at best. Gertrude stooped and plucked a large handful of grass. She'd soon have to come up with another way of feeding the guinea pigs when grass wasn't as plentiful in the winter months. Maybe the livery owner would let her purchase a bale of hay. It couldn't be that different than grass and hadn't seemed to hurt Squeakers or Gideon when they'd escaped.

A door slammed somewhere down the alley.

"We gotta be more careful, or he'll be on to us." A male voice sounded familiar, but she couldn't place it.

"Shut up. We've got nothing to worry about. Just do what you were hired to do. If you don't, we'll find someone else who will."

Her pulse spiked.

What were they talking about? She crept closer to the alley. Holding her breath for a few seconds, she tried to work up her courage to see who the men were. But by the time she did so, the alleyway was empty.

Gertrude shook off her concern. Nothing sinister would happen in Burrton Springs.

The sight of Enoch lying face down in the dirt flashed before her eyes. It had been an accident, right? Nobody she knew would have a reason to hurt him.

By the time she opened the back door, she'd convinced herself her imagination had gotten the better of her. As she walked down the hallway she called, "I have some grass for you and your family, Squeakers."

She entered her shop, and the grass fell from her fingers.

Enoch.

~*~

Everything Enoch had been planning to say to Gertrude evaporated as soon as she entered the shop. It was a mistake coming in when he couldn't tell her what was going on. In his limited experience with women, they weren't happy when you withheld something from them.

She didn't say anything to him, instead stooping to pick up the grass she'd dropped on the floor when she'd seen him.

Should he help her?

She completed the task, walked over to the cage, and dropped the grass in the cage.

The guinea pigs whistled and squealed as they ate the food she'd supplied.

He never heard creatures be so noisy while they feasted. "They sure do like it, don't they?"

She nodded. Her lips pinched together.

He withdrew the bouquet of wildflowers from behind his back that he'd picked earlier. "Thought these might help today."

Still nothing.

She didn't even reach for them.

"I was surprised to hear about the new shop."

Something flickered in her eyes.

"I'm sure you have nothing to worry about. Folks will see the value of what you've created here." He motioned. Several petals fluttered to the floor.

She glanced at it.

Enoch bent to pick them up. When he stood, she busied herself with straightening a pile of shirts. He tamped down his frustration. He deserved her censure. Setting the flowers on the counter he said, "I'll just leave these here. If you need anything, you know where to find me."

As he opened the door, her soft words fluttered to him.

"I won't."

He'd prefer being stabbed over her losing faith in him.

Lord, help me to be able to make things right after the troublemakers are in jail.

But what if that never happened? What then?

~*~

Enoch stood outside the front window of Gertrude's shop for a few moments without moving. Was he thinking about coming inside again? Did she want him to? Gertrude glanced at the flowers.

How did he always find a way to do something nice for her when nobody else seemed to notice her struggles?

"Just because he's thoughtful doesn't mean he has any feelings for me."

Squeakers stopped chewing and cocked his head, looking her way.

The creature likely wondered why she was talking to herself. Or maybe he figured she was talking to him.

"Probably was feeling sorry for me, right Squeakers?"

The guinea pig whistled.

Right. Best to keep busy and keep her mind off the sheriff. She spent the next few hours putting the store in order and finishing the order for Sarah Brown. At some point she'd have to make the shirt she'd promised Enoch. Gertrude didn't look forward to having to deliver it to him.

Just as she prepared to close early for the day Sarah entered the store. "Hello, Gertrude. Figured I'd stop in since I was in town." The mother-to-be smiled.

The woman likely had been checking out the dress shop but had the decency not to mention it.

"I'm glad you came in. I finished your dress a little bit ago." She crossed to a hook where she had the dress hanging. Gertrude held it in front of her. "What do you think?"

Sarah came closer and fingered the full skirt. "Oh, Gertrude, you've outdone yourself. It's beautiful. I can't wait to show if off to David. He'll be so surprised. I'm sure he'll like it."

"He'll appreciate it because you're wearing it."

The young mother blushed.

"I can wrap it for you." She pulled out a length of paper.

"That would be wonderful. I wouldn't want him to see it until our anniversary."

Gertrude wrapped the dress in the paper, tying it with a piece of twine. "There you go. Please let me know if you have anything else you'd like me to make you sometime."

"I'll keep it in mind." She squeezed Gertrude's hand. "Thank you so much. I'd better get back home, or David will worry about me. Joel will soon be up from his nap. Goodbye."

After Sarah left, Gertrude went over to the sign on her door and flipped it to say CLOSED. Might as well spy on her competition. No, not spy. See if she could discover some ways to make her shop more exclusive to the needs of the entire community instead of just the women.

By the time she stepped outside, there was no longer a line waiting to get into Betty's new shop. She paced by the store a few times before she gathered enough nerve to go inside.

Beatrice Smith stood on a small pedestal wearing the dress Betty had made. A gaggle of ladies were around her oohing and aahing.

Gertrude shifted away from the commotion. Beautifully stitched and designed dresses stretched across the length of room and along the back wall. She made her way along the perimeter studying each one. Her gut churned. Each creation was more spectacular. She shook her head. How had Betty sewn so many in the short time she'd been in town?

"Hello, dear." Betty's aunt Mary came to stand beside her. "I'm surprised to see you here."

"Mmm." What else could she say?

"I begged her to leave well enough alone." The gray-haired woman frowned. "She was taught better than this."

How should she respond to that kind of statement?

"I told her it was despicable."

What was the woman talking about? Gertrude swallowed. She wasn't sure she wanted to inquire what the older lady found despicable.

"You've seen it, haven't you?"

"There you are, Aunt Mary. I could use your assistance when you have a moment." Betty appeared beside them, breathless as if she'd been running a race.

"I'll be there in a minute, dear."

Betty nodded and went over to a small counter.

"I'm sorry, Miss Miller. I wish she hadn't done it."

She glanced at Betty's aunt. "I'm afraid I'm not following what you're saying. What did Betty do that's so despicable?"

The older woman wrung her hands and then indicated a dress in the back corner.

The gown was identical to the wedding dress Gertrude had made for herself and was still on display in her shop.

32

Gertrude forced her hands to lay still on her lap. After Enoch's unusual drop by the shop yesterday, and seeing her wedding dress duplicated in Betty's shop, she'd thought twice about making an appearance at church service this morning. Would everyone be talking about the new shop and her foolhardiness in having a business of her own?

"Good morning." Pastor Drew stood behind the small podium set on a table. "What a glorious day to be celebrating our Lord and Savior."

Gertrude didn't know that she'd call it glorious.

"Let's talk about Second Corinthians chapter four, verses seventeen and eighteen. 'For our light affliction, which is but for a moment, worketh for us a far more exceeding and eternal weight of glory; While we look not at the things which are seen, but at the things which are not seen: for the things which are seen are temporal; but the things which are not seen are eternal.'" Drew glanced around the room. "You may find yourself in the midst of troubles."

She sat up a little taller in her seat. Had he heard about all her struggles?

"Perhaps you can't tell which way is up right now because you're in the middle of a storm, or you feel like a wave has overpowered you, and you're floundering in the water trying to catch your breath. Do you remember the story of Jesus walking on the water to meet His disciples who were already on the ship? They were afraid and thought He was a spirit."

"I know that story, Pa." Elizabeth whispered loud enough for the congregation to hear.

A chuckle flowed through the room like a wave.

Drew smiled. "I imagine most of you have heard the story before.

But did you ever wonder why Jesus didn't calm the wind and waves until He and Peter were back in the boat? Here in Matthew fourteen, it says, 'But when he saw the wind boisterous, he was afraid; and beginning to sink, he cried, saying, Lord, save me. And immediately Jesus stretched forth His hand, and caught him, and said unto him, O thou of little faith, wherefore didst thou doubt? And when they were come into the ship, the wind ceased.'"

Gertrude could relate to being in the middle of a storm.

"Peter cried out for Jesus to help him. I can imagine he was terrified seeing the wind make the waves even stronger. He was afraid to drown." Drew chuckled. "I'm sure I would've been afraid too if I were in that situation."

She nodded.

"You could say Peter didn't have any peace about what was happening. He went from believing he could walk on water like Jesus, to starting to sink in a split second. What made the difference do you think?"

The room was quiet. Not even the babies stirred or made a sound.

"He took his eyes off Jesus and studied the situation around him. Peter went from trusting to doubting. Maybe you're in a similar place right now where it's hard to trust God." Drew bent and picked up a paper wrapped package tied with red yarn. "I have a gift for one of you today."

The children all raised their hands. Some called out. "Ooh, pick me, Pastor Drew."

He chuckled. "Elizabeth Wheeler, come up here for a minute."

"He picked me, Pa." She stumbled in her haste to get to the front of the room.

"Careful there." Drew put out a hand to halt her from falling. "I have something for you, Elizabeth, but first I need you to do something for me."

"Yes sir." She grinned.

"I want you to close your hands tight into a fist." He demonstrated.

Elizabeth did what he said.

"I have a gift for you, Elizabeth. You can only have it if you can hold onto it and not drop it, but I don't want you to open your hands."

Each time she tried to reach for it, the package fell to the floor.

Pastor Drew put his hand on her shoulder and turned her to the congregation. "You weren't able to receive the gift, were you, Elizabeth?"

She shook her head.

"I can tell you want what I have for you."

Elizabeth nodded.

"What would you need to do to get the gift?"

She shrugged. "Open my hands?"

He beamed. "That's right. You may open your fists now." He handed her the package, and she took it. The pastor hugged the girl and whispered to her.

She took the gift back to her seat.

"God wants to give you a gift too. When we're in the middle of a storm, He desires to give us His peace. But we don't always accept His gift. We want to hold some things back. Actually, He desires for us to know, understand, and move in His peace all of the time. But sometimes we think we know better than God. Which is silly. We don't open our hands and trust Him to fill them. You can't fully walk in His peace in your life until you learn to let go."

Murmurs filled the room.

"But in order to receive the gift, your hands can't be closed. Sometimes we hold tight to our worry, doubt, unforgiveness, or other things we're refusing to give to God. We block the flow of the goodness He wants to bestow on us when we hang onto things." He grinned. "I don't know about you, but I don't want to get in the way of all the goodness God wants for me. I'm sure you don't either."

"When Peter realized he couldn't keep himself from falling beneath the waves, he cried out to Jesus to save Him. Friend, I pray you don't wait until you're sinking in the water to call to Him. Instead, each day ask the Lord to help you to experience the peace He promised. The kind of peace He mentioned in this verse from the gospel of John. 'Peace I leave with you, my peace I give unto you: not as the world giveth, give I unto you. Let not your heart be troubled, neither let it be afraid.'" Pastor Drew closed his Bible and studied the congregation before bowing his head for the final prayer.

Gertrude's heart constricted. How many times would she hear the verse before she started believing it? Tears blurred her vision.

~*~

Enoch squirmed in his seat. He hadn't experienced peace ever since he made the decision to keep information from Gertrude. Once things were settled, would she believe he'd withheld things to keep her safe or would she see it otherwise? Would she doubt his integrity?

His gaze swung to where she sat two rows ahead of him. Enoch's senses had been aware as soon as she'd entered the building before the service began. If she saw him earlier, she'd given no indication.

Am I trying to provide for her safety instead of trusting You to take care of her, Lord? He wasn't sure he wanted to take the time to examine his heart on the matter. Maybe he wouldn't like what he discovered. *Is it wrong of me to want to protect her? Didn't You make men to be the protectors?*

"Folks, before the picnic begins, I wanted the opportunity to introduce everyone to our new teacher. He arrived on the stagecoach yesterday afternoon. I hope you all will make him feel welcome. Stephen, come up here." Pastor Drew motioned to someone on the left side of the room.

Folks murmured as a tall, red-haired man walked to the front of the room. His hair was parted in the middle. He wore a black jacket and pressed pants. Not a wrinkle in sight.

Pastor Drew clapped the man on the back. "Please welcome, Stephen Arnold. We're excited to have you here and look forward to getting to know you better. For all you parents, in case you hadn't heard, Mr. Arnold will be starting classes tomorrow morning."

Some of the children groaned.

Enoch caught sight of one of the mother's grabbing her son by the ear. Must've been one of the complainers. He hid his smile behind his hand. The man would have some troublemakers on his hands.

The congregation stood and clapped.

The pastor held up a hand for silence. "I know we're all getting hungry. Please make a point of introducing yourselves to Mr. Arnold. Before we head outside, let me say a blessing on the food." He bowed his head and everyone else followed suit. "Dear Lord, thank You for Your provisions. One of those is Mr. Arnold. I pray You be with him as he adjusts to life in a new place. Help us to do whatever we can to make the transition smooth for him. Thank You too for the food everyone has provided. Bless it to nourish our bodies so we can become the people You want us to be. Guide and direct our daily walk with You so others can see You through us. In Jesus's name we pray, amen." Drew looked up. "If some of you men will help set up sawhorses and boards, the ladies will be able to get the food set on tables for us. Thank you all and have a great day."

Enoch moved to assist with the set up, but he was hemmed in on both sides as folks took their time chatting to each other. A steady stream of people went forward to make the new teacher welcome.

Gertrude made her way to the front, standing in line to talk to the newcomer. She spent a few minutes speaking with the pastor before it was her turn to say something to the teacher.

The man took her hand in his, lifted it to his lips, and kissed the back of her knuckles.

Color filled her cheeks, and her eyes fluttered a few times.

A few minutes passed before the newcomer let go of her hand. Or did it just feel like a few minutes? Enoch couldn't tell for sure.

She wasn't interested in the man, was she? She took a step closer as he said something in her ear.

Enoch's gut twisted.

There was no reason for that. Sure, the chatter in the room was getting a might loud but she was standing close to the man. Too close.

The fella said something again, and she tipped back her head and laughed. The man joined her merriment.

Enoch scowled. He'd never seen her act that way with anyone before, not even George. Of course, he hadn't seen the man until after he'd been arrested and swindled money from her.

Their conversation kept going until the man behind Gertrude

tapped her shoulder. She smiled and said something else to the new teacher before she finally left him.

Enoch's chest eased as she started walking away.

A smile spread across her cheeks, a becoming pink on her face made her more beautiful than he'd ever seen her…except for the fact she was probably thinking about the fella she'd just met.

His gut churned again. He'd lost his appetite.

Her gaze met his for a second before she glanced down.

Not wanting to see more, he shoved past the couple blocking his way. "Excuse me." He didn't wait to hear what they said in response.

Outside, he got busy tossing boards on the sawhorses that had already been set up by someone else. The task was completed long before he'd worked off his frustration.

Josh came up beside him. "Something bothering you?"

"What gave you that idea?"

"Oh, no reason." Josh chuckled and indicated various folks standing and staring at him.

He sighed.

"I'm guessing you weren't too happy with Gertrude taking her time greeting the new guy?"

So he wasn't the only one to think that. No use saying it though.

"Can't blame her. After all, she hasn't had many men glancing her way."

"The fellas from your town are loco then." He crossed his arms.

"Is that so?" Josh grinned.

"Said it many times." Oh, no. Shouldn't have mentioned that. Josh would never let him hear the end of it.

His friend's brows waggled. "You've been glancing at her ever since you took the job as deputy. Now you're the sheriff and bought your own place. So what's holding you back from making your intentions known to her?"

"Who said I have intentions for Gertrude?"

"I just did."

"I'm not saying I do or don't, but I'd be a fool to get her involved with me until things have simmered down." He glanced around and lowered his voice.

"Maybe. Maybe not."

Enoch ran a hand along his stiff neck muscles. "What do you mean?"

Josh didn't answer right away. He glanced at the door to the church, but Gertrude still hadn't come outside yet. "The way I see it, there'll always be some sort of trouble here in town."

"You said nothing ever happened." Enoch glared at Josh.

His friend held up his hand. "I didn't say that. If I recall, I said things *usually* don't happen. Guess I never told you about the shoot out when Annie was in jail. Or the time Jules was kidnapped."

Enoch's mouth gaped. He shook his head. "Wait. What? When did this happen? You never told me about either of those. Are you holding out on me?"

Josh chuckled. "No. Just been too busy to get around to telling you about it. When things slow down, I'll share the full story."

"I'll hold you to that."

"Just as my brother-in-law said in the service this morning, you can't keep holding onto things thinking you can control them. Sure we try and take care of what we can, but the rest we have to leave with God since He knows what's best for us. I'm convinced if you're sensing God has led you to Gertrude, He'll provide what she needs whether you're there or not." He clapped Enoch on the back. "Don't keep your life on hold until things settle down, or you'll find there's always something that crops up for you to attend to."

"You think?"

Josh nodded. "I do, or I wouldn't have said it." A twinkle flitted in his eyes. "Pray about it and see what God's telling you to do but don't base your decision on what you can do to keep her safe. Trust God with her. Give her to Him."

His chest eased. "I guess I have been trying to control the situation."

"I know you have."

Enoch glanced at the doorway again. Still no Gertrude.

"I've known from the start, you're the man who can woo Gertrude. She hasn't paid attention to the fellas here because they didn't have that special spark she's been looking for." He poked

Enoch's chest. "But you do, Enoch Valentine."

Warmth spread through his chest. *I'd be blessed to have a special woman like Gertrude in my life, Lord.* His gaze strayed to the doorway like a magnet. *Who am I kidding, Lord? I don't want a woman like Gertrude in my life. I want Gertrude Miller.*

Laughter snagged his attention. He saw a flash of her skirt before he saw Gertrude. Enoch smiled anticipating talking to her.

She stepped out of the church…

On the arm of the new teacher.

33

Gertrude's finger barely touched the crook of Mr. Arnold's arm. When he'd asked if she'd linger to accompany him outside, she hadn't wanted to refuse and appear rude in the process. Her gaze flitted to Enoch's. She'd prefer to be with him, but for whatever reason he'd decided to build a wall between them. Not knowing what it would take to break it down, she stayed with someone safe—a newcomer who needed a friend to navigate the ins and outs of his new community. It was the least she could do.

Enoch looked as though he'd eaten a bite of a sour peach. He stared at her a moment longer before he turned away. What was that about?

She stumbled.

Mr. Arnold's grip tightened on her arm. "Are you injured, Miss Miller?"

Her face warmed. "No. I'm fine. Just not watching where I'm going."

He patted her hand. "Stay with me, and I'll make sure nothing harms you."

"Yes…well…I appreciate your kindness."

"Just trying to be the gentleman my mother raised me to be." A smile stretched on his freckled face.

She smiled in return. "I'm sure she's proud of you. Is your family living close by?"

He shook his head. "No. Back in Illinois. I was a schoolmaster for ten years."

"Oh? What made you decide to move west?"

"All the years of teaching my students about the land west of the Mississippi River. I've read about Louis and Clark's travels extensively through the years. It's always fascinated me. I finally decided to take the plunge and see some of the area firsthand."

"I hope you aren't disappointed." She chuckled.

"On the contrary. I look forward to trekking around the countryside and perhaps taking my students into the field as well. Perhaps you'd like to join us sometime." He halted and stared at her.

Her mouth went dry, and she coughed.

"Please. Allow me to get you something to drink." He excused himself. With determination in each step, he walked to where one of the ladies was serving water. A moment later he returned and handed her the tin mug, his fingers grazing hers.

Was the day growing warm or was it just her? She fanned herself and took a big gulp of the liquid. It went down wrong, and she sputtered and coughed. Gertrude gasped trying to get air.

Mr. Arnold's eyes filled with concern. He looked as though he didn't know whether to whack her on the back or make his excuses and take his leave. Did he think she had something catching?

Josh hurried over giving her a firm thump between her shoulder blades. "You all right, Gertrude?" He slipped his fingers around her wrist.

She sucked in a big breath, pulling her arm away. "I'm fine." She prayed her gaze implored him to take her word instead of drawing more attention to herself.

"Gertrude? I heard you coughing." Her mother hurried over. "Of course, everyone has heard you by now."

She coughed again, her eyes watering. Waving, she was finally able to catch her breath. "I'm well. No need to worry yourselves. Just got water down the wrong pipe." Her cheeks flamed. *Please Lord, let them all go away.*

"If you're sure…" Mr. Arnold hovered.

Mama thrust her hand towards the new teacher. "Hello, I'm Mrs. Miller, Gertrude's mother. We'd love for you to join us on our blanket for the picnic."

Oh, no. She had to make some sort of excuse. She had no intention of spending the afternoon having her mother share all of Gertrude's abilities as if she were trying to sell a prized livestock. She'd lived with it through the years and had no desire to have it inflicted again.

Especially when her mother was so blatant in her quest to find a husband for Gertrude. "If you'll excuse me, it looks as though they could use some assistance getting the food ready." She scurried away before anyone protested.

A minute later she slid behind the makeshift tables as several of the married women helped to arrange the food. "Where can I help?"

Sarah Brown blew a stray hair from her forehead. "You're a godsend, Gertrude. Little Joel needs to be nursed, and I just made Jules sit since she was having pains."

She sucked in a noisy breath. "It's not her time, is it?"

"I don't think so. She's been overdoing with the twins."

Gertrude chuckled. "I'm sure they keep her busy." She motioned. "I've got this covered. Go take care of your little one."

Sarah squeezed her hand. "Thank you. David has been frantic trying to hold Joel off until I found someone to relieve me."

"No problem."

The next quarter of an hour was a flurry of activity. She was handed more and more food. More than she had room for. When she thought the tables couldn't hold anymore, Pastor Montgomery called for their attention.

"Looks as if we have plenty to eat, folks. Help yourself and don't forget to introduce yourselves to our new teacher if you haven't yet. We've already prayed, so have at it."

She kept track of the table, removing dishes that were emptied and shifting others forward. She used the responsibility as an excuse to not socialize. Folks could've made their way through the line without her being there. After the line dwindled, she wasn't sure what she'd do.

Her gaze flitted to the blanket Mr. Arnold shared with her folks. There was no way she planned to join them. Question was, who could she sit with so as not to draw attention to herself? Last thing she needed was to be the center of gossip again.

She glanced around where folks were sitting with family and friends. Too bad Ellie Lou hadn't attended today, or she'd sit with her.

Betty Hadler sat beside her aunt. Several men were situated

beside the young woman listening with rapt attention.

Gertrude sighed. Who else could she sit with?

A throat cleared and the sound drew her back to her serving responsibilities. "I'm sorry. I was…"

Enoch's hat was in his hand. "I've been meaning to talk to you about something."

~*~

Enoch balanced a laden plate trying to work up the nerve to convey to Gertrude what was in his heart.

She fiddled with the spoon in a dish of stewed apples, scraping and re-scraping the sides. Had she heard him?

He shifted the plate, keeping an eye on two boys tossing a ball back and forth.

"That's a good one, Leroy," one of the boys called. At least they were having fun.

"Here's a long one," Leroy yelled back to his companion.

Something thumped hard into his back. His grip on the plate slipped a second later as a small body bumped into his arm with enough force to launch the platter against Gertrude's chest. Mashed potatoes squished against the fabric as gravy ran a path down the front of her skirt.

Her eyes widened as she watched it.

"Gertrude, I'm so sorry." He hurried around to where she stood, whipping out his handkerchief and starting to brush the food off her skirt.

Her cheeks flamed bright red.

Realizing where his hands were, he looked up into her angry gaze. His ears blazed. He handed her the cloth.

She shook her head, lifted her skirt a smidgen, and took off at brisk walk.

He wadded up the handkerchief and scurried after her.

"Enoch. Hold up there." Josh grabbed him by the arm.

He shook him off. "No, I need to talk to her."

His friend's hand settled on Enoch's shoulder. "Best to wait on that conversation, especially if it's the one I said you should be having."

He turned toward Josh. "What's up with you? First you tell me to have the discussion with her and when I try to, you stop me."

Josh grinned. "I've always found it best to talk to a gal when she's not covered in food, especially when you're the one who caused it."

"It wasn't my fault." He shoved his hands through his hair.

A slow chuckle didn't help to dispel his mood.

"It's not funny."

Josh sobered. "Sorry. You'll thank me later. I know it wasn't your fault. I saw the boy overthrow and the other little guy wasn't watching when he plowed into you. Gertrude had her head down and didn't see how it happened. Don't want her blaming you. Figured you needed to share your heart when she's in the right frame of mind."

"Share my heart. Now you're sounding like a gal."

"Just wait until you get married. You'll find yourself sounding more and more like your wife the longer you're wed."

Enoch snorted. "At this rate, I won't ever be married."

"Now don't be thinking that way."

He scrubbed a hand along his jawline. "You're right." He hefted a sigh. "Didn't ever figure on marrying until I met her."

Josh chuckled. "Then you're like most men. There's always a filly who comes along and snags our attention when we least expect it."

"Speaking of fillies, maybe I should go check on Miz Williams. It's been almost a week since I stopped by the ranch. Best to make sure she hasn't been having any problems."

His friend clapped him on the back. "Good idea. Maybe by the time you return to town, Gertrude will be ready to talk to you."

Enoch thrust his hand out. "Thanks, Josh. Appreciate you looking out for me."

He shook it. "Any time."

As he walked through town, Enoch didn't see anyone lingering around. Whoever wasn't at the picnic must be settled in their homes for the day. He strolled to the jail where he'd tied Fee when he got to town earlier. Often, he would've ridden straight to church, but he'd forgotten to file some papers yesterday and hadn't wanted to wait until tomorrow morning to do so. Instead, he'd taken the brief detour.

Fee snorted as he got closer.

"I didn't forget about you, girl."

She bobbed her head.

He patted her before swinging up onto her back. Turning her head, he tapped her sides with the heels of his boots. "G'dyup."

She surged into motion as if she was as anxious to get moving as he was. The mare always had a way of sensing his moods. He allowed her to set the pace. She galloped for a couple miles before she slowed to a walk.

Dry grass spread out on either side of the dirt trail. The wildflower patch he'd found earlier in the summer now was dried, the petals all but gone. Birds swooped and called to each other. A prairie dog poked his head from his home. Probably preparing for the winter months ahead.

Calm descended.

I sure messed that up, didn't I, Lord? He patted Fee's neck. *Think she'll ever forgive me, God? Can You make her more open the next time I try and talk to her? I want her in my life. I want to share my days with her.* His chest tightened. *Guess that's why You said to Adam it was best if he wasn't alone and why You made him a help meet. Help Gertrude to see marriage can be a good thing. Can You make her to want to spend the rest of her life with me instead of running away like today? And Lord, can You keep her safe when I can't? I don't want to trust in myself and my abilities but instead give them up to You to use as You see fit. Above all else, I want to be in the center of Your will.*

The clip clop of Fee's hooves was all he could hear.

I want to be in the center of Your will…even if it means You don't want Gertrude and me to be together. But, Lord, I'm asking You to allow it if at all possible. She makes me feel things I never have before. I want to marry her, God. But I'll wait until You give me the go ahead to talk to her. He sighed. *Help me not to rush ahead and do things on my timing. Help me to wait on You, Lord even when the waiting and relying on You is hard. And God, could You make her start thinking more about me?*

34

Gertrude couldn't stop thinking about Enoch as she stripped off the food splattered dress, placed it in a bucket to soak, and pulled on a worn but comfortable calico dress. What had gotten into him to throw his plate at her? Had he intended to do so, or could it have been an accident? Maybe he hadn't liked seeing her on Mr. Arnold's arm. She snorted. "As if he'd be jealous when he's never given any indication of desiring a future with me." She sat down on her overstuffed chair, propping her feet on the stool.

A knock sounded.

Gertrude hurried downstairs, hesitating by the back door. She wasn't ready to talk to Enoch. He wouldn't come here, would he? She took a deep breath and opened the door a slit.

"It's me."

A female voice.

Air whooshed from Gertrude's lungs. "Come in, Sarah." She opened the door wider. "Can I get you something to drink?"

Sarah smiled and handed her a laden plate. "David told me what happened. I feel just terrible since you were filling in for me."

"Nonsense. I'm glad it didn't happen to you." Of course, she would've appreciated not having it happen to her either. "Can you stay for a few minutes?"

"Yes. I told David you might like some company after what occurred, unless I can persuade you to come back to the church?"

Gertrude shook her head and motioned to the stairs. "No, I think it's best if I stay here for now. Wouldn't want to give En-Mr. Valentine another opportunity to—"

Sarah halted at the top of the steps. "You do realize it was an accident, don't you?"

Gertrude indicated the soft chair for her guest, went to the kitchen, and brought back one of the wooden chairs to her small sitting room. "I assume so, but—"

"David said the boys were tossing a ball back and forth. One of the boys threw the ball hard and when the other one jumped to catch it, he slammed into the sheriff's arm. Unfortunately, it was the one holding his plate full of food. I know he must've felt terrible about the whole thing." Sarah settled on the seat.

She fiddled with the frayed cuff of her sleeve. "What makes you think that?"

"Because he tried to follow you. Would have too, but Joshua Walker stopped him."

"He stopped Enoch?" Why?

Sarah nodded. "He sure did, and the new sheriff didn't look so happy about it."

Enoch's words flashed through her memory. What had he wanted to discuss with her before they were interrupted? She swallowed past the lump in her throat, not sure if she wanted to find out. Question was, why did Josh feel the need to stop Enoch from pursuing her? All right. Not pursuing–at least not in a romantic sort of way.

"Gertrude? Are you sure…that is…is something wrong?"

She swung her gaze back to the young woman. "Sorry. Just woolgathering. I'm fine. Just don't feel like going back to the festivities. Thank you for bringing me some food. I appreciate your thoughtfulness."

"I saw you had the opportunity to talk with Mr. Arnold." Sarah smiled. "I hope he'll stay for a while. Maybe having a male teacher will make a difference. I know the children loved Annie when she taught, but as soon as she married and started a family of her own the children have been without a teacher. Maybe Mr. Arnold will stay longer if he finds a bride here." She glanced at Gertrude. "You wouldn't be interested in him, would you?"

"Umm. I uh…that is…" She swallowed.

"Forgive me. I can be too direct sometimes. Of course, maybe you're not interested in getting married. I'm sure your shop keeps you busy." Sarah smoothed her skirt. "I should get back."

Gertrude stood. "Before you go, can I ask you something?"

"Of course." Sarah smiled at her.

"When, that is, how did you know David was the one for you?" She cleared her throat. "I'm so sorry. That was too personal of a question. Please don't feel the need to respond."

"Nonsense. Feel free to ask whatever you'd like." Sarah perched on the edge of the chair. "I've known David all of my life. When we were in our final school year, all the other girls were buzzing around him like bees after flowers. I had liked him for a long time but didn't think he'd noticed me. At the time, I was rather timid."

"How did that change?"

"We had a box social. He asked Drew how I'd decorated my basket, so David would know which one to bid on. Turned out he'd been interested in me as well. He'd done little things for me through the years – carrying my books, explaining schoolwork I didn't understand, picking a flower and placing it on my desk. At the time, I thought he was nice like that to all the girls. Apparently, he'd only had eyes for me. He didn't tell me until we shared our box lunch."

"That's so sweet."

"He was showing his love for me in those little things he'd done through the years. It just took me a while to realize it." Sarah stood again. "It seems men often don't know how to express their love in words. When they're afraid of being rejected they test the waters by doing little things for a girl. I recognized later it was those small gestures that started opening my heart to his love." She chuckled. "Good thing I did too or there would've never been a Joel or this little one." Sarah rested her hand on her still flat stomach and smiled. "I thank God every day for using those small acts to bring David and I together."

Could it be true? Had Enoch been trying to say the same thing the past few months even though his words said otherwise?

~*~

How could Enoch share his love for Gertrude in a way she'd understand? He swung down from Fee and still hadn't come up with an answer to the question. Patting his mare, he led her into the barn at the Williams's ranch. "You in here, Jim?"

The place was quiet.

He refrained from climbing the steps to the loft above reminding himself he didn't live here anymore. Best to check the paddock. Maybe he'd missed seeing the ranch hand there.

The door to the main house opened. "Jim, you got a minute?" Miz Williams popped her head out. "Enoch." She came outside. "I thought maybe Jim had returned."

"He's not here?" Enoch glanced around. Sure enough, the man's horse wasn't in the enclosure.

"No. Said he had something to do today." She folded her arms across her chest. "Didn't say what it was, just mentioned he wouldn't be able to escort me to church in Hutchinson this morning."

"You should've sent word. I would have gone with you. After all, I promised the boss and we still haven't caught our troublemaker." He removed his Stetson and twirled it in his hands.

She laughed. "I think it's high time you called me Ellie Lou, Enoch. Charles is gone, and I'm no longer your boss. Besides, we've known each other for a long time."

"True enough."

"Why don't you come inside, and I'll brew some coffee?" She opened the door and motioned him to follow.

"Yes'm."

Her brows rose.

"That is, I'd be much obliged, Ellie Lou." The name felt wrong to say.

She grinned. "There now. Wasn't so hard to do, was it?"

He didn't answer.

Quiet settled as she puttered around the kitchen, setting the coffee to brew. A little while later, she set a steaming mug in front of him. "There you go."

"Mmm. Thank you." He blew across the hot liquid and took a small sip.

"What's new in Burrton Springs?" She sat down in the chair across from him.

"New schoolteacher arrived yesterday." He took another swallow.

"Is that so? I imagine all the fellas lined up to meet her at church today."

Enoch chuckled. "Him. Not Her. Mr. Stephen Arnold starts teaching tomorrow."

"Oh. A male teacher. Been a little while since they had one, I believe." She smiled. "I suppose he caused a stir. What can you tell me about him?"

"Not much." Should he mention Gertrude had taken a fancy to him?

"I bet all the single women lined up to meet him. Course the families with children would as well. Were you introduced to him?"

He shook his head. "Didn't get a chance to."

"I'm surprised with you being the new sheriff. Thought you'd make introductions."

He shifted on his chair and fiddled with the handle on his mug.

"Enoch? Did something happen?"

He hefted a sigh. "Guess you could say that."

She reached over and rested her hand on top of his, halting his fidgeting. "Do you want to talk about it?"

Yes. And no. He puffed out another breath.

"Sometimes it helps to get it off your chest."

Visions of the food plastered against Gertrude's chest flitted through his brain. He shoved it aside. Oh, what could it hurt? In as few words as possible he relayed the interchange with Gertrude outside the church.

"Oh, my. Definitely not the way to win her hand."

How did she know about that? He hadn't said anything.

Ellie Lou flipped her hand back and forth. "You didn't have to tell me. I've known for a while. I'm sure she won't hold it against you. Accidents happen. But I'm guessing something else occurred you haven't told me about." Her brows lifted. "Am I right?"

He refused to squirm. He nodded.

"I'm here if you need some advice." She took a long sip of her coffee, just staring at him.

He shoved the coffee aside. "Gertrude made a point of meeting the new schoolteacher."

"I'm not surprised. The girl has a caring spirit. She wants others to feel welcome because she struggles with not knowing where she fits into the community."

Enoch nodded. Her sweet spirit had drawn him from the start. He tapped a finger on the rim of the mug. The coffee had cooled.

Ellie Lou's eyes sparkled. "You're not jealous, are you?"

He bristled. "Of course not."

She chuckled. "You sure? It seems as if you are."

"I just don't know why she'd fall for his fawning over her hand and slobbering on it."

"What?"

"Nothing." He shoved to his feet and paced the small enclosure.

"Come sit down, Enoch. You're making me dizzy."

"Yes'm." She didn't correct him this time.

"It's perfectly acceptable for a man to kiss the back of a woman's hand when they're introduced."

Except Ellie Lou hadn't seen how long the man held Gertrude's hand. It wasn't appropriate.

"Perhaps you've waited too long to let her know how you feel about her."

He closed his eyes. *Please help it not to be true, Lord.*

"That is, if you do have special feelings for her…"

"I do." He snapped his mouth shut.

"I suggest you tell her before it's too late."

Too late? So, Ellie Lou thought Gertrude's head could be swayed so easily?

She patted his hand. "No, I'm not saying she doesn't care for you, but sometimes a woman will accept a man's suit when she feels there's no chance of the fella she really cares about noticing her."

"Gertrude isn't fickle like that. Besides, she's said she doesn't want to marry."

"I know, but at times a woman can be wooed into thinking differently."

"Do you suppose…"

"Do I think she'd be open to you wooing her?"

Heat rushed up his neck.

"Most definitely. Just don't wait too long to do so. Especially when there's new competition in town."

He'd find a way to tell her the next time he saw her. *Help her not to say no, Lord.*

35

Enoch's day hadn't gone at all the way he'd intended. He'd tossed and turned for hours on end throughout the night only to fall asleep just before sunrise. By the time he awakened again, the sun had been up for hours. He yawned as he pulled on his pants.

Something clattered outside.

Enoch reached for his gun. In his haste, he slammed his toe against the corner post of his bed. He sank to the mattress, holding the throbbing appendage. He was as skittish as a colt. *Lord, I need Your patience today. You know I wanted to be up early so I could talk to Gertrude. Sure would be nice to have some sort of noise that can wake a person each morning.* A rooster would create noise to wake up to, and fresh eggs from the hens would be nice too. The Zellers had already built a coop on the property. It only needed cleaning, and it'd be ready for new occupants. Worth stopping at the Brown farm on the way to town to see if David had some chickens he was willing to part with.

Decision made, Enoch pulled on his socks and carefully pushed his foot into his boot, wincing when he stood. He bit back a groan.

In the kitchen, he prayed before yanking off a hunk from the loaf of bread Ellie Lou had insisted he take along home yesterday. His stomach growled. At some point, he'd need to pick up staples at the general store.

A few minutes later, he strapped on his gun belt and put on his Stetson. He opened his door and glanced at the darkening sky. Looked like rain. Enoch whistled for Fee, but the pasture was empty. Odd. He hadn't put the mare in the barn, had he?

He sauntered to the building. A piece of paper fluttered from a nail tacked to the wood door. It wasn't there last evening when he'd returned. He ripped it off and read the short note.

You didn't stay away. Now you'll pay.

Enoch shoved the note in his pocket, moved the bar, and opened the barn door. He let out another whistle, but no answering whinny came.

He trotted outside, ignoring the pain in his toe. Climbing the pasture fence, he walked to the crest of the hill, but Fee was nowhere to be seen. She wouldn't have run off which left only one scenario. Someone had stolen his horse.

Really, Lord? Of all days…

He hopped the fence.

A gun fired.

He hit the dirt and withdrew his pistol.

Another shot sounded.

Heart pounding, he crawled to the water trough, lowered behind it, and prayed he was out of bullet range.

The next few minutes dragged by as he waited and listened. No voices. No sounds other than the wind rustling through the leaves on the tree.

A birdcall.

Enoch cocked his head. Was it a signal or an actual bird? He couldn't tell for sure. Holding his breath, he lifted his head above the trough. Another shot whizzed by him, knocking his Stetson to the dirt. He ducked.

Lord, I could use some help here. I'm pinned down and don't have a way of getting away. Without Fee, I have no way of making a fast getaway.

If he could come up with a distraction, he could make it to the house. No. That wouldn't do any good either. Then he'd be trapped in the house with only one way of escaping.

I'm second guessing my decision to become the sheriff, Lord.

A shot pinged off the metal beside him.

His pulse sped up as he shifted to make sure all of his body was completely behind the scant protective cover.

If only he could see where the shooter was, then he'd be able to figure which way to crawl.

Another shot rang out. How many was that now? Enoch had lost count.

He whistled again in case Fee happened to be in the area. If the horse heard him, she'd come.

Nothing.

He tried again.

No answering whinny.

Are You hearing my prayers, Lord? Sure don't feel like You're listening to me today.

A Bible verse he'd memorized as a child, filtered through his memory. *'In the day of my trouble I will call upon Thee: for Thou wilt answer me.'* He couldn't recall where it was in the Scriptures.

Thank You, God for reminding me of Your Word. I guess that's why You say about Your Word not returning void. Well, Lord, I'm asking You to show Yourself by helping me in my day of trouble. Because this is one of those. I'm at a loss here and have no idea what I can do to save myself. He released a breath. *I guess that's the point. I have no idea how to do this on my own, so I'm calling on You and trusting You'll answer me.*

Another shot ricocheted off the trough.

If only he could figure out where the shooter was hiding. Which direction the bullets were coming from.

Too bad the Kansas prairie didn't lend itself to many places to hide.

Hide.

Enoch did a quick mental tour of his new property. Where could a person hole up? Beside the house or barn? The stand of trees across the pasture? He racked his brain but couldn't come up with anything else.

Still too many places to be hiding, Lord. I'll need Your help here.

~*~

Gertrude finished the last seam on the shirt she'd promised to Enoch. She hoped he'd like it. He hadn't picked out a bolt of fabric he favored, so she'd chosen a deep blue that would be a stark contrast to his dark eyes and hair. Tying a knot, she snipped the thread. She folded the shirt and set it aside.

The bell chimed. The shop had been busier than she'd anticipated especially with Betty's store opening the past weekend. Apparently the first day of school meant the ladies in town were anxious to shop without little ones under foot.

A very pregnant Jules waddled in with her twins in tow.

Gertrude smiled and reached for Emily. "I can hold one of them for you. What can I do for you today?"

The little girl popped her thumb in her mouth and leaned her head on Gertrude's shoulder.

Her heart melted.

Jules stooped and lifted Elliot. He pointed at his sister. "She's just fine." Jules patted his back. "He gets concerned when someone other than me or Drew holds Emily."

"Oh, I don't have to." She started to set the little girl on the floor.

"She's just fine. Don't you worry none about Elliot." Jules shifted the child to her hip causing her stomach to bulge more. "These two are growin' faster than I can keep up with. Any chance you have somethin' stitched up for their sizes?"

"Of course. Right over here." Gertrude headed in that direction.

"You know I've never been overly handy with a needle." Jules grinned. "This new young'un is wearin' me out, and he hasn't even made an appearance yet. It's hard enough keepin' track of these two. What one doesn't think to do, the other does. They have me runnin' all day long until they're in bed at night. By the time that happens, I'm ready for bed too." She yawned. "Never seems to be enough hours in the day to get everythin' done that needs doin'."

"I think you should find a few things you might like here." She pointed to a small stack of dresses, pants, and little shirts she had on hand. If Jules bought some, Gertrude would have to stitch some more.

The sound of Emily's soft, even breathing puffed in Gertrude's ear. "You can always hold a dress up to Emily to see if it will fit."

Jules glanced her way. "I reckon you have the touch, Gertrude. Never saw her take to someone so quick like and fall asleep like that. You'll make a fine mother one day."

Why did people keep telling her that? Didn't they know she didn't even have a man interested in her?

Jules set Elliot on the ground.

His little lip puckered.

"Hush now. Yer mama has to look for some clothes for you." She rifled through the stack.

Elliot plopped on his bottom and stared up at his mother.

It didn't take Jules long. She held a few dresses up to Emily's back as Gertrude held the child.

"I think these three will work for her." Jules set them aside and stooped beside her son, holding small shirts and pants in front of him.

He reached for them.

Jules shifted them away. "Not just yet, son."

His lip puckered again.

Gertrude held back a smile.

"I think that's it for today." Jules stood. "How much do I owe you?"

She quoted a price.

Jules handed her some coins.

Gertrude went to the small drawer where she held change. It was a little difficult with Emily still on one arm, but she managed. "There you go. Let me wrap these up for you so they'll be easier to carry."

"I appreciate it. Hard enough keepin' track of these two." Jules reached for Emily.

The trio no sooner left when the bell chimed again.

Sarah, holding young Joel, stepped inside and smiled. "Hello, Gertrude. I thought I'd check in and see how you're doing after your encounter with the sheriff yesterday."

"You just missed your sister-in-law." Gertrude closed the money drawer.

"I'll go see her after I'm finished here." Sarah stroked the brim of a bonnet Gertrude finished stitching last week.

"I'm doing well. No harm done." She smiled. "Although it took some doing to get all the food from my dress."

"I can imagine. How much is this bonnet?"

Gertrude pointed to the sign above them.

"Silly me. I don't know where my head is this morning." Sarah chuckled. "My bonnet is getting frayed, and David said I should look for a new one when I came to town next."

"The one you're holding will go with many different colored

dresses, especially your new one." Gertrude winked at her.

The young mother's cheeks colored.

Joel thrust his fingers in his mouth, chewing on them.

"I see he's still teething?"

"Yes, poor boy." Sarah patted Joel's cheek. "I'll be glad when these last teeth cut through the surface."

"I can imagine." She couldn't really, but the mother didn't need to hear that.

Sarah settled on her purchase and waved goodbye.

The door no sooner closed when Melissa and Amelia Evans stepped inside. Gertrude headed in their direction as Doc Adams, Beatrice Smith, and another gentleman entered the shop.

She no sooner looked after one customer when another was needing her assistance. Customers continued to come and go throughout the morning hours.

Squeakers whistled with each chime of the bell. Some of the customers made a point of checking out the guinea pig family while others avoided them.

Mrs. Montgomery arrived and made a beeline towards Gertrude. "I debated about coming back or not. I see you still have those rodents." She sniffed and held a handkerchief to her nose. "I need a new cape. Stopped by Miss Hadler's boutique but she said she is sticking strictly to dresses and nothing more which means I had no other choice than to come here since I do not have time to run to Hutchinson."

Gertrude pinched her lips together to halt herself from saying something she'd later regret.

"I want something stylish that will keep me warm while also looking nice. Do you think you can accomplish the task?" The woman waved her handkerchief back and forth.

The bell rang out again.

Two more ladies entered.

"I'll be with you in a minute," Gertrude called.

"No problem." One of them smiled. "We'll just browse until you're available."

"Now, back to my cape." Mrs. Montgomery's gaze narrowed. "I

assume you will be able to sew it?"

She spent the next few moments helping to find fabric the woman deemed suitable.

The two other ladies must've gotten tired of waiting because they ended up leaving before Gertrude finished assisting Mrs. Montgomery.

Her shoulders relaxed when the woman left and the store was empty.

Squeakers made his presence known again.

"What is it, boy?" She strolled over to the cage.

A white piece of paper was propped beside the enclosure. It hadn't been there before.

Gertrude picked it up. Her name was scrawled across the outside.

Odd someone would leave it there without saying anything. She flipped it open and read.

Gertrude, I need your help. Come right away. It's a matter of life or death.

~ Ellie Lou

36

Enoch lost track of how long he'd hunkered behind the water trough. If he didn't move soon, he wouldn't be able to. There hadn't been any shooting for quite some time now. He glanced around and glimpsed a long stick about a body's length away from him. Should he risk it? Decision made, he shifted an inch.

No sound of gunfire.

He shifted two inches.

Still no gunfire.

Three more inches.

His heart pounded. Was someone coming? He couldn't tell over the sound of his heart in his ears.

He willed it to slow.

No, it definitely sounded like a horse. He shifted his head to get a better glimpse of the trail. Sure enough. They were too far away yet to see who it was. How could he warn them? He shifted his pistol and shot in the air.

The horse and rider picked up speed as they raced towards him. He waved, trying to warn them to hold up.

They kept coming.

"Get down!"

His words were lost over the thundering hooves.

"Enoch?" The man reined the horse to a halt and jumped to the ground. "What're you doing in the dirt? Are you injured?"

"Get down!"

Josh stared at him as if he'd taken to talking nonsense.

"There's a shooter."

His friend quickly stooped low and whipped out his pistol. "Where? I don't see anyone."

"Not sure. Started shooting at me a while back. Couldn't tell where they were. Been praying for God to send help. Didn't figure it'd be you."

Josh half-stood, keeping an eye while digging through his saddle bag.

"What're you doing?" Enoch's words came out in a hiss.

"Getting my binoculars." He stopped as soon as he had the item. It took a couple minutes for him to adjust them and scan the area. "I don't see anyone. I'm guessing whoever shot at you is long gone now. You can get up."

Enoch stood and dusted the dirt from his pants and shirt. "Fine sheriff I am." He put his finger through the bullet hole in his Stetson.

"You are a good sheriff, Enoch. From the looks of it, you held your ground."

He snorted. "If you count lying in the dirt behind a feed trough holding my ground, then yes, I did a good job." He shoved his hat on.

"No use getting touchy."

"Sorry. Just been one of those days." He pulled the note from his pocket and handed it to Josh. "What do you think?"

He read the slip of paper. "Where did you get it?"

"It was tacked to the barn door. Found it this morning when I went looking for my mare and couldn't find her."

Josh whistled. "They stole your horse too?"

He nodded.

"They sure are getting more bold. What did you do after you left the picnic?"

"Not sure why it matters, but I went to the ranch to check on Ellie Lou Williams." He ran a hand along his jaw. "She hasn't been having any more trouble. Maybe the events aren't related."

"Just seems too coincidental though." Josh stared at the pasture. "My gut says otherwise."

"Mine too." He kicked at a clod of dirt and winced. "Now what? Any recommendations? Besides, what were you doing out this way?"

"One of the Smith children has a fever. Martha wanted me to come check on him to make sure it wasn't something catchy."

"Is it?"

He shook his head. "Don't think so. Told her to keep him home from school. Don't want to take a chance." Josh massaged his neck muscles. "I'm not sure what the next step should be of our investigation. This one has me stumped. I still say the Williams brothers have the most to gain, but those two are lazy. There's no way they've been doing all these shenanigans."

"Maybe they have an accomplice. Somebody working with them."

He nodded. "Someone doing what they don't want to get their hands dirty with."

"Question is, who? Who else would benefit from getting Ellie Lou to leave the ranch?"

"What about the fella who was fighting with the Williams brothers way back when I broke up the fight at the saloon?" Enoch motioned to the house. "Did you want to come inside?"

Josh nodded. "But let's check out the pasture first. I have a feeling whoever shot at you was holed up in the stand of trees over there."

He should've thought of checking the area. Enoch puffed a sigh. "That's what I narrowed it down to as well. Thought they could be either at the edge of the house or barn, but it didn't seem as likely. Every time I tried to put my head up to see, I got shot at."

Josh stared at him. "From the looks of it, you came close to losing your head. If that bullet had been an inch lower, you probably would've been dead."

He swallowed.

It didn't take long to walk to the stand of trees. Sure enough, shell cartridges littered the ground.

"Whoever it is, they're getting sloppy." Josh stooped and picked them up. "Most folks would take these with them to make re-loads. Could be the fella from the bar fight was in cahoots with the Williams's. Only problem is we haven't seen the other man since then."

"Maybe he's been hiding out somewhere in the countryside."

Josh nodded. "You're right. Good chance of that. Besides, if someone local was working with them, we'd have seen them together."

"Never did get a good feeling about the saloon owner though

either. Do you think he could be working with them?"

"Jeb?" Josh headed toward the house.

Enoch lengthened his stride to keep up with him. "Yes."

"I wouldn't think so. The man's always been a bit odd, but I've never seen him being overly friendly with the two."

"True. But neither of us frequent the saloon either."

Josh swung onto his horse. "We'd best get to town. Barabbas should be able to handle both of our weights since it's not far."

"I'd appreciate it." He reached for his friend's hand and swung up behind him. Enoch couldn't quiet the feeling that Gertrude needed him.

~*~

Gertrude dropped the note and ran, flinging the door to her shop open. Lifting her skirt, she scurried down the street to the livery. "Henry? I need a horse quick."

"Miss Miller that you? What'd you say?" The balding man poked his head from one of the stalls.

"I need to rent a horse. Hurry please. It's a matter of life or death." She scurried down the aisle, grabbed his hand and tugged.

"Give me a minute, and I'll have Bessy saddled for you." He lifted a saddle from the floor.

She paced as he worked, willing him to go faster.

"There you go." He tugged the reins. "Let me help you up, Miss Miller."

Gertrude waved him aside, hiked her skirt, and put a foot in the stirrup. She hopped with the other, launching herself onto the back of the horse. "Giddy up."

Her heart thudded in tempo with the mare's hoofbeats. The miles between town and the Williams's ranch seemed to take longer than normal. *Dear God, be with Ellie Lou. Protect her. Help me to be able to assist in whatever she needs.*

As soon as she got close to Ellie Lou's home, Gertrude sawed on the reins, bringing the horse to a halt, her sides heaving. "Sorry, girl." She patted the mare and swung down.

Lifting her skirts she ran to the back door, pounding on it. "Ellie Lou? Are you in there? I got your note, and I'm here."

No sound came from inside the house.

She banged hard with her fist. "Ellie Lou. Open up!"

Still no response. Maybe she was in the barn.

Gertrude trotted the short distance to it. Despite the overcast day, her eyes took a minute to adjust to the dim interior. "Ellie Lou? You here?"

She went along the long aisle, glancing in each stall. They were all empty and smelled as though they hadn't been cleaned in a while.

Now what, Lord?

Back at the house, she knocked again. Waiting a minute longer, she decided to try the doorknob. It turned in her hands. Opening the door, she stepped into the cool interior. "Ellie Lou? Are you here? It's Gertrude. I got your note."

Still nothing.

A piece of paper on the kitchen table snagged her attention. She glanced at it, debating if she should read it. Indecision filled her. Gertrude stepped closer to it. Maybe Ellie Lou had left another note for her. Decision made, she picked it up and read the short missive.

The propertee doesn't belong to you. Leave or else.

Her throat closed. *Dear God.* The paper fluttered to the floor.

"Ellie Lou?" She stepped into the sitting room.

Chills ran down her spine.

Ellie Lou sat on the fainting couch with a cloth tied around her mouth. Her arms were behind her back. A masked man stood beside her with a pistol pointed to her head.

"Get in here and have a seat beside your friend there." He motioned with the gun.

Ellie Lou's gaze swung to hers. Tears welled in her eyes, soaking the cloth tied beneath her nose.

"I don't understand."

"Sit down and shut up. Didn't ask you to understand." He set the gun down. "Don't try to do something stupid or my partners will make sure you don't live long enough to tell anyone." He withdrew a piece of rope and tied Gertrude's hands behind her back. After completing the task, he shoved her to the couch. Fishing in his pocket, he yanked out a handkerchief and wrapped it tight around her mouth.

Her pulse stuttered. Why hadn't she left a note in case someone stopped in the shop? They'd never know where to look for her.

The sound of the ticking clock on the mantel was the only noise in the room.

Gertrude racked her brain for a way to escape. Hadn't she caught sight of another ranch hand the times she'd visited when Enoch still lived here? She didn't think she'd ever met the man though. Maybe he'd stop by the house and come to their rescue. *Please, Lord.*

Their captor paced back and forth. "You should've left when troubles started, but no, you had to wait it out. Same as your husband."

Ellie Lou's body stiffened.

The man cackled. "You thought he was sick."

Her friend's eyes widened.

Was the man saying Charles Williams hadn't gotten sick? That his death had been intentional?

Dear God, send someone to save us from this madman. Her limbs trembled. *Help me to be brave. Lord, provide Your peace even in the middle of this storm. The waves are blasting against me and Ellie Lou. We need You to calm the sea.* She sniffed. *Give us Your peace even when we can't feel it. I want to learn to walk in Your peace, Lord instead of trying to solve problems on my own. I've been doing that for too long. Forgive me. I'm giving everything to You, Lord. Help me to trust You to provide even when I can't see the answer. Above all else, I know You love me and want what's best for me and Ellie Lou. I choose to trust You, Lord. Help me not to be afraid.*

Ellie Lou leaned against Gertrude's shoulder. The warmth of her friend brought a measure of comfort and peace. Somehow God would get them through this. How, she didn't know, but she trusted God to be with them no matter what they faced in the coming minutes.

A bird call sounded outside and was repeated a couple times. The clip clop of horse hooves filtered through the open window.

Who was coming? Their captor's partners or someone else?

"That's the sign. Time to move you two to somewhere safe. Need to do so before the sheriff gets here."

Enoch. What did they plan to do to him?

37

Enoch jumped from Barabbas's back. "Thanks for the ride to town, Josh."

"No problem. Let me know if you need anything." He waved as he turned his horse in the direction of the doctor's office. "I'll keep an eye on things too."

"Appreciate it." He waved.

Josh's horse had no sooner trotted down the street when the sound of shrill whistles could be heard. What on earth? He cocked his head. That sounded like the adult male guinea pig – the one called Squeakers. Enoch glanced toward Gertrude's shop. The door stood open.

Odd.

He didn't think he'd ever seen the door wide open like that. His heartbeat stalled.

The guinea pig continued to call.

He sprinted toward the shop. *Please let her be there, Lord.* "Gertrude, you here?"

Squeakers whistled again.

He made his way over to him. "What is it, boy?"

The critter stood on his hind legs, front paws resting on the wooden slats. His small body thrummed with each sound he made.

Enoch checked the hallway beside the shop, but she wasn't there. He stepped out the back, calling for her, even checking the outhouse. Still no sign of her. Inside again, he scurried upstairs. "Gertrude, honey, are you here?"

Nothing. No noise. No Gertrude.

Where can she be, Lord? He hurried downstairs. *Give me some sort of sign of where to look for her, Lord.*

Squeakers was still going at it when he entered the shop.

"What's gotten into you, boy? What're you trying to tell me?"

The guinea pig squeaked again and meandered to the end of the cage, standing on his hind legs again.

What was that paper on the counter near the cage? Gertrude always kept things tidy and neat. He picked it up and read, his blood running cold. *I'm coming, honey.* He ran to the door, closing it behind him. Someone slammed into him.

"Enoch, I'm so sorry. I wasn't watching where I was going." Annie Walker adjusted her hat.

"Tell Josh I need him out at the Williams's ranch. Make sure he knows not to delay." Before he could run off, Annie grabbed him by the arm.

"Wait. He's not in town."

"But I just was with him no more than ten minutes ago."

"He got called to set a bone. One of the Sanson boys fell out of a tree and broke his arm."

Enoch lifted his Stetson and shoved his hand through his hair before clapping the hat back in place. "Can you get word to him to come to the ranch as soon as he's finished? I gotta go. Ellie Lou's in danger. Gertrude may be too." He didn't wait for her response, sprinting towards the livery.

A saddled horse stood in front of the building. He swung onto it.

"You can't just take it." The bald-headed owner frowned.

"Got to. It's a matter of life or death."

"Wonder if that's what Miss Miller was facing too." The man scratched his head.

"Gertrude? She was here?"

The man nodded.

"How long ago?"

"Probably close to an hour now. She was in an all-fired hurry like you."

"Did she say where she was going?"

He shook his head. "No, sir."

"Thanks." He turned the stallion's head. Enoch dug his heels in the horse's side. "H'yah." *How will I protect both of them, Lord? Send Josh as soon as possible, will You?* He continued to pray over the long miles to the ranch.

As soon as he got within a quarter mile, he slowed the stallion. Best not to go in with guns blazing or one of the women would get hurt. Providing his hunch was right and Gertrude had come here. She wouldn't avoid an obvious call for assistance, no matter who it came from. In fact, maybe it'd be better to walk the rest of the way on foot. No sense riding into a trap. He may not have been a sheriff long enough to know the ins and outs of identifying what motivated an outlaw, and if he was wrong about this, he'd turn in his badge. He'd seen Ellie Lou's handwriting before and the note at Gertrude's hadn't been written by his former boss. He'd count on it.

Enoch tied the stallion to a grove of trees not within vision of the house. He dropped to the ground and low crawled to the top of the slight rise. The house and barn stood quiet. Not a single movement. He studied the outlying pastures. Not a single person or horse in sight. The small herd should be there, unless Jim had moved them farther away. Where was he? Why would he have moved the horses or was he doing so now? Did he think all the trouble was past and they had nothing to worry about anymore? Enoch shook his head. It made no sense. There wasn't time to concentrate on that now. He had ladies who needed rescuing…or he thought that was the case.

Am I wrong here, Lord? Why do I find it so easy to doubt myself and my abilities? He puffed out a breath. *Give me wisdom here, Lord, so I do the right thing and don't get anyone hurt in the process. Give me Your peace.*

If he came to the house from the east side, they wouldn't be able to see him since no windows were on that side. No one would be able to see from the barn either since the door and loft window opened on the west side of the building. Decision made, he withdrew his pistol and checked the chamber. Spare cartridges were on his gun belt within easy reach.

Enoch crept forward one foot at a time. After each foot he paused and held his breath, watching, waiting, and listening for any type of movement. He worked to control his breathing, so it didn't give him away.

Ten feet to go.

Five.

Four.

Two.

A shot rang out, and he lunged for cover in a bush at the edge of the house.

~*~

Gertrude strained against the restraints at her hands and feet. No good. The knots seemed to tighten every time she struggled to untie them. If only there was some way she could warn Enoch. He wouldn't know about their captor, let alone the two men working with him. All three were holed up at various spots in the barn, house, and in the big white oak tree below where they'd tied her and Ellie Lou. Tears slipped down her cheeks, soaking the handkerchief at her mouth. If she didn't find a way to warn him, she'd never get the chance to tell him how she felt about him. That she loved him. Wanted to spend the rest of her life with him if he'd have her. If they got out of this unscathed, would he be offended if she proposed to him?

She rested her head against the rough bark of the tree. *Keep him safe, God. You know how much I've come to care for him. How much I love him. I don't know what I'd do if something happens to him. Please keep him safe.*

Gertrude rubbed her cheek against the bark again. The gag shifted a smidgen.

Where had Enoch gotten to? Was he still behind the bush?

Another shot rang out, stirring dirt beside the shrub.

Her heart stilled.

They'd seen where he'd gone.

She had to warn him. Scraping her face against the tree, tears sprang to her eyes as several layers of skin were ripped from her cheek. The material slipped a little more down her face. One more try and she'd hopefully have it out of her mouth.

The outlaw below her shifted, aiming at Enoch.

Enoch's Stetson poked above the bush for a second.

Gertrude strained, grinding her face against the bark. The gag gave way. She spat it out of her mouth. "Enoch, watch out. In the tree."

The man below her fired again.

"No!" Her heartbeat stalled.

~*~

Enoch's hat flew from his head. He scowled and ducked deeper into the bush. Being shot at twice in one day was more than enough to anger a man.

Movement in the tree dragged his gaze there. He squinted. Was that Gertrude and Ellie Lou in the tree? Why were they there? The gunfire had come from that direction.

His heart squeezed. *Dear God. The rabble rouser is there too, isn't he?* She hadn't been letting him know she and Ellie Lou were there, she was trying to tell him it was where one of the outlaws were. *Keep her safe, Lord.*

The man fired again, the bullet ricocheting off the clapboard just above Enoch's head.

He sucked in a breath, released it partway, and pulled the trigger.

The man howled and fell from the tree. His body crumpled on the ground.

Enoch watched him for a full minute to make sure the fella wasn't playing possum. He sneaked out from his hiding place and ran towards the tree, picking up the masked man's gun and tucking it into the back of his belt. He pulled the mask down. George Williams. The man stared unseeing. Enoch closed the man's eyelids.

"Enoch." Tears streaked Gertrude's face. Blood ran down her cheek. "Be careful. There's one in the barn and one in the house unless the man in the barn escaped."

He nodded and crept to the corner of the house, staying right up along the edge. When Enoch got near the sitting room window, he peeked inside, ducking when he spotted Charlie Williams resting on the fainting couch with his dirty boots propped on the flowered fabric. No gun was in sight.

Taking a deep breath, he lifted a leg and crawled through the window, dropping to the floor. He rushed forward. His gun drawn. "Hands up. You're under arrest."

Charlie's eyes fluttered open. "Why, Sheriff. Glad you can join the party."

"Sit up." Enoch fished the restraints from his pocket, locking them on Charlie's wrists. "Stay there."

"Sure, Sheriff. Whatever you say." The man grinned.

He should've brought rope to truss up the outlaw. Why was the fella not surprised to see Enoch? It didn't make sense.

"We knew your gal would come running to see what was wrong with Ellie Lou. Didn't take long to figure you'd come scurrying here too if you thought Miss Miller was in trouble. You two are too predictable."

"I wouldn't say that. At least your brother wouldn't."

Charlie scowled. "What's George got to do with anything?"

He shook his head. "He doesn't. At least not anymore."

The outlaw surged to his feet. "You didn't."

"I'm afraid so. Now sit back down again."

The scoundrel barreled toward him, his head down.

Before Enoch had time to react, his body slammed against the wall, knocking the wind out of him. He was temporarily dazed.

Despite being handcuffed, Charlie wrestled him, trying to snatch the gun that had been thrown from Enoch's hand. He scurried to reach it first, grabbing hold of it. Just as he did, Charlie seized the gun in the back of Enoch's belt, leveling it on him.

He chuckled. "Well, well, well. Looks like the tables have turned, Sheriff." He motioned with the gun. "Get on that side of the room where I can keep an eye on you."

Enoch thumbed the hammer on his gun. "You back up. I don't want to shoot you, Charlie, but I will if I have to. You don't want to end up like your brother did." Maybe if he could keep the man talking, Enoch could find a way out of the mess without any more loss of life.

Charlie pulled the hammer on George's gun. The one Enoch had recovered.

Enoch's mouth went dry.

Dear God, don't let it end like this.

"I suggest you do what Charlie says if you want to keep that pretty gal of yours from getting hurt."

Enoch's gaze swung to the doorway. He knew that voice.

38

Enoch spun around, his gun trained on the masked man in the doorway. "No use wearing a mask, Jim, I know who you are."

"Place your gun on the ground and kick it over here."

Enoch un-cocked his pistol and stooped to place it on the ground. Instead of kicking it towards the outlaws, he booted it in the opposite direction.

The ranch hand scowled at him. "Took you long enough to get here."

"Would've made it sooner if someone hadn't stolen my horse and shot at me before I could leave my house today." He glanced at Charlie. The man still had his gun aimed at Enoch. "You better not have done anything to Fee."

"Fee." Jim snorted. "What kind of name is that for a horse? Never did understand you. Your mare's fine. I put her somewhere safe."

At least the horse hadn't been harmed. "So, was it you this morning?"

The ranch hand grinned. "You sure are a late riser since you got your own place. Didn't think you'd ever get up." He waved his gun. "Once this place is mine, I plan to do some sleeping in too."

"Hey. Wait a minute. You said you were helping George and me get this place from Ellie Lou. It's ours…" Charlie sniffed. "I mean mine. We never said we'd give it to you."

Jim laughed. "That's what I wanted you to think."

The pieces fell into place. "You've been orchestrating things from the very beginning, haven't you?" Enoch asked.

He thrust his chest out. "You aren't the sharpest saw in the toolbox, Enoch. Maybe you should think twice about your job as sheriff. Not that it will matter since I'll be getting rid of you all once Ellie Lou signs the ranch over to me."

Charlie took a step toward Jim. "You mean when Ellie Lou signs it over to me."

Jim shook his head. "Looks like Enoch already took care of killing one of you off. Leaves me less work to clean up this mess."

A dark look flashed across Charlie's face.

"You'll never get away with it." Enoch glanced at Charlie who kept inching closer to the ranch hand.

Jim leaned against the doorframe, crossing one leg over the other. "I'll just tell the sheriff-turned-doctor that George killed Ellie Lou and Gertrude and that you, Charlie, and George got shot in the aftermath. Course, the missus will need to deed the ranch to me first since I'm her only loyal employee."

"He'll never believe it," Enoch said.

"Now hold on there. I didn't have a problem with you killing my cousin and setting this whole thing in motion, but you promised that George and I wouldn't get hurt in the process." Charlie shifted again, scowling. "My brother was all I had left in this world."

"I didn't kill your brother. He did." Jim pointed at Enoch.

Enoch needed to distract Charlie. "How did you kill our boss?"

A half-crazed look settled on Jim's countenance. "Slowly started poisoning him. Missus just thought he was getting sick. Ended up having to kill him sooner than I wanted because he discovered the can of poison in the barn."

Dear God. Give me wisdom on how to get out of this alive.

The two outlaws weren't paying attention to him. Enoch shifted toward both of them. If he could get close enough, maybe he'd find a way to disarm them.

"Charlie, don't you want to get even for the new sheriff killing your brother?" Jim grinned again.

The older man glanced at Enoch. His hand holding the pistol trembled. "It's not right that you killed my brother."

"I didn't want to." He swallowed. "It was self-defense. He would've killed me."

A tear slid down Charlie's cheek. "I don't know what to do without my brother."

"You should kill Enoch." Jim stepped closer to Charlie. "George would want you to get even for him."

Charlie glanced at Enoch and then back to Jim.

Lord, help me here. "Don't listen to him, Charlie. He just wants you to take the blame for killing a lawman because he knows if he's caught, he'll spend the rest of his life in prison."

"I don't want that." Charlie started to lower his gun.

"You're weak." Jim spit out the words.

Charlie glared, his gun dipping more. "I'm not. Just tired of the killing. George and I were wrong to have you do something to our cousin so we could get the ranch. It's not worth it. Not without George here to be with me. I won't do any killing for you, Jim." He tucked the pistol in his belt.

The weight on Enoch's chest eased a bit. One down. One to go. *Give me an idea on how to get out of this, Lord.*

The faint sound of horse hooves drifted through the open window. A few seconds later he heard a whinny. Enoch bit back a smile. He'd know that sound anywhere. He let out a shrill whistle.

"What're you doing?" Jim scowled. "Back up."

Fee poked her head through the window, snorting.

As Jim's gaze swung to see what the disturbance was, Enoch charged him, knocking the man to the floor. Jim's pistol went flying. Jim tackled Enoch, and they both fell to the floor. Enoch rolled, pinning Jim to the ground. Using all his strength, he hauled back and slugged the ranch hand in the jaw. Enoch pulled out his second set of handcuffs, and after slapping them on Jim's wrists, Enoch hauled him to his feet.

The gun. He'd forgotten all about Jim's gun.

Charlie scrambled to pick it up. He raised it.

"Put the gun down. You don't want to do this." Enoch held onto one of Jim's arms and reached toward Charlie.

Charlie shifted the pistol, so the barrel was facing down. "I wasn't going to shoot you, Sheriff. Just wanted to make sure he wasn't going anywhere. I know better than to kill a lawman." He handed the gun to Enoch.

"Both of you, over on the sofa." He motioned them with his weapon. "Stay still and don't move."

They shuffled over to the couch and sat down.

"Enoch? You in here?"

"Josh?" He sent a quick glimpse to the doorway.

The former sheriff stepped into the room. "From the looks of it, you have things in hand here. Guess you didn't need my help after all." He glanced at the window where Fee still had her head poked through. "I see she found you. She was tied to a fencepost in the far pasture. Found her when I took a shortcut across the ranch to get here faster. No sooner untied her and she took off at a run. Almost as if she knew you were in trouble." He laughed. "I've always been partial to Barabbas, but your horse is one to behold."

"Would you mind keeping an eye on these two? I have some ladies who need saving."

~*~

Gertrude's limbs trembled from being tied to the tree for so long. Worst of all was not knowing what was happening in the house. Ever since Enoch had gone around the corner of Ellie Lou's home, they hadn't been able to see what was going on. The not knowing was killing her.

Lord, I know You're with him. I'm choosing to trust You. I'm choosing to walk by faith on the water as Peter did. I don't want to sink beneath the waves. Help me to keep my eyes on You. I want to walk in Your peace no matter what the outcome is.

The sound of the front door flying open and smacking against the house traveled to her ears. She shifted her head to catch a glimpse of whoever was coming.

Enoch.

Her heart thrummed as he ran towards the tree. "Oh, Enoch. You're alive. Praise God."

Ellie Lou mumbled something, but the gag kept her from being understood.

"I'm here." He started climbing the tree.

Her pulse quickened as he got closer and closer. Finally, he was at the branch right below her and Ellie Lou.

He boosted himself, easing the handkerchief from Ellie Lou's mouth. "Are you two hurt?"

"We're uninjured." Gertrude's throat tightened and tears welled in her eyes.

"Thank you." Ellie Lou's voice was hoarse. "If you cut these ropes, I can climb down on my own. Climbed many a tree as a girl, and I doubt I've forgotten how to get down from one." She winked. "Besides, I think Gertrude could use your help more than mine."

"Yes, ma'am." He withdrew a knife from his boot and slit Ellie Lou's bindings. "You sure you'll be fine on your own?"

She nodded. "And don't forget, it's Ellie Lou." She smiled and started descending.

Enoch's brown eyed gaze sought Gertrude's. He ran a finger along her scraped cheek. His touch was as light as a butterfly sending shivers down her spine. "Thought you said you weren't injured."

She licked her lips. "This is nothing."

His gaze settled on her lips. "Hold on tight, darling. Wouldn't want you to fall."

Darling? Dare she hope he cared for her? Her limbs quaked as she held tight. As soon as the rope fell away, her strength waned, and she started to slip.

Enoch vaulted to the branch, securing her body between his and the tree. "I've got you, sweetheart. Let's get you down from here."

The next few minutes were a blur as they made their slow, deliberate path down the tree. As soon as they got to the bottom, Enoch turned her toward him. He brushed his fingers along her jawline, tipping her head.

Her pulse thudded in her neck as he dipped his head. His lips met hers. First as soft as a feather, then with more urgency. Wrapping her arms around his back, she pressed him a little closer to her, not wanting him to ever get away.

A throat being cleared caused them both to pull apart.

Gertrude immediately felt a loss.

"Guess you two have things in hand." Josh grinned.

"What happened to George's body?" Enoch glanced around as if he'd just noticed it was gone.

"Josh came over to investigate when he got here. I told him you were inside the house. He shifted George's body out of the sun." Gertrude shuddered.

Enoch's hand found hers.

"Figured if they came out before I made it inside, I'd move the body to throw them off. Thought it would help to keep the women safe if they had no reason to go by the tree." Josh grinned. "Well, I'll take care of carting these two to the jail now. Ellie Lou said she'd come along and make a statement. Figured the least I could do was start on the paperwork for you, Enoch." He winked at them. "I suppose you and Gertrude have a little 'discussing' to do. I'll leave you to it."

"What was he talking about?" She asked as soon as the trio departed.

Enoch pulled her into his arms again, kissing her mouth, chin, and neck.

Her heart pattered as if she'd ran all the way here from town. She could get used to the feeling. She laughed. "Is this the talking you wanted to do?"

A twinkle flickered in his brown eyes. "Part of it." He ran a finger along her jawline again.

She shivered.

"I know you didn't want to marry, Gertrude, but I can't imagine my life with you not in it. At my table, working by my side, warming my bed at night." His tanned cheeks flushed. "I love you, Gertrude. I hope you'll come to love me too and one day want to marry me."

She rose on her toes and kissed him for all she was worth.

When they came up for air he said, "Does that mean you'll marry me, Gertrude?"

"Yes. Oh, yes. If you hadn't asked me, I was going to ask you." She nestled in his arms.

The sound of his rich laughter reverberated in his chest, where her head lay.

"I love you, Gertrude Miller."

"And I love you, Enoch Valentine."

EPILOGUE

Gertrude flipped the sign and closed the door behind her. She scurried to the church. Buggies, horses, and wagons were tied outside. Enoch stood waiting.

His brow furrowed when he saw her. "Gertrude? I was afraid you weren't coming."

"As if I'd forget our wedding day." She kissed his cheek. "Sorry I'm late. I have a surprise for you. It, I mean, they got delayed. They were supposed to be here yesterday."

"What are you talking about, sweetheart?"

She motioned to the older couple standing behind one of the trees.

Enoch turned to see. "Ma? Pa? W-what're you doing here?"

His parents moved toward him. His mother had tears streaming down her cheeks. "Oh, Enoch." She hugged him.

His father wrapped his arms around Enoch and his wife. "We're sorry, son."

Tears pricked Gertrude's eyes.

"But how did you know where I was?" Enoch's brow wrinkled.

"Gertrude wrote to us a while back. Asked us to come. Asked us to forgive you. Told us how we needed to cling to each other in our missing Anna instead of staying apart." His ma gripped Gertrude's hand. "She was right. It's time to put the blaming aside. We should've never pushed you away in the first place."

His pa's Adam's apple bobbed. "We were wrong, son. Please forgive us."

Tears ran down Enoch's face. "Of course, I forgive you." His gaze found Gertrude's. "I-I don't know how to thank you, sweetheart."

She smiled. "I'm sure I can find a way." Her cheeks immediately flamed as her thoughts sprang to what it would be like to be husband

and wife.

"We're just glad she reached out to us again so we could be here in time for the wedding." His pa touched Gertrude's arm. "We'll never forget what you've done for us."

The door to the church opened, and Ellie Lou stepped onto the porch. "You two better get in here. People are starting to get restless."

"That's right. We've got a wedding to attend." His pa winked at her and put his elbow out for his wife. "Coming, dear?"

His ma kissed Gertrude's cheek and squeezed her hand. "Thank you. We're so glad to have a daughter again."

The couple trooped up the steps.

Enoch's arms wrapped around Gertrude. She could get used to this feeling.

"I'm so glad I decided to woo you."

She hugged him tight. "Me, too. Me, too."

A Devotional Moment

Peace I leave with you, my peace I give unto you: not as the world giveth, give I unto you. Let not your heart be troubled, neither let it be afraid. ~ John 14:27

Sometimes when life overwhelms, Christians struggle with calming themselves, and allowing God to work. They believe, but see no end to the troubles that plague their lives. It's hard to trust others when life has betrayed you, and many times, Christians include God in that mistrust. Christians are supposed to stand for their beliefs, not cave to pressure. But part of that resolve is to let God handle it.

In **Wooing Gertrude**, past misdeeds of others have overwhelmed both protagonists. Both feel their past is a detriment to any happiness they wish to have. Meanwhile, they rush to solve a mysterious mischief-maker who has targeted their livelihoods and their homes. But they have to work within the confines of the law while trying to figure out who is wrecking their peace, their trust in God, and each other. As they sort out the clues and reach out to others, their hope in God is at first weak, and then strengthens as good friends help them to rely on God and His plan for their future. In accepting His grace, they find that the peace that God brings strengthens both from within.

Have you ever felt so overwhelmed by circumstance that you couldn't see any resolution to the situation? When things are complicated or seem to impact you negatively, it's difficult to stand still and let an invisible God work. But, even though letting go and trusting God with everything that stands against you is a hard lesson to learn sometimes, it's imperative to your wellbeing—physical, mental and spiritual wellbeing—to do so. When you surrender, you'll find the peace to weather the storms that life tosses you.

LORD, HELP ME TO RELY ON YOU ALWAYS, EVEN WHEN IT'S DIFFICULT AND EVEN WHEN IT SEEMS AS THOUGH YOU'RE NOT ON MY SIDE. HELP ME ALWAYS TO TRUST IN YOU AS AN ALL-KNOWING, ALL-CARING FATHER AND TO FIND THE PEACE YOU PROMISE. IN JESUS' NAME, I PRAY. AMEN.

Thank you

We appreciate you reading this White Rose Publishing title. For other inspirational stories, please visit our on-line bookstore at www.pelicanbookgroup.com.

For questions or more information, contact us at customer@pelicanbookgroup.com.

White Rose Publishing
Where Faith is the Cornerstone of Love™
an imprint of Pelican Book Group
www.PelicanBookGroup.com

Connect with Us
www.facebook.com/Pelicanbookgroup
www.twitter.com/pelicanbookgrp

To receive news and specials, subscribe to our bulletin
http://pelink.us/bulletin

May God's glory shine through
this inspirational work of fiction.

AMDG

You Can Help!

At Pelican Book Group it is our mission to entertain readers with fiction that uplifts the Gospel. It is our privilege to spend time with you awhile as you read our stories.

We believe you can help us to bring Christ into the lives of people across the globe. And you don't have to open your wallet or even leave your house!

Here are 3 simple things you can do to help us bring illuminating fiction™ to people everywhere.

1) If you enjoyed this book, write a positive review. Post it at online retailers and websites where readers gather. And share your review with us at reviews@pelicanbookgroup.com (this does give us permission to reprint your review in whole or in part.)

2) If you enjoyed this book, recommend it to a friend in person, at a book club or on social media.

3) If you have suggestions on how we can improve or expand our selection, let us know. We value your opinion. Use the contact form on our web site or e-mail us at customer@pelicanbookgroup.com

God Can Help!

Are you in need? The Almighty can do great things for you. Holy is His Name! He has mercy in every generation. He can lift up the lowly and accomplish all things. Reach out today.

Do not fear: I am with you; do not be anxious: I am your God. I will strengthen you, I will help you, I will uphold you with my victorious right hand.

~Isaiah 41:10 (NAB)

We pray daily, and we especially pray for everyone connected to Pelican Book Group—that includes you! If you have a specific need, we welcome the opportunity to pray for you. Share your needs or praise reports at http://pelink.us/pray4us

Free eBook Offer

We're looking for booklovers like you to partner with us! Join our team of influencers today and periodically receive free eBooks!

For more information
Visit http://pelicanbookgroup.com/booklovers

How About Free Audiobooks?

We're looking for audiobook lovers, too! Partner with us as an audiobook lover and periodically receive free audiobooks!

For more information
Visit http://pelicanbookgroup.com/booklovers/freeaudio.html

or e-mail
booklovers@pelicanbookgroup.com

www.ingramcontent.com/pod-product-compliance
Lightning Source LLC
Chambersburg PA
CBHW030357310726
48979CB00001B/339

* 9 7 8 1 5 2 2 3 0 4 3 2 6 *